The Horseman's Frontier Family

KAREN KIRST

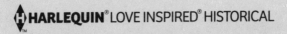
HARLEQUIN® LOVE INSPIRED® HISTORICAL

Special thanks and acknowledgment are given to Karen Kirst
for her contribution to the Bridegroom Brothers miniseries.

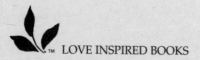

Recycling programs
for this product may
not exist in your area.

LOVE INSPIRED BOOKS

ISBN-13: 978-0-373-28263-0

THE HORSEMAN'S FRONTIER FAMILY

Copyright © 2014 by Harlequin Books S.A.

www.Harlequin.com

Printed in U.S.A.

In his heart a man plans his course,
but the Lord determines his steps.
—*Proverbs* 16:9

"Until the case goes to court, this is my land," Gideon said slowly. **"I don't want you making any changes without my approval. Understand?"**

Scrambling up, Evelyn matched his stance. "You've conveniently forgotten whose name is on the stake, Mr. Thornton. Just because you've been living here longer and have made improvements doesn't make it yours. I can do whatever I want. Understand?"

"My stake was in the ground when I left to get help for your husband. Someone switched it. Drake was the only one here."

"He was dying!"

"Your brothers came around to collect his body. In the chaos, my brothers and I weren't watching the stake...."

"What exactly are you insinuating?" she pushed out through clenched teeth.

"Think hard. I'm sure you'll figure it out. Unless you're incapable of thinking for yourself, that is."

How dare he! The outrage churning inside bubbled up. That was the second and last time he insinuated she was a brainless female. Seizing the pail of water she'd brought with her, she dumped it over his head.

* * *

Bridegroom Brothers: True love awaits three siblings in the Oklahoma Land Rush

The Preacher's Bride Claim—Laurie Kingery, April 2014

The Horseman's Frontier Family—Karen Kirst, May 2014

The Lawman's Oklahoma Sweetheart—Allie Pleiter, June 2014

Books by Karen Kirst

Love Inspired Historical

*The Reluctant Outlaw
*The Bridal Swap
  The Gift of Family
    *"Smoky Mountain Christmas"
*His Mountain Miss
*The Husband Hunt
  The Horseman's Frontier Family

*Smoky Mountain Matches

KAREN KIRST

was born and raised in East Tennessee near the Great
Smoky Mountains. A lifelong lover of books, it wasn't
until after college that she had the grand idea to write
one herself. Now she divides her time between being
a wife, homeschooling mom and romance writer. Her
favorite pastimes are reading, visiting tearooms and
watching romantic comedies.

Chapter One

Brave Rock, Oklahoma
May 1889

Gideon couldn't have heard right. His ears must be clogged. Or he was dehydrated, which would explain why he'd misunderstood the cavalry officer. Extreme thirst and heat could do that to a man.

Glaring at the fortyish man who'd introduced himself as Private Jesse Wellington, he demanded he repeat his previous statement.

The polished buttons marching down the middle of Wellington's navy blue uniform rose and fell with his long-suffering sigh. Tall and distinguished, the officer had streaks of silver at his temples that lent him a sage air. "I'm here to inform you that your claim to this land has been challenged."

Challenged? "You're joking, right?" After all, he'd planted his stake deep into the earth with his own two hands.

On April 22, the day of the land rush, thousands of settlers had raced to claim a piece of this Oklahoma prairie for themselves. Thanks to President Cleveland and his decision to make the Unassigned Lands available to settlers, scores of people from all parts of the country had seized the opportunity to start over, to build new and better lives for themselves and their families, he and his brothers included.

The private smirked. "The United States Army isn't in the habit of *joking* about such matters, Mr. Thornton. Mrs. Evelyn Chaucer Montgomery, along with her brothers, Theodore, Brett and Reid Chaucer, are disputing your claim."

His gut knotted up below his sternum. Chaucer. A name embedded in his consciousness, going as far back as his toddler years to the time of the war between the states, a name associated with trouble and turmoil, hatred and discord. The Chaucers—Southern sympathizers to the core—despised his family for their loyalty to the North and its cause. That they had turned up here, in this start-up community of Brave Rock, struck him as downright suspicious.

Beyond Wellington's left shoulder, three men stood shoulder to shoulder, their olive skin and European features marking them as Chaucers. Because they were familiar to him and uninteresting, he skipped right over them to focus on the slender female dressed in head-to-toe black. Her head was bent so that her bonnet's brim hid the top half of her face.

Gauging from her gold-kissed skin and the black-brown hair whispering against her nape, Chaucer blood ran through her veins. The vague recollection of a twin sister drifted through his memory. Before he could pin it down, however, he noticed another member of their party. A small child. A boy with disheveled black hair and huge brown eyes in a face that hadn't yet lost the fullness of toddlerhood. A boy around the same age as his Maggie….

Shying away from the life-sucking grief, Gideon slammed the gateway to the past shut. Wrested his gaze away from the small figure clinging to his ma's skirts and planted it firmly onto the soldier.

"I've been here eight days, Private. Why are they just now disputing the claim?"

"Because we had a funeral to arrange, you—" Theo leaned forward. Brett put up an arm to block him.

"You've wasted your time. These people have misled you."

Wellington didn't so much as blink. "They contend that Mrs. Montgomery's late husband, Drake, staked this plot and that it rightfully belongs to her and her son, Walter."

Montgomery. The inexperienced rider who'd foolishly followed him the day of the land rush? His gaze flew to the widow's face, now fully visible beneath the curved brim, delving into eyes the color of thick, sticky molasses. The exotic beauty countered his scrutiny with open challenge, her dainty chin uplifted and her high forehead lined with determination. Slashing black brows arched above flashing, thick-lashed eyes, and rounded cheekbones were balanced by a lush pink mouth. Disdain radiated from her bristling stance.

"I'm sorry for your loss, ma'am," he said directly to her, with effort not allowing his gaze to lower to the boy at her side, "but you're mistaken. Before the land rush, I studied the maps carefully and chose this plot because of its distance from town and proximity to this offshoot stream. I discovered a shortcut, a path hazardous for anyone who isn't a strong rider."

He recalled the exact moment he'd realized someone

was trailing him. The surprise. The urgency, the drive to reach the land first. He had waited too long for this opportunity, hadn't been about to let it slip through his fingers. "I planted my stake. When I looked back, I saw Montgomery's horse stumble and pitch sideways. He was crushed."

A quiet gasp drew his attention once more to the female. A small hand pressed against her son's back tucked him closer to her, as if her touch alone were enough to spare him life's harsh realities.

Eager to be done with this unpleasant scene, Gideon pushed out the rest of the story. "I checked on him. Saw that he was alive and in desperate need of medical help, so I sought out my brother's fiancée, Alice Hawthorne. She's a skilled nurse. I thought—" He scraped a hand along his unshaven jaw, the bloody images coming into focus. "We were too late to save him. By the time we returned, Mr. Montgomery had already passed."

"You're lying." Her voice was huskier, deeper than he'd expected.

His spine stiffened. "Be very careful, madam. That's a serious accusation to levy at a complete stranger."

Rather than cower at the current of steely warning in his voice, she took a step forward. "I want to see the stake."

"As do I." Theodore glared at Gideon, the heat of old rivalries stirring to life in his dark eyes, punctuated by the once-straight nose that was now slightly offset.

Ignoring him, Gideon looked at Wellington, who nodded in agreement. "In order to sort this out, we need to see it. Shall we walk or ride?"

He weighed his options. Refusal didn't appear to be one of them. Besides, the sooner he proved his case, the sooner he'd be rid of the Chaucers. "It's about fifteen acres south of here. We'll ride."

Spinning on his heel, he strode over to the corral and, ducking between the rails, signaled Star. The two-year-old palomino lifted his head and met him at the gate. After a brief touch on his muzzle, Gideon swung up onto his broad, bare back.

A light breeze carrying the scents of sunbaked earth, hardy grass and sweet hyacinths gave him a brief respite from the overhead sun's scorching heat. The near-constant breeze was one of the first things he'd noticed about his new home in central Oklahoma. Whether it was due to his proximity to the Cimarron River slicing through the grasslands or the absence of substantial hills in this area, he didn't know and didn't care. In his opinion, he and his brothers couldn't have picked a better place to start fresh. Ruggedly beautiful countryside, fertile land and, best of all, remote. With 160 acres to call his own, he didn't have to see another living soul until he wanted to.

Unless folks chose to drop in on him unannounced. A scowl created deep lines around his mouth as he waited for the group to pile into their wagon.

He led them south, away from the Cimarron, through verdant pastures thick with yellow and orange flowers, along the stream bank dotted with sweeping cottonwood trees to the place where he'd staked his claim. Very near to where Mrs. Evelyn Chaucer Montgomery's husband had perished.

For a brief moment he allowed himself to feel compassion for the young widow. He knew all too well how it felt to lose a spouse with absolutely no warning. No preparation. *She must be in shock still.*

Then he shoved it aside. She'd labeled him a *liar.* He should expect no less from a Chaucer.

Sliding smoothly to the ground, he waited for the rest to catch up, anticipating their reaction to the proof. The officer perused his surroundings with keen interest. He wondered what misdeeds the man might've committed to have robbed him of his rightful rank; a man of his age and experience was not a mere army private for no reason.

The Chaucer brothers' hungry gazes gobbled up his land, Theodore in particular wearing a too-confident expression. Taller and leaner than the other two, he had sandy hair that set him apart from his siblings. The second eldest, Brett, was shorter, broader and less aggressive, but still a pain. Reid was Gideon's least favorite. Cocky. Short fused. Unpredictable.

Once out of the wagon, Mrs. Montgomery handed the boy off to Reid and strode for the wooden stake sticking out of the ground beneath a hackberry tree. The sweep of her full black skirts through the tall grass frightened a pair of cottontails that scurried in the opposite direction. She was oblivious, however, to all else save that stake.

Too bad she was in for a disappointment.

But when she yanked it out of the ground and read the name, the satisfaction and relief flashing across her expressive face did not indicate disappointment at all. Confused, Gideon walked toward her as if in a dream, his feet reluctant to carry him where he wanted to go.

"It's Drake's," she said in a triumphant whoosh, holding it up above her head like a torch.

"I knew it." White teeth flashed in Brett's face as he looped an arm about her waist and whirled her in a circle.

Pulse sluggish, thoughts muddled, Gideon extended a flat palm. "Let me see that."

Laughter fading, Brett lowered her but didn't release her. Her big brown eyes locked on to him, and the brief moment of rejoicing leached from her countenance. She extended the stake without a word.

He took it. Studied the scrawled letters.

Montgomery, Drake Sutton.

"This can't be right." Stunned, Gideon stared at the hole in the ground. Cast about the surrounding ground for answers. Where was *his* stake?

Wellington asked to see it.

"I don't understand." Gideon numbly passed it to the officer.

Wandering to the steep bank where his opponent had lost control of his horse, he rehashed the events of that day. There'd been only the two of them. Land rush rules stated that once a man's stake of possession was planted in the 160-acre tract of his choice, he had to hold that claim and defend it against other settlers. Leaving to fetch help meant Gideon had risked losing his plot. He hadn't been able to ignore a dying man's need, however. He hadn't hesitated to make the right choice.

His brothers, Elijah and Clint, had accompanied Alice. Clint had gone to alert the authorities, and hours later Theodore and Brett had arrived to confirm the deceased man's identity and take the body for burial.

Returning to the group, he addressed Wellington. "My stake was here when I left. Montgomery must've somehow removed it and replaced it with his own before he died."

"That's preposterous!" The widow pushed out of her brother's arms. "You honestly expect us to believe a dying man cared one way or another who got this land? Drake would've conserved his energy. He would've waited for help to come. He certainly wouldn't have risked aggravating his injuries."

Staring down at her, he pulled in a bracing breath. "I understand you're hurting right now—"

"Don't patronize me, Mr. Thornton." She faced off against him. "I know all about you and your family, how you cheat and scheme your way through life, not caring who you trample on your way to the top. I know exactly what happened here the day my husband died." Lifting her chin, she condemned him without a trace of evidence. "You saw an opportunity to steal the land and you took it. In your arrogance, you didn't even bother to change out Drake's stake with your own. You didn't expect us to challenge you, did you?"

Gideon opened his mouth to speak. No words came out. First she'd called him a liar. Now she was accusing him of being a thief? Outrage churned in his gut. The independence he'd dreamed of for so long, worked so hard for, was suddenly in jeopardy.

All because of this woman.

Evelyn wasn't about to let this mountain of a man intimidate her. "This land belongs to me and my son. It's Walt's rightful inheritance. I won't let you take that away from him."

Bringing his face near hers, the man bared his teeth. Glacial gray eyes impaled her. "This is *my* land." He jammed a thumb to his broad chest. "I'm not simply going to hand it over to you."

Gideon Thornton spoke slowly and with great deliberation. But beneath the facade of control, she detected the smoldering anger in him, a river of molten lava scrambling to be unleashed. Taller than her by a good three inches, he had a powerful body that looked as though it had been carved from stone and hands that could no doubt easily hoist her into the air and carry her to parts unknown. He was one impressive male.

All right. Maybe she was a smidge intimidated. She'd never let it show, though. Had learned her lessons early. Growing up with three brothers had toughened her, forced her to fight tooth and nail for everything she'd ever wanted. Though she'd sometimes bemoaned her lot—was one sister too much to ask?—there were times her experience came in handy.

This was one of those times. One of the most important. This land meant independence. A future for her and Walt. No way was a Thornton going to rip it from her grasp.

"I'd appreciate it if you'd cease with the name slinging." With his face this close as he spoke, she couldn't ignore the overall impression of wolfish magnificence. The chiseled cheekbones, strong nose, firm mouth. Eloquent brown brows—the only refined feature in his wild appearance—framed cold, glittering eyes the color of rainy skies. From the dark scruff along his hard jaws and chin, it was clear he'd misplaced his straight razor. "I'm neither a liar nor a thief," he said through clenched teeth. "Your parents and brothers have fed you a pack of lies about us."

"My parents were God-fearing, decent people." *Unlike your traitor of a father.*

As if he'd read her mind, his brows slammed together. Whatever stinging retort he'd had planned was cut off by Theo.

"Private Wellington, you've seen the proof. Kick this trespasser off my sister's property."

Wellington held up a hand. "I can't do that."

"Why not? We have the stake. Surely—"

"I don't have the authority to settle your dispute. At this point it is my responsibility to suggest you work together to reach a compromise."

"Compromise? You have no idea what you're asking." Theo shook his head. "I wouldn't give a Thornton the satisfaction."

"Then your dispute will have to be taken up in court. Unfortunately, there's a backlog of cases. There's no way of knowing how long it will be before your case can be heard. It would be best for all of you to vacate the land until the dispute is settled."

"Out of the question." Gideon looked as unmovable as a mountain.

"I have no intention of leaving," Evelyn shot back.

"If you both insist on staying, you'll have to share it while you wait for the judge to hear your case."

"That's not acceptable," Brett clipped out, his hand slicing through the air. "You've seen the stake. Thornton is clearly taking advantage of the situation."

As her brothers argued with the older officer, Evelyn and Gideon glared at each other, locked in a silent battle of wills. No way was she sharing Walt's inheritance with this man. For his part, her nemesis appeared equally appalled at the prospect.

When the arguments grew heated, Wellington held up both hands. "Enough." His sharp command rendered the group silent, his cool blue eyes touching on each person. "However much you all dislike the situation, there's no other alternative. I suggest you make the best of it."

Reid came to stand beside her, Walt still held securely in his arms. "I'm not leaving my sister here alone with Gideon Thornton."

Of all her brothers, her twin was the most protective. Maybe it was the age thing or the special bond they shared. Still, it rankled. Why couldn't he accept that she was a capable adult?

Resting a hand in the crook of his elbow, she said, "I can take care of myself."

"Other cavalry officers will periodically stop by to ensure they are sharing the land peacefully." Wellington sized up Gideon. "Besides, if anything were to happen to Mrs. Montgomery or her son, everyone in Brave Rock would know whom to suspect."

Theo scowled. "You're forgetting the nearest claims are held by Gideon's brothers, as well as town members who've been tricked into thinking the Thorntons are decent and honorable men. If Gideon turned against her, these people wouldn't rush to her aid. They'd support Gideon. They've gone so far as to entrust their spiritual well-being to Elijah and their safety to Clint, whom they've named sheriff."

Gideon visibly bristled. "No need to worry. I have absolutely no reason to go near this woman."

Spinning about, he skirted the group and, greeting his beautiful palomino with a gentle touch, mounted with a grace and ease that belied his brawny build. And without a saddle, too. Moving as one, horse and rider traversed the fields until they faded from view.

Of all the insolent, rude—

"Our business here is concluded, gentlemen. Time to get a move on." Wellington's long legs ate up the distance to the wagon.

With a troubled light in his coffee-colored eyes, Reid sidled closer to his twin sister. "I'll stay here with you."

"We can take turns." Nodding, Brett looked to his oldest brother for confirmation.

"Out of the question." Evelyn planted her hands on her hips. "You have your own claims to tend to."

Theo shouldered closer, his hair falling in his eyes. "The Thorntons—"

"Are not murderers, Theo. I'm in no danger here. You heard the officer. Gideon Thornton would be an idiot to try anything." All three men's eyes narrowed dangerously. "Not that he would," she rushed to say. "You saw the way he acted. I doubt we'll exchange so much as a single word."

"I don't like this."

"I'm not a little girl anymore, Reid," she reminded him quietly, determined not to be railroaded.

For the first time in five years, since her wedding to Drake, she felt free. It was a liberating feeling, buoyant and carefree, but not without a measure of guilt. Her husband was dead, after all. Shouldn't she be mourning his absence? Her lack of reaction confounded her brothers. All three had been watching her since the funeral, expecting her to dissolve in a heap of tears. She'd even heard Theo mention the word *shock*.

How can I mourn a man who found fault with my every move?

Her five-year-old son watched them with wide, solemn eyes, unnaturally silent. Reaching out, she caressed his silken cheek. When was the last time he'd smiled? Or uttered a word? Always a quiet child, he'd stopped speaking altogether the day of Drake's death.

How can Walt miss a father who'd basically ignored him?

Determination pulsed through her veins, washing away the doubts, the fears.

She would move heaven and earth to help her precious child. Her hope was that a new home, a change in routine and surroundings, would draw him out. While her brothers meant well, they didn't know what was best for her son. They would not be allowed to sabotage Walt's chance at a normal life.

When she held out her hands, he lurched forward into her arms. Soon he would be too heavy for her. Settling his familiar, reassuring weight against her hip, she half turned so that all three could see her face, see she meant business. "It's my decision to make, and I choose to stay here and wait it out. Alone."

The memory of Gideon Thornton's ice-cold eyes sent a shiver of foreboding down her spine. May she not come to regret this decision.

Chapter Two

Temper boiling over, Gideon kicked an empty pail and sent it sailing through the air to bounce across the yard. Beneath the anger and resentment churned very real concern. What if the judge ruled in her favor?

A lifetime of living at the mercy of other men's whims had sparked within his soul a desperate craving for independence. For control. The chance to shape his own destiny. And now, thanks to the Chaucers, his dream of running his own ranch was being threatened.

His gaze touched on the corral and the partially-built stable, the trees he'd felled and readied for use. All this effort—the planning, the sweat and toil and time— would've been for nothing.

His hunger forgotten, repressed energy making him jittery, he stalked around back and lugged another log closer to the rear wall. While he worked, he pondered the stakes. If Drake had indeed summoned the strength to switch them, where had Gideon's disappeared to? Just didn't make any sense.

He'd tried to help a dying man and his repayment was this—a problem he couldn't readily fix, one he couldn't have foreseen. Yet another tangle with the troublesome

Chaucers. A year and a half ago, he would've gotten on his knees and sought God's direction. Not now.

He was itching to inform his brothers of this new trouble. True to form, Lije would suggest he pray about the situation. Not happening. Lawman Clint would be more inclined to action, but what could be done? As much as he needed to mull this over with them, he didn't feel right leaving his claim just yet, not when the Chaucers were sure to return with the widow and her son.

Wedging another log into place, he caught his thumb in the indented corner. With a muttered oath, he tugged the glove off and sucked on the throbbing finger. Should he abandon the project? After all, there was a very real chance he was actually building this shelter not for himself but for a hateful family who did nothing but point their fingers at him and his brothers, unfairly blaming them for their own misfortune.

But he'd never been a quitter. Call it determination or plain old stubbornness—he wouldn't give up, wouldn't stop fighting for his dream until the judge gave his ruling.

Two hours later he was downing a quick lunch of buffalo jerky and two-day-old biscuits he'd snagged from Alice's table when Mrs. Evelyn Montgomery returned with a mountain of belongings. Trunks and barrels and carpet bags were piled into the wagon driven by her twin, Reid. Where did she think she was gonna stow all that?

Perched on an upended crate near his tent's opening, the towering cottonwoods high, crooked branches providing welcome shade, he did not go out to welcome them. His dogs, Lion, a golden-haired beauty with a wise face, and Shadow, a shaggy black mutt with a playful spirit, lifted their heads from their outstretched paws.

Bringing them to Oklahoma had been the right decision. The dogs were good companions, loyal to a fault.

Reid stopped the wagon in front of the stable and, after assisting his sister and nephew down, began to unload her stuff.

"Where will you sleep?" Reid's question carried on the breeze.

She glanced Gideon's way and, catching him staring, arched a provoking eyebrow. "Mr. Thornton and I will sort that out."

Seeing the direction of her gaze, her brother tossed him a scowl. "I wish you'd let me help you get settled at least."

She turned her back and her response was lost. Burrowed into her skirt, the raven-haired boy twisted his head to stare at Gideon. The absence of animation on his face was unnerving. He was what? Four? Five? For certain he was missing his pa but the watchful stillness wasn't typical of a child that age. Especially a boy.

Gideon found he couldn't look away. Memories burst into his mind. A little girl's giggles as he twirled her up in the air. The sweet scent that clung to her blond curls and skin as she nestled in his lap for a bedtime story.

Surging to his feet, he discarded the now-cold coffee behind the tree and rinsed his mug in the stream, deliberately blanking his mind. He'd spent little time around children in the past year or so. Only natural that the boy's presence would resurrect the past.

Best thing to do is keep your distance. Let the two of them tend to their own business while you focus on yours. It's not like you have extra time on your hands anyway.

"Mr. Thornton?"

He stiffened, turned to see mother and son standing by his stone-encircled fire pit. Beyond them the wagon ambled in the direction of the hastily-constructed town, which so far consisted of a single bank, mercantile, café and jail.

So. This was it. They were well and truly stuck with each other.

"I see you haven't built a cabin." She indicated the undulating fields around her with a sweep of her arm. "Where do you suggest we sleep?"

At odds with her military-like posture and assertive manner, she kept a tight hold on the boy, the white in her knuckles betraying her unease.

"Got a tent somewhere in all that baggage?"

Studying his tent with distaste, she reluctantly admitted, "I'm certain I do."

"You don't know for sure?"

"You don't think I packed every single container myself, do you?"

Noting the sun's lowered position in the sky, he picked up his Stetson and, brushing dust from the black felt, dropped it on his head. "I suggest you start searching, then, Mrs. Montgomery. Only a few more hours left before sunset. Wouldn't want to be caught outdoors overnight without shelter. Coyotes pass through these parts on their way to the Cimarron."

The boy's jaw dropped and his fingers bunched in her black skirts.

"It's all right, Walt," she soothed, all the while shooting daggers at him over the child's head that screamed, *How dare you?* Her silent reproach hit its mark with accuracy.

He'd spoken without a thought to Walt's feelings. That was the first and last time.

He cleared his throat. "But they stay away from the tents because of Lion and Shadow." Pointing to the dogs, he looked Walt in the eye, man-to-man style. "They're my guardians. Now that you're here, they'll watch out for you, too."

Walt tilted his head back and stared at Evelyn. A tender smile curved her lips, the intense love and affection shining in her eyes knocking Gideon back a step. He'd witnessed that look before, the shared unbreakable bond between a mother and her child. He felt the absence of it keenly. An image of two graves side by side with twin handmade crosses tormented him.

As desperately as he craved space, there was something he had to do first.

He bent a knee to the ground. "Lion. Shadow." Immediately the dogs came to stand on either side. Resting his hands on their backs, he addressed the boy. "Would you like to come and meet them?"

Cautious interest bloomed in Walt's dark eyes. Again he looked to his mother but remained silent.

Lightly squeezing his shoulder, she nodded. "It's okay."

Walt slowly approached, his focus on the animals sitting on their haunches and waiting patiently to be introduced.

"Walt, this here is Lion," he said, indicating the yellow-haired one. "He's intelligent and extremely loyal. Shadow is younger and a bit more playful." He patted the shaggy black head. "Hold out your hand and let them smell you first. Then you can pet them all you want."

He did as he was told, gingerly at first. When Shadow licked his fingers, a tiny smile flickered. Gideon's gaze shot to Evelyn. Concern tugged her thick brows together, and she'd pressed her hands together, covering her mouth and nose.

What was going on here? He sensed something deeper

than grief had affected Walt Montgomery. *Mind your own business. Don't get involved. Remain detached.* His formula for avoiding any more pain.

Easing to his feet, he said, "Boys, you stay here with Walt. I've got work to do." Inclining his head a fraction as he passed her, he said, "Mrs. Montgomery."

Striding away, he felt the weight of her scrutiny sizzling the exposed strip of skin above his collar. He wouldn't have a bit of trouble maintaining his distance from the woman. All he had to do was remind himself of her reason for being here. The boy, he feared, was another matter altogether.

"How hard can erecting one tent be?" Evelyn muttered, the pads of her fingers sore from trying to force the too-large buttons through the hand-worked holes along the peak. Hot, sweaty and thirsty, she regretted not accepting Reid's offer of assistance.

Pushing errant strands behind her ears, she observed her son for a moment. Perched on a flat rock beside the stream, he sat between the dogs, his arms slung about their necks. He'd taken off his shoes and socks, rolled his charcoal pants up to his knees and submerged his feet and ankles in the meandering water.

A smile surfaced. If there was one good thing to come out of this dreadful arrangement, this was it—companions for Walt.

When the obtuse Gideon Thornton had goaded her about the coyotes, she'd been livid. The last thing she needed was for her son to entertain nightmares of rabid beasts ripping through their tent and carrying him off into the night. But then the unexpected had happened. He'd realized his blunder and remedied it.

Not that one kind gesture could soften her opinion of him. *Land robber.*

Sighing, longing for the days of honest-to-goodness baths—luxurious soaks in full-length tin basins—she took hold of the nearest stick and maneuvered herself underneath the thick white canvas. Holding the rear of the tent with a hand above her head, she attempted to lodge the makeshift pole into the hard ground. It refused to cooperate. She really needed both hands and perhaps a trowel, but she couldn't do that without the canvas collapsing in on her.

Oppressive heat quickly filled the space. Her itchy bonnet had been discarded an hour ago while rifling through the trunks searching for the tent. Her heavy hair strained the pins holding it in place, which occasionally poked her scalp.

Deciding to let the canvas rest on her shoulders, she curled her fingers around the thick stick and tried jamming it as hard as she could. Unladylike grunts slipped out as she repeated the action. At last it was deep enough. When she successfully angled the pole up to support the top, she sat back with a satisfied sigh.

When it tipped over and the whole thing collapsed in on her, she let out a frustrated yelp. She swatted the material engulfing her.

Suddenly, steel-like vises gripped her shoulders through the canvas. "Hold still."

"Get your hands off me!" Embarrassment flooding her cheeks, she tried to twist out of his grip.

"It'd be a whole lot easier to get off if you'd stop fighting me."

The suffocating feeling intensifying, she stilled, and within seconds the white canvas was pulled away. Welcome sunlight and fresh air washed over her.

"If you'll step over to the side—" Gideon's controlled voice snapped her eyes open "—I'll have this set up in a jiffy."

Crouched a scant yard away, he was on eye level with her, his cool gray eyes sober. Watchful. The fact that he wasn't laughing at her predicament came as a surprise. Her brothers would've laughed and teased her mercilessly. Drake would've lectured, pointing out her lack of forethought and overall incompetence.

A curl tumbled over her forehead and tickled her nose. Lifting a hand to her hair, she belatedly wondered what a tangle with the tent had done to her appearance. Her focus shifted to the left, to the half-built stable and her belongings now strewn about the grass. Her hand mirror was there. Somewhere.

Not that she cared one whit what a Thornton thought about her.

Dislodging the irritating curl, she rose to her feet as gracefully as she could and, shaking out her skirts, stepped over the wadded-up canvas. Her stiff boots chafed her heels. She wished she could join Walt at the stream but there was too much work yet to do.

With her out of the way, Gideon went to work. Beneath faded cotton the same hue as the sky above, his back and shoulder muscles rippled and tensed as he plunged the poles deep into the soil. Every move was calculated. Deliberate. No wasted energy here. Despite his size, he was very much in control of his body.

He intrigued her when she had no business being intrigued. *Enemy, remember?*

With a flick of his wrists, the canvas billowed out and settled over the poles. He then straightened the sides and tied up the door flaps.

He stepped back and surveyed his work. "All finished."

"Thank you." It wasn't easy expressing gratitude to this man.

He looked at her. "Point me to your necessities and I'll bring them over first."

"I don't need any further assistance from you, Mr. Thornton."

Squinting, he studied the horizon, where the sun was dipping closer to the distant plains. "It'd be a shame if you and the boy had to bed down in the grass. Not easy to sleep on an empty stomach, either."

Pursing her lips, she ran a finger beneath her scratchy collar. There was much left to do before nightfall. What was more important in this instance? Heeding her brothers' warnings or seeing to Walt's needs?

Easy choice. "I'll accept your help, Mr. Thornton. This time."

She'd gone five steps when she noticed he wasn't following her. Halting, she twisted around. He hadn't moved. Spine straight, shoulders set and hands at his sides, he watched her with his unnerving gaze.

She quirked a questioning brow.

"It's Gideon."

"Fine. Gideon." She pressed a hand to her bodice, the intricate beadwork digging into her palm. "Evelyn."

His gaze openly roamed her features, probing, as if attempting to unearth answers to puzzling questions. The intense focus made her skin prickle. While she was accustomed to men's appraisals of her appearance, this went deeper. To her mind, her very soul. It made her feel exposed.

Turning her back on him, she marched across the field and, with a scant glance at the handsome horses grazing in the expansive corral, began searching for the trunk containing their bedding. He joined her but did not jump in and start rifling through her things. Instead, he hung back, awaiting her direction. Gideon touched only those things she pointed out to him, and she felt a grudging appreciation for the respect he showed her.

The transfer of personal items, as well as cooking essentials and preserved foods, took half an hour. He did the majority of the work. Evelyn tried her best not to be awed by his effortless strength. Tried and failed.

After checking on Walt, who was now knee-deep in the stream searching for bugs, she shoved her hair out of her eyes and, planting her hands on her hips, confronted Gideon.

"Why are you helping me? What's it to you whether or not we eat? Where we sleep?"

Lowering her portable iron stove to the ground between a small barrel of eggs packed in sawdust and a trunk filled with clothes, he straightened and mirrored her stance, large hands gripping his denim-clad waist. A muscle ticked in his granite jaw.

"What exactly has your family told you about me?"

Refuse to be intimidated. Lifting her chin, she met his smoldering gaze head-on. "I know that right before the war, your father took you and your brothers and, like a coward, fled north in the middle of the night. You betrayed your neighbors, your friends and your state. Indeed, the entire Southern way of life. And yet you prospered, were rewarded for your traitorous actions, while we, despite our loyalty to our traditions, had our home sold out from beneath us by your beloved North."

His nostrils flared. "You keep saying *'you.'* You're forgetting I was a child when the war between the states began and so were you."

He was right. She didn't remember wearing expensive frocks or attending parties. Nor did she recall the grand plantation home where she'd been born. All she'd ever known was the reality of living in crowded quarters with other unfortunate relatives, of sitting down to humble meals and wearing cast-off clothing. Oh, but her parents had regaled her and her brothers with stories of their former life, showing them the single remaining photograph of Rose Hill, describing the plantation in such minute detail that it came alive for her.

Her mother's words echoed through her mind and she spoke them. "The North robbed us. Because of people like you and your father, we lost everything."

"I'm not to blame for your family's misfortune," he bit out.

"You come from a family of traitors." She found herself repeating Theo's often-spouted remarks about the hateful Thorntons. "You're not to be trusted."

"Hogwash."

"I know you're a brawler. I know you broke Theo's nose."

Clouds passed over his face. "I will accept the blame for that."

The minute the Thornton brothers had returned to their defeated Virginia town after the war, the threat of trouble lurked in the shadows, infected conversations and dogged everyone's thoughts. The once-beloved Thorntons had become hated for their escape of the war's repercussions while local families loyal to the South had lost everything. They had betrayed the South and had been handsomely rewarded for it, their ancestral home having been restored to them by the Reconstructionist government. The townsfolk had made it plain they weren't welcome. Two months after their arrival, a brawl had erupted between them and her brothers. While Evelyn hadn't been told the details of the fight, the Thorntons' abrupt departure afterward had told her everything she'd needed to know. As had Theodore's broken nose. They were at fault.

He lifted his chin. "I had trouble controlling my temper when I was younger."

"And you're in total control of it now?"

"No." His face became pinched. "Not entirely."

He was admitting to a fault? "I—"

Walt ran up and tugged on her skirt. Smoothing his ruffled raven locks, she summoned a smile. "What is it, sweetheart?"

He cupped his throat, a signal he'd devised to express thirst. Oh, how she missed hearing his sweet voice. When would he speak again? What if he never— No. She couldn't entertain such a horrific thought.

"You want some water?"

Frowning, he shook his head.

"Milk?"

At his firm nod, she shot Gideon a quick glance. He was observing them with a studied frown, confusion wrinkling his brow.

Self-conscious, she knelt to Walt's level and tried to explain about the milk cow. "We had to leave Mirabelle at Uncle Reid's, remember?"

His frown turned into a scowl. Of course he would miss having milk on hand. Evelyn hadn't had time to think through all the ramifications of this move. Now she worried his health might suffer if their case didn't come to trial in a timely manner. *Please, Lord, don't allow this situation to stretch on interminably. I can't abide this man. Not after what he did to Drake and what he's trying to do to us.*

Gideon's measured voice broke the silence. "There are wild strawberries on the other side of the stream. Maybe he'd like to pick some."

Irrationally perturbed at his intrusion and that the solution was a good one, she watched Walt's somber expression change to one of eager anticipation.

"I'll get you a container to put them in." Straightening, she sent Gideon a "good riddance" look. "Thank you again for your help. I can take it from here."

"Of course." Touching the brim of his hat, he gave her a stiff nod and strode off, leaving her to her work. She breathed easier after he'd gone.

Chapter Three

"They accused you of *what?*" Above the pewter mug suspended halfway to his mouth, the gold flecks in Clint's brown eyes shimmered with disbelief.

Cradling his mug of steaming coffee, Elijah leaned back in his chair and sighed. "This shouldn't come as a surprise. We're all aware of the Chaucers' opinion of us." He looked across the table at Gideon. "I'm just sorry that coming to a man's aid has placed you in this position."

Gideon traced lazy circles on the coarse tabletop. Even if he could've foreseen the outcome, he wouldn't have left Montgomery to die. His brothers knew that. Still, the situation he found himself in rankled.

Despite his fatigue, he'd passed a restless night, his mind on the occupants of the tent a quarter acre upstream. Visible yet far enough away he couldn't hear their conversations. *They don't have conversations, though, do they?* Not for the first time, he pondered the boy's continuing silence.

"We don't know much about Evelyn Montgomery. Is she as disagreeable as her brothers?" Clint asked.

His brother's appointment as sheriff of Brave Rock had become more than just a job. It had become a call-

ing, an honorable mission to maintain the peace of this
Oklahoma town birthed from dreams of independence
and the grit and determination to see them into reality.
With a keen, observant mind and commitment to uphold-
ing the law, he was the best man for it.

"Evelyn—" her given name sounded odd on his lips
"—can be difficult."

"Which is another word for stubborn, like some people I know." A knowing grin hovered about Lije's mouth.

"Contrary is a better word," Gideon shot back, thinking of her resistance to his every attempt to make life
easier for her. Why he even tried he hadn't a clue. "She's
good with her son, though. Protective." The immense
love she possessed for him was evident in every look,
every touch.

Seated across the table in Lije's cabin, his brothers
exchanged a quick, telling glance. He knew by Clint's
cautious expression and the sympathy in Lije's hazel eyes
they were thinking of Susannah and Maggie.

"You have my constant prayers, brother. In time, God
will sort this out the way He sees fit."

Gideon pressed his lips together, cutting off the stinging retort. As a preacher, Lije centered his whole life
around the things of God. Comforting folks, praying
for them and encouraging them in difficult times came
as second nature to the eldest Thornton brother. Gideon
wanted no part of it. Not anymore. The grief stemming
from the loss of his wife and daughter had transformed
into resentment and anger at the all-powerful God he'd
once served.

He could've spared them and yet chose not to. Every
time he felt the urge to pray or dust off his Bible, he reminded himself of that fact.

Pushing to his feet, he set his cup in the dry sink behind him and crossed to the door, retrieving his hat from the row of hooks. "I've gotta go. Got errands in town to tend to."

Lije stood, as well. "And I have to meet the work crew. We're framing the chapel windows this morning."

Work on the official Brave Rock church—which would also be used as a meeting house—had commenced a couple days ago on the western edge of Lije's claim closest to town. Residents were working in shifts so that everyone shared the load and families weren't taken from their planting and the building of their own cabins for very long.

"I can spare a few hours this afternoon," Gideon told Elijah.

The preacher's jaw dropped. "You're offering to work on the church?"

Aware of Gideon's aversion to spiritual matters, his brother hadn't asked him to pitch in. But Lije worked his fingers to the bone seeing to the needs of this town. Swinging a hammer for a few hours was the least Gideon could do. Besides, it would gain him a reprieve from the feisty widow Montgomery.

"I am. Unless you don't need me."

Clint watched the exchange with interest.

Lije picked up his jaw. "Oh, we need you, little brother." Clapping a hand on Gideon's shoulder, he grinned big. "What time should we expect you?"

"Around one o'clock. How's that?"

"Perfect. The men will be returning from lunch then."

Gideon opened the door.

"Hold up a second."

Clint shoved his chair back. The gold star pinned to his vest winked in the morning sunlight streaming through the curtainless window. The last shingle of Lije's one-room cabin had been nailed into place last week, and it lacked those little touches that made a dwelling into a home. Wouldn't be this way for long, however. He'd seen Alice hemming blue-and-white-checked curtains in preparation for her and Lije's upcoming nuptials. If the bouquet of daffodils gracing the table—the only spot of color in the room—was any indication, the sweet-natured redhead would have these sparse quarters looking more like a home in no time.

"You should know we've had more trouble," Clint said. "The Ramseys' barn burned down last night. It was a total loss."

Lije's expression turned grave. "There weren't any fatalities, thank the good Lord."

Gideon shook his head in disgust. "Did they get all the animals out?"

"All but a milk cow," Clint supplied. "They were fortunate."

"Any idea how it started?"

"Not yet. Lars and I are looking into it." His younger brother's features hardened. "If it turns out it wasn't an accident, we'll find out who the perpetrators are and go after them."

"These incidents are stirring up suspicion amongst the townsfolk, which is the last thing we need." Sighing, Lije wearily massaged his neck. If Gideon knew his brother, he'd probably stayed up half the night tending to the Ramsey family's needs. "Without unity and a sense of brotherhood, what kind of town will Brave Rock be?"

Not a place any decent folk would want to live, Gideon answered silently. If he were still a praying man, he'd ask God for assistance. Since he wasn't, he'd just have to trust Clint's prediction. The troublemakers would make a mistake eventually, which would lead to their arrest and, ultimately, peace for Brave Rock's residents. Hopefully sooner rather than later, before someone got hurt or outright killed.

"Hold him steady. I'm almost done." Evelyn's pencil scraped across the page in light strokes. "I think this one is some type of earless lizard. We'll look it up tonight before bed."

Fortunately, she knew exactly which trunk contained their books. Drake had argued against bringing them out here, saying she wouldn't have time for such unnecessary luxuries, but she'd been adamant. Walt enjoyed studying the pictures in the encyclopedia and almanac. And she wouldn't dream of leaving her journals behind. They contained drawings and descriptions of all sorts of things—Rose Hill, their church in Virginia, flowers, butterflies and birds she'd encountered—a pictorial history of her life. Of course, Drake hadn't seen any value in them.

"Done." She snapped the book closed.

Walt raised the bluish-gray-and-black lizard closer to his face, ran a finger along its spindly spine and gingerly set it on the sloping bank, watching intently as it scurried behind the rocks. Shrugging, he turned to her. Red ringed his mouth, evidence of the berries he'd eaten for dessert. She picked up the basin of dirty dishes and carried it to the stream. Crouching beside him, she dipped a rag in the cool water. "Let's clean your face, sweetheart. It's a wonder you didn't get a tummy ache from all those strawberries."

Wearing a long-suffering expression, he stood still and let her work. Affection bubbled up in her. He was so beautiful, her little boy. His olive skin, dark, expressive eyes and distinctive features had been handed down from his Russian grandmother, Nancy Petrov Chaucer, just as they had been to Evelyn and her brothers. There wasn't a single sign of his Montgomery heritage. Was that the reason Drake hadn't bonded with him?

Sighing, she kissed his cheek, which he rewarded with a tight hug. When he stiffened against her, she leaned back. His eyes were huge. "What's wrong?"

Twisting, balancing her weight with a splayed hand in the grass, she spotted Gideon's wagon slowly approaching. There, trailing behind it, was a Guernsey cow much like the one they'd left at Reid's. That wasn't Mirabelle, however.

Taking Walt's hand, she stood and watched as the aloof cowboy eased his team to a stop in front of the stable. After setting the brake, he climbed down and, striding to the cow, untethered her and led her across the field in their direction. *What in the world?*

The brim of his black Stetson cast his eyes in shadow; his stubble-covered jaw and chin were set in grim lines. As if she exuded a foul stench, he stopped a ways out, his mouth unsmiling. Gloved hands gripping the lines, he extended them to her.

"This is Petra."

"That's a Russian name."

A sigh lifted his vest-clad chest. "Bought her from a Russian family."

"There are Russians here?" During their stay in Boomer Town, the tent city that had sprung up along the border of Unassigned Lands in the weeks preceding the land rush, she'd encountered Poles and Czechs but no Russians. "My mother came to America when she was a little girl. She taught me the language. What are their names?"

"Kozlov."

"Where is their claim? Can you take me?" Excitement shimmered through her. Her brothers hadn't cared to learn the language. She'd enjoy conversing with native speakers again.

He gave her a long measuring look. "I reckon I could do that."

"Forget I asked." *What's gotten into you, Evelyn? To willingly accompany this man anywhere would be unthinkable.* "I'll locate them on my own."

Jerking a thumb over his shoulder, he said, "I've got supplies to unload. Can you take her now?" Again he lifted the leads.

"What do you expect *me* to do with her?"

"Take care of her. She's your milk cow, after all."

"Mine?" Her gaze volleyed between the cowboy and the russet-hued beast. "I don't understand. Did my brothers—"

"They have nothing to do with this." He shoved up his brim, revealing those piercing wolf's eyes, a turbulent, stormy gray. "Your son needs milk."

As if that were enough justification for a gesture such as this. "You can't mean to tell me that you purchased Petra for us?"

Gideon's gaze flickered to Walt, and his face altered. *Pain-ravaged* was the best word to describe him. Tormented. Jaw working, he dragged his attention back to her.

"For Walt."

Dazed by what she'd seen, Evelyn took halting steps forward. He veered back, maintaining distance as he transferred the leads to her. Then he left.

Evelyn stared after him. A thousand bewildered questions skated through her mind with no clear-cut answers.

Petra shifted, straining to reach the grass. A milk cow. Gideon Thornton had brought them a milk cow. He'd become aware of their need and met it, no questions asked, no payment demanded.

Something was very wrong here.

"Can't you see what he's doing?" Reid paced a trail in the grass, his gestures stiff and jerky, while she scrubbed her single black dress in the wash basin. "He's obviously trying to make you think he's one of the good guys, someone to be trusted."

Evelyn paused, soap bar resting against the ridged washboard, and gazed at Petra grazing contently in the field, then at Gideon heaving another log into place. Even from this distance, the man's impressive strength was on display. His biceps had to be as large as small tree trunks! "Why would he care what I think?"

Her brother shot her a dubious look. "Please tell me you're not really that naive. What do you have that he wants?"

The name on the stake. "Rightful ownership of this claim."

"Exactly." He snapped his fingers.

"Let me get this straight. You think he bought the cow not as an act of kindness but as a bribe. He's going to try and convince me not to contest the claim."

"That's right."

Resuming her task, she mopped her forehead with her sleeve. "Doesn't sound like something he'd do."

"Oh, what, now that you've spent a whole day in his company you know what kind of person he is?"

"No, of course not. It just doesn't seem like he'd put forth that kind of energy on a plan that isn't foolproof. He's rather busy, if you can't tell."

Glancing toward the stable, Reid smirked. "Yeah, well, his single-mindedness will only benefit us. When all is said and done, that will be *your* stable, sis. Yours and Walt's. It'll save us from having to build it later."

Her gaze once again drawn to the taciturn middle Thornton brother, she experienced a pinprick of disquiet. How would she feel if she'd worked that hard on something only to have to leave it behind?

"Oh, no, you don't." Her twin was suddenly squatting in front of her, his coffee-colored eyes boring into hers. His ivory felt hat sat at a rakish angle on his head. "Don't feel sorry for the guy. He doesn't deserve your compassion, Evelyn. Remember, he's trying to steal Walt's inheritance. He's taking advantage of a widow and her fatherless child."

She disliked it when Reid read her mind like that. Some things a girl preferred to keep private. Lifting her chin, she met him stare for stare. "I could never forget that."

Studying her with narrowed eyes, he finally nodded, then frowned again at her navy blue skirt and white scoop-necked blouse. No doubt he disapproved of her not wearing proper mourning clothes.

"Before you say it, I own only one appropriate outfit." She lifted the long-sleeved, too-elegant-for-everyday-use black blouse out of the sudsy water. Aware of Evelyn's scant wardrobe, her mother-in-law had made her several outfits to wear to church services. Not a fan of black, she'd rarely worn this particular one. "I have to wash it sometime. Besides, it shouldn't matter what I wear out here when there's no one around to see."

Again, a long, slow perusal. "Evelyn, I—" Frowning, he stared at the ground beneath his dusty boots. "I've wanted to ask you about Drake ever since..." Cautious eyes met hers. "Look, the accident shocked us all. I know you have a huge burden to shoulder. Walt's silence adds to that, I'm sure, but I'm worried about you. We all are."

Laying the soap aside, she rinsed the material and wrung out the excess water. "There's no need to worry. I assure you I'm fine."

For her brothers' sakes, she'd tried her best to hide her unhappy marital state. After all, Theo had introduced her to Drake Montgomery, and all three brothers had encouraged her to accept his proposal. If they'd discovered the true state of affairs between her and her husband, they would've blamed themselves. And perhaps intervened, which could have ended in violence. So she'd playacted.

Reid followed her to the rope she'd strung up between two oaks. "That's the problem. A woman who's just lost her husband should not be fine."

"Everyone grieves differently." Hooking the clothespins in place, she checked to see that Walt was still cavorting with Lion and Shadow along the stream bank. "Besides, I've a lot to keep me busy these days. There isn't time to dwell on our loss."

"You were inconsolable after Ma and Pa died," he pointed out, following her back to the pile of laundry awaiting her attention.

"That was different."

"Evelyn—"

"Reid." Holding up a hand, she shot him a quelling look. "No more. Please."

He opened his mouth to speak, shook his head and snapped it shut again. As she bent to her task, relief speared through her. Her brother could be relentless. Somehow she doubted this was the last time she'd hear of this.

"I'd better go."

"Thanks for the rabbits. I'll make a nice stew for supper."

"That's nice."

Hearing the note of distraction in his voice, she looked up and caught him staring in Gideon's direction, a troublesome glint in his eyes.

Popping up, she slipped her arm through his. "I'll walk you to your horse."

Unfortunately, they had to walk past the stable to where Rusty was tethered to the corral fence. Just as they came abreast of the door opening, Gideon emerged and bumped into Reid.

"Sorry," Gideon muttered.

Shaking free of her hold, Reid sidestepped to block his exit. "Why don't you watch where you're going, Thornton?"

"It was an accident," he clipped out, holding himself erect. Aloof. "No need to make more of it than it is."

Although about the same height, Gideon had at least forty pounds of solid muscle on her brother. The outcome of an altercation between the two men wasn't difficult to envision.

Reid poked a finger in Gideon's chest. "Nice try with the milk cow. But I'm wise to your schemes, and so is Evelyn. Don't think you can charm your way into keeping what doesn't belong to you."

Gideon's head reared back. His icy gaze slammed into her, silently accusing. "My motivation had nothing to do with the dispute."

Was he speaking the truth? Or was he just a clever actor?

Aware of the ratcheting tension, Evelyn tugged on her brother's forearm. "Reid, please. Let it go."

"Steer clear of my sister and nephew, you filthy cur."

Color climbed up Gideon's neck. His massive hands curling into fists, he stuck his face close to Reid's. "Or what?"

Oh, no. Gideon's legendary temper was about to be unleashed.

"Oh, you'll find out what," Reid sneered.

"I don't cotton to threats, especially from a man who's trespassing on my land."

"Why, you—"

"Don't do this." Evelyn hauled on Reid's arm with all her might but couldn't budge him. "Think of Walt."

Beneath her fingertips, she felt his thick muscle quiver, and she thought Reid would shake her off again. He surprised her, however. With a parting promise that this conversation wasn't finished, he guided her to the corral. A sigh gusted from her lungs. Crisis averted.

This time. What will happen the next time your brothers come to check on you? What if she couldn't talk them down? Theo, Brett and Reid loathed the Thornton brothers. Now that Gideon stood in the way of her inheritance, the state of affairs would only deteriorate.

Someone was likely to get hurt, which would only serve to traumatize Walt further.

No matter what, she couldn't let that happen.

Chapter Four

"I want a word with you."

Gideon gritted his teeth as he walked along the stream. Why couldn't the Montgomery woman leave him alone? Didn't she have the common sense to know not to provoke a riled beast? The rage coursing through his body made him feel more beast than human. This lightning-quick temper was a curse that had originated in childhood, about the time his father dumped him and his brothers at Cousin Obadiah's, went off to fight for the North and never returned. With God's help he'd learned to control it. There'd been exceptions, of course, like the time he broke Theo Chaucer's nose.

Lately, that control was slipping more often. Despite his antipathy toward the Lord, he recognized he wasn't strong enough to master it by relying on his own strength.

He glided his hat along the surface of the water, scooping a fair amount into the crown. Then he upturned it over his head, the cool liquid shocking the anger out of his system. Slowly rising, he turned and climbed the gently sloping bank to where she stood waiting beneath the cottonwood branches, her black boot tapping out an impatient rhythm. Her molten-molasses gaze accused him of all sorts of ills. *May as well get this over with.*

"I'm listening."

"You almost lost it just now, didn't you? I could tell you wanted to plant your fist in my brother's face. Well, I'm warning you right now I won't stand for violence. Not in front of my son."

Shame flooded him. Not once had he lost his temper in front of a woman. Not even his wife. Whenever he and Susannah had quarreled, he'd gone off alone to sort through his feelings. He wouldn't dream of doing so in front of a child.

"I won't do anything to worry Walt. You have my word."

One thick brow arched in disbelief. "According to my brothers, that's not worth much."

The nerve of her. Spine rigid, Gideon turned his back on her as his ire stirred anew. He'd taken quite enough from this mouthy female. She'd questioned his honor at every turn.

Like a dog worrying a bone, she darted around him, forcing him to hear her out. "Until our case goes to court, my brothers will be coming out here regularly to check on us. How can I trust you won't resort to violence?"

"Maybe you should revisit what just happened here. It's your brother you should be lecturing, not me."

She batted at a stray curl that had escaped the pins holding her shiny locks in place. She wasn't wearing mourning black, he noted. The pure white blouse lit her skin with a healthy glow, accentuating her waist where it tucked into her billowing navy skirt.

"Look, I know you don't give a fig about me or my family. I know that we're on opposite sides of a feud that began many, many years ago, and when it comes to this land, we both want it for ourselves. But I'm begging you—" her husky voice wavered as she flung a hand toward the field where her son played "—have compassion on that little boy out there. He's been through a lot in his short lifetime, more than any child should have to endure. All I want is for him to be happy and free of worry."

The sheen of tears in her expressive eyes startled him. This was the first sign of vulnerable emotion he'd glimpsed in the fierce widow. Walt had recently lost his father. To what else was she referring?

He opened his mouth to question her, recalling in the nick of time that it wasn't his concern. Their past was their business, not his. Soon they would be out of his hair. An unfortunate reminder of a troublesome time.

Anxiety pinched her features.

As a father, he had no trouble identifying with what she was feeling. Good parents desired the best for their children, instinctively strove to protect and nurture.

Attempting to soothe her unease, he spoke quietly and surely, injected confidence in his stance. "The boy has nothing to do with our troubles. I won't do anything to traumatize him."

Lips compressing, she studied him, gauging his sincerity. Finally, she nodded.

"I will warn you, however. I won't stand idly by if provoked beyond reason. I will defend myself. I suggest you make sure your brothers understand that."

Spinning on his heel, he left her there with her mouth hanging open. He mentally shrugged. Wasn't his fault if she caught a fly.

Gideon stirred awake to the sound of the stream trickling past on its course to the Cimarron River. The tent stretching above him was washed in orangey-pink, evi-

dence of dawn's arrival. Woodpeckers scouted for breakfast in the elms stationed midway between his tent and
the stable, and a frog chirruped a throaty greeting.

Easing to a sitting position, he leaned forward and
parted the tent flaps to soak in the prairie's serene beauty.
Buttery light gilded each individual blade of grass, every
wildflower tilting its face eastward, every glossy leaf
dangling from the trees, so that it seemed to him a vista
of pure golden goodness. He'd grown accustomed to this.
The thought of leaving it—and the dreams it nursed like
a greedy infant—made his insides seize up something
terrible.

There was nothing else to do but continue his work
and, when the time came, present his case and attempt
to convince the judge of his rightful ownership.

Dressing quickly in denims and a blue-and-white-
striped shirt, he straightened his pallet and pillow and
retrieved the bulging laundry sack from the corner.
These were his last pair of clean trousers, which meant
he couldn't put off a trip into town any longer. He tried
to space them out as much as possible. In general, people
drained the life out of him. Their nosiness and frivolous
chatter gave him a headache. He was an oddity, he knew.
A lone wolf who craved solitude and space to think. *Does
not get along with others,* his teacher had once observed
to his ward, Cousin Obadiah. *Possesses a superior attitude.* Gideon grimaced. That had earned him twenty
lashes and a week of bread and water for supper.

Elijah and Clint were the only ones who really understood him. They accepted him. Didn't try to change
him like Susannah—

Shoving to his feet, he strode to the stream and
splashed his face and neck and wet his collar-length hair.

Tying on a neckerchief, his fingers brushed the scruff on the underside of his chin. Time for a shave and haircut.

As he stirred the fire and set the scuffed tin pot to boil, he kept a watchful eye on the other tent, hoping she'd prove to be a late riser. Conversation anytime was a stretch. Before breakfast bordered on criminal. What was more, he couldn't fudge his way through. Evelyn Montgomery required all the focus and concentration he could muster.

Low on provisions, he made due with corn mush that was about as tasteless as tree bark but filled his belly. He carried his coffee with him to the stable, stopping to greet Star and Snowball, a three-year-old gray he'd bought shortly after his arrival in Boomer Town. Their friendly greetings never failed to soothe him. Horses didn't judge him or push him to be something he wasn't. He understood animals better than he did most people. Actually preferred their company, if truth be told.

Star nudged his shoulder.

"Searching for treats, huh?" he ran a hand through her mane. "You're outta luck. But I'll see if I can't scrounge up a carrot or two in town. How about that?"

She dipped her head, seeming to agree with him. A fleeting smile lifted his lips.

"Gotta go." He pushed away from the fence. "The faster I get this stable up, the sooner you'll have a roof over your heads."

Inside the structure, he surveyed his progress. The walls reached his waist. Since he couldn't physically lift the logs any higher without help, he'd have to rig a pulley system.

The sound of feet shuffling in the dirt behind him had him spinning about, hot coffee sloshing over the mug's rim. His heart settled back into a somewhat normal rhythm when he spied his pint-size visitor.

"Walt."

The boy hovered just inside the opening, his hands twisting behind his back, large, dark eyes surveying the interior with interest. His shirt buttons were off-center, the wrinkled hems uneven, and his wavy hair hadn't yet seen a comb this day.

Gideon searched the field beyond the opening, suddenly desperate for Evelyn's presence. He did not want to be here alone with a walking reminder of his dead child.

"Where's your ma?" he croaked, throat muddy with trepidation.

Pointless question. He hadn't heard Walt Montgomery emit a squeak, let alone an intelligible response. Not that the child was slow-witted. Far from it. Intelligence shone in those Chaucer eyes.

He pointed a chubby finger in the tent's direction.

"Is she making breakfast?"

Walt shook his head, folded his hands and pressed them against his cheek.

"She's still asleep?"

When he nodded and wandered over to the neat piles of tack—saddles, blankets, bridles and more—Gideon tamped down panic. "Uh, maybe you should go back to your tent. Your ma will worry if she wakes and finds you gone."

The little boy ignored his suggestion, touching a hesitant finger to this item and that, bending at the knees, peering closer. Inquisitive as well as intelligent.

And without a father. Just as Gideon had been at that age.

Drake Montgomery's image resurfaced in his mind. Gideon could clearly recall the expression of hatred, of reckless resolve that drove him to push himself and his mount beyond their limits. He could still hear the frantic pleas for help as he lay writhing in pain. What kind of man had he been? What kind of husband? Father?

Taking another swallow of the bitter coffee, Gideon dislodged the misplaced curiosity. Not his business, remember?

Still standing in the same spot, he watched as Walt drifted over to the corner where the building tools were stacked. He picked up a hammer, tentatively testing its weight. When the boy lifted a beseeching gaze to him, Gideon was hurtled backward in time, to before the war that divided the nation and ripped his father from him, to a time when things were simple and good. His father had taught him how to pound nails into wood. How proud Gideon had been to be his helper.

Spurred by poignant memories, he set the mug on the ground and, retrieving a discarded wood round, located the box of nails. He could spare a few minutes for a lonely little boy, even if it meant resurrecting pain that would devour him from the inside out if he let it.

Evelyn woke with the distinct feeling that something was off. But what? She lay motionless for a long moment, not breathing, trying to pinpoint the source of her unease. *Breathing.* Walt's soft breathing wasn't filling the tent's cramped interior. The absence of it aroused all sorts of dire imaginings.

Bolting upright, she called his name, lifting the blue-and-yellow-swirled quilt even though it was obvious he wasn't here.

She shoved her arms into the thin cotton housecoat, tugged on her boots without bothering to lace them. Stumbling outside, she searched both sides of the stream.

The fields were empty. Tethered to the nearest tree, Petra turned her head and let out a welcoming bawl.

"Walt?"

Where could he be? Surely not with Gideon. To a shy kid like him, the man must seem like a giant. A big, brawny, intimidating giant. Clutching her housecoat lapels, she strode across the field, dewdrops wiping away yesterday's dust from her boots.

The steel-swathed-in-velvet voice slowed her steps. Patience marked Gideon's words as he explained the safest way to wield a hammer. Amazing how soothing and, yes, even pleasant, he could sound when he wasn't defensive or tense or angry as he was around her.

Edging to the doorway, she caught sight of man and boy crouched close together. Walt had a tight grip on the handle, a look of intense concentration on his face, lower lip tucked in tight. The cowboy's capable-looking hands gently covered his, mimicking the movements.

Oh, Walt. Evelyn's throat constricted. Anyone could see he was soaking up the attention.

She must've made a sound, because Gideon's head whipped up, the force of his gray gaze slamming into her. While his voice and expression were easy, his eyes told a different story. Misery was reflected there. Desolation. Whatever had happened to this man had come close to destroying him, had robbed him of hope and life and trust.

Blinking, he severed eye contact, then dipped his head. "Look who's here."

Walt's blinding grin sidetracked her train of thought. How long had it been since he'd been this animated? Silently animated, she amended, drawn farther into the sunny space. This time when Gideon looked at her, his eyes were clear of turmoil as they did a slow inspection of her hair, her clothing and her unlaced boots.

Heat traveled to her cheeks. They were practically strangers, and here she was in her nightclothes, her hair arranged in a haphazard, sleep-tousled braid.

Tightly bunching the material at her neck, she held out her hand to her son. "Let's leave Mr. Thornton to his work, sweetheart."

This suggestion did not sit well with Walt, who jutted his chin at a stubborn angle.

"I don't mind if he stays a little longer," Gideon said, surprising her. "We're not quite finished with our lesson."

Finished or not, Evelyn had to stamp out the adoration taking root in Walt's eyes. He could not be allowed to become attached to her family's sworn enemy.

"You'll have to finish it later."

Pushing to his feet, Gideon approached, a defensive slope to his broad shoulders. "What's the problem, Evelyn?" He spoke quietly. "Surely you don't believe a few minutes in my company will sully your son?"

She fought the urge to take a step back. He was too close, his manly scent—a combination of campfire and leather—luring her closer. The wide, solid planes of his chest looked like the perfect place of refuge, a place to rest her head and, for a brief moment, give up control. Lean on someone else's strength. The sweetness of that prospect had her swaying toward him.

His sleek brows furrowed in response.

"I—" She scrambled for something sensible to say, stunned at herself. Gideon Thornton was the last person on earth she should be seeking support from.

Liar. Thief. Adversary.

Gentle. Patient. Kind.

Before she could unravel her thoughts, he clamped his

jaw. "No need to say anything else. Your opinion of me is quite clear." He motioned for Walt. "Breakfast time, kiddo. Go help your ma."

The joy leached from Walt's face. Small shoulders drooping, he trudged across the dirt floor. Indecision knotted her insides. Was she wrong to interrupt? Of course she didn't actually think Gideon posed a threat to her son, but a lifetime of warnings could not easily be brushed aside.

Hunkering down to Walt's level, she took his hand and caressed a thumb over his soft skin. "How would you like to help me make flapjacks?"

He kicked up a shoulder. Dug the rounded toe of his boot in the reddish dirt.

"I found our crock of maple syrup. That would taste good on top, don't you think?"

He nodded, but no smile appeared. He didn't want to leave Gideon. Swallowing a sigh, she shot the cowboy a parting look, which he missed because he'd already turned away to tidy up the space. Judging from his ruler-straight spine and careful movements, he wasn't any happier than Walt was.

On the walk back to the campsite, one disconcerting question drummed through her mind. How could someone so distasteful, so despicable—according to her brothers—treat her son better than his own father had?

Even if her husband were around to defend himself, he wouldn't see the need to answer to her or anyone else. Drake had been the center of his own universe. His goals and his comforts were all that had mattered. Whenever she'd asked him to pay more attention to their son, he'd shrugged her off. *A toddler isn't worth my time. When he's old enough to understand grown-up stuff, then I'll take him under my wing.* Infuriating, foolish man. He died not knowing the treasure he'd rejected.

Sitting on a low stool at Petra's side, she situated Walt between her knees and showed him how to direct the milk into the pail at their feet. His initial hesitation gradually faded, and when the cow's tail swished against his ear, he giggled. The carefree laughter, like a bubbling spring, made her yearn for more. To hear him say "Mama" and "I love you." To hear him sing again in his pure, lighter-than-air voice.

Theo had warned her not to push him, and she'd taken his advice. It hadn't been easy. Living with this unnatural silence, wondering if he'd ever speak again, had filled her with troubling anger. This was Drake's fault. She wanted to rant and rave and vent her frustration at a dead man. What did that say about her as a person?

"All done," she said, masking the unpleasantness boiling inside. "Good job, sweetie. Now let's go make flapjacks. I'm hungry as a bear, aren't you?"

By the time the fluffy cakes were stacked in trenchers with a hefty slathering of syrup, Walt's earlier unhappiness was forgotten. He dug into the meal with gusto. With logs for seats and no table to speak of, they ate with the trenchers in their laps, the great outdoors their dining room. Couldn't ask for a nicer view. The birds whistling overhead and the rush of water were nice touches. However, she could do without the pesky flies.

Her gaze drifted to the stable, where Gideon had his head bent to an unknown task. He hadn't worked on the walls so far this morning, despite the fact there was a pile of logs behind the structure ready for use. Unusual that he'd chosen to erect the animals' shelter before his own. If his cabin had already been built, would he have given up his living quarters for them? Not for her, but for Walt? The question was an unnecessary one but interesting. If not for his purchase of Petra, she would've said outright that Gideon Thornton giving up his home for the likes of her was about as likely as a wolf giving up his prey. Now she wasn't so sure.

Chapter Five

Gideon was in the middle of assembling the pulley system when an unexpected sound mingled with the birdsong, swelling above the horses' nickers and the breeze rippling through the high grass. Evelyn. Singing. Her smoky voice belted out a lively tune, one he didn't recognize, in a language he didn't understand. Her playful tone told him this was a happy song, maybe even a silly one.

Unable to resist a peek, he set aside the rope coil and wheel and, standing, went to lean against the half wall. At the stream cleaning their breakfast dishes, she serenaded the boy in an attempt to draw him out. And although Walt smiled and bobbed his head, he didn't join in.

Yearning for what he could never have captured him in its torturous grip, and he wished them far from there. Resentment curdled his stomach. Why did they have to intrude upon his much-needed solitude?

"I see you have company," an accented voice said from the doorway.

Gideon half turned, not surprised his friend had managed to approach without his realizing it. Lars Brinkerhoff might have been Danish by birth, but his years with the Cheyenne had molded him into an adept hunter and trapper, able to blend in with his surroundings.

"You spoke to Elijah and Clint, I take it."

"*Ja,* that I did." The big Dane nodded, cornflower-blue eyes bright with concern in his tanned face. "I am sorry to hear about this complication."

Lars joined him at the wall, his arms poised along the roughened edge. He tipped his head in Evelyn's direction. "Beautiful song."

Gideon didn't comment.

"Is the widow Russian?"

"Her ancestors are." He dragged his gaze from her animated form to the man at his side. "Do you understand what she's saying?"

"She is singing about a cat and mouse who, though natural enemies, have become the best of friends."

Enemies who became friends. He'd been right. It was a ridiculous song.

"Any news on the cause of the Ramsey fire?" He sought to get his mind off the intriguing widow and onto more neutral matters.

Lars frowned deeply. "Clint and I sifted through the debris and found a kerosene container. Someone set that fire, no doubt about that."

It was beginning to look as if the recent string of accidents weren't accidents at all. They must be connected somehow. "Who would do this and why?"

His friend's beefy hand settled heavily on his shoulder. "We are going to get to the bottom of this mystery. In the meantime, be on your guard. We have not been able to establish a pattern, which means any one of us is a potential target."

Gideon ground his back teeth together. His future was

already being threatened by Mrs. Evelyn Montgomery. Now he had an unknown menace to worry about?

"There is nothing to be done in this moment, but there is plenty we can do about your animals' shelter. Winona is not expecting me for her language lesson until midafternoon. I will help you, but first, why not introduce me to your land mate?"

Land mate? While Lars's English was very good, he had a funny way of phrasing things.

"Let's get this over with," he muttered, leading the way to her tent site.

The dishes already cleaned and put away, she was now reciting the alphabet. As they drew closer, he saw that Walt was tracing letters in the dirt with a stick.

Evelyn lifted her head, her eyes going wide at the sight of his companion. He recalled his first impression of Lars, who, with his shoulder-length blond hair, fringed buckskin clothing and moccasin-style boots, looked like no one he'd ever seen.

Swiftly rising, she stepped in front of her son, blocking him from view. The protective lioness guarding her cub.

"Evelyn, this is Lars Brinkerhoff, a good friend of mine." His *only* friend in Brave Rock, as Gideon wasn't one to seek out relationships. From their first meeting shortly after their arrival in this unsettled slice of Oklahoma territory, Lars had gone out of his way to strike up a friendship. "Lars, meet Mrs. Evelyn Chaucer Montgomery."

He wasn't sure why he'd inserted her maiden name. His brothers would've told Lars about her connection to the Chaucer men, who'd made it their mission to poison the townsfolk's minds against them.

The Dane extended his hand. Evelyn reluctantly allowed hers to be swallowed by his oversize grip, apprehension snaking across her features. Of course she would be uncertain. She was a woman alone with her enemy and his friend.

"Pleasure to meet you, Mrs. Montgomery."

Her dark eyes shot to Gideon. The flash of vulnerability made him want to reassure her that she had nothing to fear. A pointless exercise, since she insisted on suspecting him of nefarious motives.

"Lars and his sister, Katrine, came over from Denmark ten years ago. They attend Elijah's church."

"'Tis true." The blond smiled broadly and, still clasping her hand, patted it reassuringly. "We would be honored if you and your little one would join us for services."

"I—I appreciate the invitation." Evelyn tugged her hand free. "I'll give it some thought."

Lars addressed him. "Gideon, you must promise to accompany Mrs. Montgomery if she wishes to attend."

He scowled. The Dane knew perfectly well Gideon hadn't once stepped foot in Lije's tent chapel. How could he, when doing so would only prod to life the latent rage inside him? God could've spared his daughter. That He hadn't still hurt so deeply Gideon couldn't even begin to process it. Instead, he boxed up his feelings and locked them up tight, hidden from the daylight, left to fester and spoil in the black caverns of his soul.

A suspicion wormed its way into his thoughts. Evelyn Montgomery was a beautiful woman, an exotic orchid among commonplace daisies. And she was available. Could Lars be interested in her?

So what if he is? A marriage between the two would solve your problem. She wouldn't be after *his* land anymore.

But what about Winona Eaglefeather? When the

Cheyenne woman came to Brave Rock in search of her runaway nephew, Dakota, Lars was able to communicate with her and help her locate the boy. And now that she and Dakota had decided to stay, he was teaching her English. To anyone watching the two adults interact, it was clear they'd grown close. Gideon got the impression his friend possessed deep feelings for the Native American beauty, but their differences held him back.

"Gideon?" Lars prompted, expression expectant.

Do the right thing.

"I suppose I could. If she makes up her mind to attend."

While Lars smiled with satisfaction and Evelyn stared as if he'd suggested something scandalous, Gideon wanted to call the words back. What in the world had possessed him to agree? He absolutely could not go. If Evelyn surprised him by agreeing to Lars's invitation, he'd deliver her to the church and wait outside to escort her home.

He knew his continued absence bothered Elijah, and he hated to cause him grief. But he couldn't go for his brother. And he certainly wouldn't go for her.

Evelyn handed the frog back to Walt with a distracted smile. She'd joined him in the stream while the rabbit stew she'd prepared for lunch simmered over hot coals. The cool water washing over her feet and ankles felt delicious in this sweltering heat. Modesty wasn't an issue since Gideon and his unusual friend were engrossed in their work half a field away. Besides, she didn't care what they thought about her.

Glancing over her shoulder, she caught sight of Mr. Brinkerhoff mounting his horse and lifting a hand in wordless goodbye. They'd accomplished a lot in a short amount of time. The stable walls now reached Gideon's shoulders.

Leaving the water, she quickly pulled on her stockings and boots, worked the large knot in her skirt free, and waited until the cotton cascaded to the ground to go and check the stew. When she lifted the lid, the thick broth's succulent aroma teased her nose. Again her gaze drifted to the stable where Gideon was still hard at work. The man had no time to prepare a decent meal. And she hadn't properly thanked him for Petra....

Acting before she could talk herself out of it, she procured a pewter bowl from her kitchenware trunk and ladled a large portion of the stew into it. "Walt." She waited for him to look over at her. "I'm going to speak with Mr. Thornton. Don't wander off, okay?"

Nodding, he returned his attention to the frog cradled in his palm.

The closer she got to her destination, the harder her heart worked to keep up with the blood tumbling through her veins. *Calming* and *refreshing* were not words she associated with their interactions. Gideon Thornton possessed the singular ability to irritate her with a mere look. Was it too much to hope this visit would proceed differently than their previous ones?

When she entered the rectangular structure through the double-wide opening, he was in the midst of hoisting a log onto the eastern side wall. Biceps bulging, forearms stiff with tension, he tugged a thick rope toward the floor, thereby lifting the log up into the air. His walnut-colored hair stuck to his temples and nape. Sweat trickled down the side of his neck and disappeared beneath the navy blue shirt collar. Scuffed boots planted far apart in the dirt, his muscled thighs strained the worn-in denim.

Evelyn stood mesmerized by this extraordinary display of strength. Breath locked in her lungs. She remained motionless, afraid to break his concentration lest the log come crashing down on him. It took about five minutes to complete the task. In between testing both ends to check the sturdiness, he flicked her a hooded glance, and she realized he'd been aware of her presence from the second she arrived.

The pewter warm against her palms, she raised her hands to draw attention to her offering. "I brought lunch. Do you like rabbit stew?"

Stepping down from the low stool on which he stood, he whipped off the deerskin gloves and stuffed them in his pocket. His gaze zeroed in on the bowl, then rose to her face. "I'm not a picky eater."

When he made no move toward her, she chose to go to him. Up close, his gray eyes contained a startling wariness. What had he to fear from her? "I assure you, it's perfectly safe to eat. I don't make it a habit of slipping poison in my food."

Those refined eyebrows lifted in surprise. "How about we test that theory?" Taking the bowl and spoon, he scooped up meat, onion and broth and brought it to her lips.

Stunned, her lips parted automatically, which he no doubt took as a sign of compliance.

Not a single part of him touched her, yet disturbing awareness danced along her nerve endings, resurrecting a longing for connection, for companionship and, yes, that dirty word, *romance*. One would've thought living with three brothers and, later, a husband who despised her would've put such naive notions to death. But there it was. Deep down where she guarded her most vulnerable secrets, she yearned to be wooed and courted, dreamed of being that one special person in a man's life. She wanted to be loved. *Truly* loved for the person she was inside.

Drake had admired her physical appearance, but the attraction had faded soon after the reality of married life set in.

She swallowed with difficulty.

Gideon's gaze was locked on her mouth, uneasiness marring his brow. Taking the spoon and bowl with him, he executed a swift turn and crossed to the corner, where he lowered himself on the stool and concentrated on the stew.

Sucking in a balancing breath, Evelyn moved in the opposite direction, knowing it was unwise to linger. The logical thing to do would be to return to her tent and leave the taciturn cowboy to his own company. But while he didn't seem to mind solitude—indeed, seemed to prefer it—she missed teasing and debating with her brothers. Talking to herself wasn't entertaining in the slightest.

Surveying the neatly stacked walls, she touched a hand to the wood, careful not to get a splinter. A rather long structure, the stable would be big enough for six or seven stalls. Four horses currently occupied the corral.

"You aren't planning a typical homestead here, are you? Most settlers get seeds in the ground before starting on shelters, yet I've seen no sign of turned earth." She pivoted toward him.

Head bent, he said between bites, "My plans are for a horse ranch. Ranching is all I know."

"How do you plan to feed yourself? Don't you like vegetables?"

He raised his head at that, and his cool gray eyes were flat. "I don't have a family to worry about. It's just me. I could care less what I eat, as long as it's filling."

Evelyn was suddenly curious why he didn't have a

wife. Why there weren't smaller versions of Gideon Thornton running around. She knew better than to ask such a personal question. Even if she hadn't glimpsed pain in him, she recognized his desire for privacy.

"I will say," he continued as his spoon scraped the bowl, "this is one fine stew. You're a good cook."

Despite the fact he'd already established his low standards where food was concerned, Evelyn couldn't ignore the pleasure his simple praise evoked. Such compliments were rare. Sure, her brothers grunted their thanks as they dug into the meals she prepared, but actual words of affirmation were few and far between.

Smoothing damp palms along her skirt front, she lowered her gaze to the reddish dirt at her feet. "Thank you."

"No, thank you for sharing with me."

He rose and walked toward her, every step a warning striking her brain. *Danger. Keep away.* Any kind word at this point in her life was a heady thing. Coming from this man, it had the power to generate traitorous thoughts. His rugged appeal, the restrained energy rippling along his muscles, the scent of leather and campfire clinging to his skin and hair drew her.

Gideon Thornton is off-limits.

As he transferred the empty bowl to her hands, his warm, calloused fingers skimmed her knuckles. Sizzling heat penetrated bone and flesh. When she imagined what those hands would feel like cradling her face, she knew she had to act fast.

"You've done a remarkable job here. It's good to know my animals will have a solid shelter once you're gone."

Breath hissed between his teeth. His jaw hardened to stone.

Bull's-eye. She was safe.

"I'm not the one who'll be leaving," he said, his eyes

narrowing to slits. "This is my land. I'll do whatever it takes to hold on to it."

"Whatever it takes? Even if that means circumventing the law?"

His hands fisted at his sides, he closed his eyes. His lips moved silently, as if he were ordering himself to be calm. Then his eyes bored into her. "You and your brothers can spread all the poisonous lies you want about me, but *I* know I'm no liar. I'm not a thief. And I don't have to prove myself to you or anyone else in this town. The judge's opinion is the only one that matters."

Evelyn attempted to absorb his words. Passion rang in his voice. Sincerity blazed in his eyes. He was either an adept actor…or he was telling the truth. And if he wasn't lying, then someone else was.

Chapter Six

Long after darkness had descended and Walt had drifted off to sleep, Evelyn reclined beside the fire, gazing up at a blue-black sky studded with brilliant stars, her thoughts unsettled. Conflicted. If Gideon was telling the truth, that meant someone in her family was lying.

While she couldn't discount his conviction, the man was a complete stranger. She knew next to nothing about him. What she did know came secondhand, and none of it was positive. She loved and trusted her brothers. And Drake… Well, he wasn't around to tell his story, was he?

Above the sound of the wood crackling and spitting came a soft *thwack, thwack*. Easing to a sitting position, she cast about for the source. What was that noise? It came again from the direction of Gideon's tent. She stood and, tucking her blouse into her waistband, peeked in on Walt. He looked peaceful as he slept, his hands nestled underneath his cheek. She wavered in the doorway. Should she ignore the sound?

Thwack.

Now that her curiosity was roused, there would be no rest until she discovered whether the cause was man or beast. Preferably not beast.

On her right moonlight glinted off the ribbon of trickling water. On the far side of the stream, impenetrable blackness cloaked the rolling fields. Up ahead the fire cast orange fingers on the elms and cottonwoods towering over his tent. There was no sign of him.

"Gideon?" She spoke quietly, praying he wasn't already asleep. Tiptoeing closer, she noticed the tent flaps were still up. His pallet was empty.

When the sounds came again in rapid succession, she ventured past the copse a little ways. A kerosene lamp swinging from a low branch outlined Gideon's unmistakable form. Slung across his back was a quiver of arrows, and in his hand he held a sleek bow. The ankle-high grass swallowed up her footfalls as she approached him. She watched wide-eyed as he brought the bow up and, anchoring it against his shoulder, fired off a shot at the paper target attached to the trunk twenty yards away. The tip sank into the wood like a knife sinking into butter. It joined five others in the black circle.

Lowering the bow, he twisted his torso in her direction. "Has no one ever told you not to sneak up on an armed man?"

Ignoring his forbidding expression, she shrugged. "I wasn't worried." Just as he'd known she was in the barn earlier, her presence here hadn't gone unnoticed. His senses were honed to perfection.

She took in his rumpled appearance—shirttails hanging out, buttons undone to reveal a white undershirt stretched across his chest and flat stomach—and decided sleep had evaded him, too. Shortly after their exchange at lunch, he'd hitched up his wagon and left without a goodbye. He must've visited the barber in town, for his hair was neatly trimmed and his cheeks smooth, the spicy scent of shaving cream teasing her nostrils. Faint lamplight cast his features in sharp relief, mysterious angles and shadows. His mouth looked like sculpted marble. Perfectly proportioned yet hard and cold and emotionless.

Suppressing a shiver, she forced her feet to approach him. Nodding at the target, she said, "You're good. You make it seem effortless, but I'm guessing it requires an inordinate amount of skill."

He stalked to the tree and removed the arrows. Replacing all but one in the quiver, he retraced his steps and stopped in front of her. "It's a good tension reliever." His wolflike gaze roamed her face, then her hair, which she'd released from its pins for the evening. The soft waves spilled over her shoulders. "You look tense. Why don't you give it a try?"

She instinctively retreated a step. "I don't think so."

Trying new things meant the possibility of failure. She'd learned not to risk the condescension. The stinging criticism. Easier to stick with what she knew and those tasks she could perform well.

With a terse nod, he said, "Suit yourself."

Then he pivoted and, without hesitation, fired off an arrow so fast her eyes could barely track it. Gideon moved with fluid grace and strength, toned muscles working together in a cohesive sequence born of hours of practice.

"Who taught you to do that?" She couldn't mask her awe.

"Lars."

"But you haven't known him very long. Your level of skill…"

"I practice a lot," he murmured without looking at her. Pacing away, he lifted a jar of water to his mouth. The light glanced off his golden throat as he swallowed.

If shooting arrows helped ease his tension, and he

was this good already, then he must be dealing with a lot of anxiety.

Fathomless eyes met hers. "Is there something in particular you wanted, Evelyn?"

She should forbid him to say her name. The way he said it—all hushed and reverent as though she were a queen or something—made her want to touch the top of her head to see if there really was a crown up there.

How utterly ridiculous, she chastised herself.

Still, she wouldn't let him run her off just yet. She wasn't ready to return to her lonely fire and even lonelier bed.

"Don't you think it's strange that in all of Oklahoma territory, both of our families chose to settle in the same start-up town?"

"You don't want my opinion on that, and I know I don't want yours." Again he snatched an arrow and, after fitting it against the bow, let it fly. *Thwack.*

"I'm curious. Why did the illustrious Thorntons choose to take part in the land rush? Wasn't there enough land and wealth to go around in Kansas?" she baited him.

The fact that they had financially benefited from the war while most of their neighbors had suffered great hardship was one of the chief reasons for her parents' hostility.

Grief gripped his features. "We were ready for a change," he pushed out on a heavy sigh. "A fresh start."

Questions bubbled up to the surface. What had happened in Kansas to make him so bereft? So closed off? So tense?

Don't ask, Evelyn. No matter what misfortune he's endured, you can't afford to feel sorry for him. Sympathy will only land you in a heap of trouble.

Feigning a yawn, she mumbled, "It's late. I'll leave you to your target practice."

Turning, she was a few paces away when he spoke.

"Good night, Evelyn. Sweet dreams."

She faltered. With a wince and a mental shake, she forged on ahead. Sweet dreams? On the contrary, she feared her dreams that night would consist of a certain cowboy calling her name.

Gideon scrubbed the scrambled-egg remains from his cast iron skillet, unable to block the sounds of Evelyn's voice and Walt's soft giggles floating downstream. Like him, they were finishing up breakfast. But while their meal was a shared experience, he'd eaten alone. In silence. *A silence that didn't use to bother you,* he reminded himself. *Not until they came along and invaded your territory.*

Their presence only served to remind him of what he'd lost, what he could never recover.

Unbidden, images of his and Susannah's modest one-room cabin assaulted him, memories of past mornings spent at the breakfast table with his wife and daughter. While Susannah hadn't been at her best at that early hour, Maggie had awoken with a smile and bright sparkle in her blue eyes, eager for the day's adventures. His little girl had been generous with her hugs and kisses and declarations of love.

Shutting his eyes tight, Gideon shook his head to dislodge the memories. Where was his ironclad control? Remembering only brought him pain and a piercing longing that refused to be assuaged. His daughter was gone. She was never coming back.

With a growl, he flung the skillet to the ground and strode for the stable. He needed a distraction. He needed action, tasks to occupy his mind and hands. Hard work and the blessed exhaustion it brought was the only relief from this incurable grief. A shame the relief was temporary.

He had almost reached the corral when a blur of brown and white barreled into his path, skidding to a stop before him and kicking up bits of dirt and grass. Walt. His small chest heaving, his hair mussed, he gazed up at Gideon with shy appeal. He pointed to the horses making their way to the fence.

No, God, I can't— He halted the mental plea, convinced asking God for help was an exercise in futility.

Where was Evelyn? Surely she would swoop in and rescue her son from his objectionable company?

Craning his head, he caught her staring in their direction. Good. He waited for her to put down the stack of dishes and storm over to rescue Walt. Only she didn't. Instead, she waved and turned back to her task.

His jaw dropped. *Now* she was extending him her approval? Now, when his insides felt as if they were being ripped apart each time he peered into Walt's innocent eyes, and he wished with everything in him it were Maggie standing before him?

The boy's tiny fingers pressed into his palm and tugged. Careful to blank his expression, Gideon reluctantly looked down. Walt was pointing to the horses again, his curious brown gaze fixed on Star.

The boy is hurting and can clearly use some extra attention, a voice inside him prodded. Not only had his father been ripped from his life, but this dispute had separated him from his uncles. No matter Gideon's opinion of the Chaucer men, he couldn't deny they appeared to genuinely care for the boy. He'd witnessed the affection that had passed between the gruff men and Walt that first day.

He cleared his throat. "Would you like to help me water the horses?"

A shy grin curved his mouth, and his head bobbed up and down.

"Let's go get some pails and fill the trough."

Walt followed him to the stable and accepted his pail with a bounce of excitement. How that emotion didn't spill over into speech he hadn't a clue. A five-year-old boy who didn't talk was downright unnatural. Pitiful, too.

Gideon determined then to question Evelyn—his no-questions rule be hanged.

They made several trips to the stream. Walt carried his half-filled pail with pride, and if most of the water landed in the dirt beneath the trough, Gideon pretended not to notice. Evelyn at last made her way over as he was introducing Walt to Peanut, a gentle mare he'd acquired from another settler the day before the land rush.

Turning, he was arrested by the unguarded contentment on her striking features. Her molasses eyes were bright with pleasure, her generous mouth curved in a loving smile. Her focus was all on her son, of course. He knew the second her attention switched to him, the veil of distrust would descend, eclipsing her radiance. It deflated a man's ego to admit this was his effect on women. *Evelyn isn't just any woman, remember? Since childhood her head has been filled with lies about you.*

"Good morning," he tossed out, just to test his theory. "Nice day, isn't it?"

Immediately, her chin went up. Her shoulders squared as if for battle. When her expressive eyes swiveled to meet his gaze, the light of happiness in the brown depths had been extinguished. Her pink lips firmed as she obliged him by taking note of the puffy clouds floating in a cerulean sky.

"I believe it will be much like yesterday. And the day before that."

"You prefer rain, then?"

"I wasn't complaining." She met his gaze squarely. "Just making an observation."

The blousy sleeves of her mint-green shirt rippled in the breeze. Her luxurious mane had been tamed into an intricate braid, rogue tendrils shiny against the pastel-hued collar. The color agreed with her. She looked cool and refreshing, like a field of wildflowers after a spring rain. He'd noticed she only wore the required black when she went into town. Was it due to practical reasons? After all, she couldn't very well do chores in that fancy dress day after day. Or did it go deeper?

Her demeanor today was collected and remote. Last night was another story. Gideon had been hard-pressed not to go near her. Maybe it was the starlight or the sense that they were alone in the vast prairie, or perhaps it was the sight of her glorious hair streaming past her shoulders combined with the huskiness of her voice when she admired his archery skills.

Long after she'd gone, his thoughts had been consumed by her. He'd awoken this morning relieved he couldn't recall a single dream, for he sensed she'd never left his mind.

Taking a step forward, he lowered his voice. "What's going on, Evelyn?"

She blinked. "What do you mean?"

"Yesterday you whisked Walt away the instant you discovered us in the barn. Today you act as if you couldn't care less. Don't tell me you've reconsidered my villain status in your fairy tale?"

"Of course not," she snapped. Then, snagging her lower lip with her teeth, she worried the soft flesh. A line appeared between her dark brows. "He's happy when he's with you. I find I can't deny him that."

"I see. So I'm still a villain, but not so bad that I can't spend time with your son. That's something, I guess."

"Gideon—" She broke off as the sound of approaching riders thundered across the plains.

Gideon recognized the riders' uniforms. Cavalry soldiers coming to check up on them. As the pair neared, he saw that Private Jesse Wellington was not one of them.

"Walt," Evelyn said as she leaned down to her son, "why don't you get your fishing pole and catch us a fish or two for lunch?"

Taking his gaze off the soldiers, Gideon caught movement in the field beyond the stream. Lion and Shadow romped in the tall grass, their heads and tails visible. Confident they'd alert him to potential trouble, he turned back to deal with their unwelcome visitors.

After the shorter man with dirty-blond hair and a thick mustache dismounted, he slowly inspected the land in all directions. With a satisfied nod, he turned and preceded his partner, a dark-haired man whose wrinkled uniform bore stains on the knees, to where Gideon and Evelyn stood waiting.

Gloved hands bracketing a slim waist, the soldier's attempt at a smile came off as more of a smirk. "Good morning to you both. I'm Private Sam McGraw. This here is Private Ryder Strafford. This is an official visit to assess how things are progressing between disputing parties." Retrieving a small pad from his jacket pocket, he flipped through the pages until he landed on the desired one. "Am I addressing Gideon Thornton and Evelyn Montgomery?"

"That's us." Gideon attempted a civil tone when what he really wanted was to boot them off his land.

As the private lifted his head, a pair of arrogant blue eyes peered at them from beneath the brim of his navy blue hat. "Would either of you like to levy a complaint?"

"No." Gideon sensed Evelyn's scrutiny. What had she expected him to say? They were making the best of the situation, weren't they?

Crossing her arms about her waist, she shook her head. "No."

Ryder Strafford edged closer to her side. "Mrs. Montgomery, I'd like to extend my condolences on your husband's death."

"I…th-thank you."

Gideon glared at the man's insensitivity. As a stranger to her, he had no business bringing up a sensitive subject. And to what aim?

"Do you have any other family here?"

She frowned, clearly uncomfortable with the nosy questions. "Three brothers."

Strafford nodded. At the sight of his superficial grin, Gideon's hands curled into fists. "That's good to hear. I would hate for a lovely woman like yourself to be out here in this wilderness alone and vulnerable."

Her eyes flashed. "I'm perfectly capable of taking care of myself, Private Strafford."

He shot a grin at McGraw. "Tell me, Mrs. Montgomery, what are your brothers' names?"

As she rattled them off, McGraw wrote in his pad.

"Why do you need that information?" Gideon demanded.

"It's important we have next-of-kin information in case misfortune were to befall the land owner."

"In that case, you'll need my information, as well," Gideon said.

McGraw looked up, meanness edging his smile. "No need, Mr. Thornton. I'm already acquainted with Brave Rock's minister and sheriff."

He supposed that wasn't unusual. The cavalry soldiers that had been dispatched to provide security during last month's land rush had stuck around to assist local law enforcement in ironing out land disputes. They would've met Clint in an official capacity. And as Brave Rock's preacher, Elijah met a great number of folks during the course of his duties.

Strafford again addressed Evelyn. "Are any of your brothers married or are they all single?"

"I hardly see how that has any bearing on our case."

McGraw's fingers tightened on the pencil poised above his pad. "Mrs. Montgomery, please allow us to do our job. You wouldn't want us to get into trouble with our superiors, would you?"

"Theo, Brett and Reid are all single."

The soldier dipped his head. "Thank you." When he'd finished, he snapped the pad shut. "I believe that will be all for today."

"Can you tell us how long before our dispute will go before the court?" Evelyn asked.

"Hard to say." He stroked his mustache. "Could be a month. Maybe two."

"Two months?"

Gideon's reaction echoed the despondency in her voice. Two months stretched out in front of him like the endless prairie with no water supply. How was he supposed to maintain crucial distance with these two around day in and day out?

When McGraw bid them good day and headed for his horse, Strafford lingered. "Mrs. Montgomery, are you familiar with where our quarters are located?"

"Behind the general store?"

His blue eyes gleamed, and his ingratiating manner irked Gideon. "That's right. If you have any need to contact me, you can find me there. I'm available day or night. No matter what the hour, I'm willing to assist you."

Gut tight with disapproval, Gideon wedged himself between the soldier and Evelyn. "Mrs. Montgomery will not be visiting the soldiers' quarters at any time. If she has a problem, you can expect a visit from one of her brothers."

Strafford's eyes flared. "You should allow the lady to speak for herself."

"And you should know better than to suggest a respectable lady visit an all-male environment on her own, no matter what the time."

Evelyn's slender fingers encircled his wrist. "Gideon, please, it's all right."

Her touch shattered all logical thought. Her skin was cool and comforting against his heated flesh. Angling his head toward her, he probed her pleading gaze and experienced an unexpected sense of oneness. For a split second, they were unified on something. Connected. And it felt amazing.

Sam McGraw beckoned to his partner. "Time to go, Strafford."

With a scowl at Gideon, the soldier doffed his hat to Evelyn. "Good day, Mrs. Montgomery." Then he pivoted on his heel and strode away.

When the men rode in the direction they'd come,

Evelyn must've realized she was still grasping his wrist.
A tiny gasp assailed his ear a second before she yanked
her hand away. Turning, he watched as she locked her
hands behind her back. Uncertainty commanded her expression.

"I'm not sorry I set him straight," he said before she
could read him the riot act. "He shouldn't have suggested
such a thing to you."

"He was impertinent. Thank you for standing up for
me."

Gideon nodded, not sure how to respond to her surprising gratitude. He studied the retreating mounts.
Something about those soldiers struck him wrong. "I
can't say why, but I don't trust them."

"Their questions did seem unnecessary."

And their manner peculiar, especially Strafford's. He
was clearly interested in the lovely widow. "Do you own
a gun?"

Her brows shot up. "I have a small derringer that Reid
gave me. Why?"

"That wouldn't subdue a cat. I'll loan you a Colt for
those times when I'm not around."

"You really think the soldiers would do something un-
lawful? They are employed by our government."

"I would hope not. They brought up a valid point,
however. A woman out here alone, without protection…"
He paused, unwilling to voice the number of horrors
slinking through his mind. He sucked in a steadying
breath. "I think it's wise to be prepared."

"And here I thought *you* were the one I shouldn't
trust."

Gideon winced. Why did she insist on ruining every
moment of peace between them?

Shading her eyes with one hand, she hitched up her

skirts and turned to search the horizon. His gaze followed hers, the quiet suddenly striking him as odd.

"Gideon," she breathed, "where's Walt?"

Chapter Seven

Evelyn broke into a jog, her frantic gaze continuously scanning the fields, the campsite, the tall trees edging both sides of the stream. There was no sign of Walt. No flash of raven hair or white shirt.

Behind her, Gideon's piercing whistles for his dogs went unanswered. That could be good or bad, she reasoned. Lion and Shadow could've gone exploring on their own, or they could've accompanied Walt wherever he'd wandered off to.

Please lead me to him, God. Help me not to imagine the worst.

Halting at the stream, she spotted his abandoned rod and pail. Her stomach knotted into a hard ball. "Okay, be reasonable, Evelyn," she whispered, her fingernails biting into her palms. Their conversation with the soldiers hadn't lasted more than fifteen minutes. He couldn't have gone far.

Gideon rode up on Star, his features set in determined lines. He extended a large tanned hand to her. "Let's find him."

She didn't hesitate. Placing her hand in his, she let him haul her up behind him onto the palomino's broad, bare back. He nudged the horse into motion. Down the sloping bank, across the pebble-dotted streambed and up the other side. Water droplets dampened her hem. Without stirrups to balance herself, she started to slide sideways.

"Put your arms around me."

She swallowed the instinctive protest. It was either do as he commanded or land in the dirt. Gingerly, Evelyn looped her arms about his waist and, locking her fingers where the buttons marched down his shirt, attempted to keep the physical contact between them to a minimum. The powerful horse's brisk trot made that all but impossible, however. Her chin dug into his shoulder and her upper body bounced off his back. The brim of his Stetson glanced off her cheek.

Gideon's chest expanded in a deep sigh. Glancing over his shoulder, he presented her with his harshly beautiful profile. "Unlock your fingers."

"What? I'll fall off."

His sculpted lips flattened. "Just trust me."

Ha! As if she'd ever do that. With an unladylike snort, she let go. His warm palm covering hers, he guided her to crisscross her arms about his middle, a move that brought her flush against the solid expanse of his back. Soft cotton brushed her cheek. Blazing heat seeped through the material, sending her temperature climbing. As he guided Star across the prairie, his taut stomach and chest muscles flexed and adjusted to every dip in the terrain.

Not since the early months of her marriage five years ago had she been this close to a man. After Walt's birth, Drake had mostly kept his distance. There'd been signs suggesting he'd found satisfaction in other women's arms, signs she'd kept silent about. What good would confronting him have done? Not only would it have incited even more strife in her sham of a marriage, it would've put her brothers in danger. If they'd had the slightest inkling about Drake's unfaithfulness, they would've killed him. And she would've been forced to watch them hang for their crime. So she'd turned a blind eye, channeled her love and affection to her son, refusing to acknowledge the loneliness suffocating her soul. Now, gliding with her as one across the sun-washed prairie, this man of contradictions—a man she was supposed to loathe—was unearthing the dangerous, almost desperate need for connection she'd fought long and hard to bury.

A tremor racked her body.

Misconstruing her reaction, his hand came to rest atop her forearm in a reassuring gesture. "We'll find him, Evelyn." His deep voice vibrated with compassion and understanding.

Furious with herself for sparing even a second on him when her precious son was missing, she clamped her jaw and nodded, forced her mind to focus on their surroundings. Rolling fields of knee-high grasses interspersed with brown-eyed Susans spread out around them; clusters of oaks and elms dotted the horizon. With every acre they traveled farther from camp, her heart shriveled a little more.

Fingers bunching in Gideon's shirt, she peered over his shoulder to study his profile. "Are coyotes active at this time of day? What about wolves? A-and snakes?" One bite from a poisonous snake would be enough to—

"Evelyn." She was startled to realize he was still cradling her hand. He angled his head to meet her troubled gaze. The clear gray pools reflected confidence. "Don't torture yourself."

I trust him. In this, at least, I trust him. The acknowledgment rippled through her like a mighty earthquake.

Gideon was a work-roughened cowboy, wise and strong and capable. If anyone could find her son, it was this man.

Gideon called Walt's name again, then Lion's and Shadow's. A hawk swooped across the sky to their right, his piercing cry the only response. Not the one he was hoping for.

Scanning the landscape, he adjusted the canteen resting against his thigh. Where could the boy have wandered off to?

Despite his reassurances to Evelyn, deep inside, a squall brewed. Very real worry swirled through his chest, driving the breath from his lungs. A small child was vulnerable out here. More than wild animals, Gideon was concerned about heat exhaustion. The sun's merciless heat made it feel more like mid-July than early May.

Behind him Evelyn had grown unnaturally quiet. He could practically feel her terror leaching into him. Still covering her hand, he stroked the silken skin with his thumb, wishing he could take away her fear, and frustrated because he was powerless to do so.

God in heaven, I know we haven't spoken in a while, but I'm not asking anything for myself. I'm asking for her. Please, protect Walt. Guide us to him.

The prayer wasn't an easy one to offer. There was no way of knowing what God's answer would be, but he had to try. He knew what it was to fear for a child's life, and he wouldn't wish that particular brand of misery on his worst enemy, not even a Chaucer.

When he slowed Star to a walk, Evelyn stiffened. "Why are we slowing?" Her voice rose. "We can't slow down. My son needs me."

"We must stop for a quick drink." He guided his

mount beneath a maple tree's branches. "I don't want you passing out on me."

This was met with silence. As soon as Star halted, Evelyn removed her arms from his midsection and slid jerkily to the ground. Gideon told himself he didn't miss her nearness, the feminine softness surrounding him, the sweet scent of gardenias that clung to her hair. In fact, the personal contact was making him antsy. He'd gone without it for too long and, if he wasn't careful, could wind up craving more, something that absolutely could not happen.

He was destined to live out the rest of his days alone.

Dismounting, he lifted the strap from his shoulder and, ducking his head under, handed her the canteen. She took a shallow sip and held it out to him.

He shook his head. "Take another drink."

"We have to save some for Walt."

"There'll be enough."

Taking another drink, she passed it to him without a word and began to pace, swatting away the tiny sweat bees hovering around. Near her ears, wisps of hair dislodged by the breeze brushed her cheekbones. A slender gold chain clung to her throat and disappeared beneath the mint-green collar. Her smooth olive skin glistened with a damp sheen.

Gideon averted his gaze, trying to ignore the fact that his lips were touching the same spot hers had just occupied. He took two swigs, recapped the canteen and settled it once more across his shoulder. "Walt wouldn't have traveled this far in the short head start he had on us. We should circle back."

Desperate hope flickered in her features. "He could already be back at camp."

"It's a possibility," he agreed, daring to share her hope.

Once more astride Star, he assisted her up. Light as a feather and agile, she settled against him as if she'd ridden bareback her entire life. A reluctant sigh tickled his ear. Then she snaked her arms around him. Her hands gripped the sides of his shirt above his waistband, small and warm and trusting.

He steeled himself against the pleasure washing over him. *Focus on the task at hand, Thornton.* "Let's go find your son."

For the next half hour, Gideon closed his mind to everything save signs that might direct them to Walt. Trampled grass, broken stalks, dog droppings. There was nothing.

Evelyn started to shake. Hearing her hitched breaths, he suspected she was giving in to her worst imaginings. He had to do something to distract her.

Taking hold of her hand, he said, "I remember one time my younger brother, Clint, wandered off during a game of hide-and-seek. Since Elijah was the oldest, he picked the best hiding places and it would take me and Clint ages to find him. I guess that day he got tired of searching and went off to explore. Of course, it was a long time before we realized he was gone, and by then it was nearing suppertime."

He recalled how frightened he and Lije had been. Didn't take much to send their cousin into a rage. Obadiah had been a hard man, bordering on cruel, who resented being saddled with his orphaned cousins. With their Southern accents and genteel ways, they represented the enemy. No matter that their father had sacrificed his life for the Union cause.

"What happened?" Her voice was muffled.

"We knew we had to find him before our cousin found out, so we begged the stable hands to help us. Lucky for us, they agreed. We finally found him at the river bordering the property, calmly tossing rocks into the water. Clint couldn't understand why we were so upset."

A rare smile played about his lips as he recalled Clint's dumbfounded expression.

"Your cousin would've punished you?" She sounded surprised and not a little disturbed.

If only she knew the lengths he would go to make them suffer. "Yes."

"But how old were you? Surely—"

Gideon straightened, thighs tensing, all senses on alert. "Did you see that?" Pointing to the northeast, he squinted. "There. A spot of black."

A minute passed. "I see it!"

Maneuvering his horse slightly to the right, he urged him into a trot. His pulse raced. *Please, God.* "I think it might be Shadow."

As they neared the copse of trees, he recognized the shaggy muzzle. Shadow's ears perked. He bounced high and twisted in midair—a display Gideon referred to as his circus routine.

"It is him!" Evelyn cried.

He wondered if she realized how tightly she was clinging to him. Doubtful.

They spotted Walt's sleeping form at the same time. He was curled up on his side, a snoozing Lion acting as his pillow, and rustling tree limbs overhead a green canopy of shade.

Gideon sagged with sweet relief. The boy was safe. When Evelyn rested her head against his shoulder, he went very still. He got the impression she was praying, giving thanks to God for reuniting her with her baby. A river of powerful emotion swept through him as past and present collided—two very different situations with different outcomes—and it took all his willpower to subdue it. She had her happy ending. That was all that mattered right now.

Evelyn scrambled down off the horse, stumbling in her haste. "Walt, sweetheart." She knelt in the grass beside him, checking his forehead for fever, smoothing his hair, caressing his tearstained cheek. He must've been so frightened. "Wake up."

Offering up a silent prayer of thanks, she barely registered Gideon's presence behind her or Shadow's wet nose nudging her wrist, his compact body quivering with excitement. Walt's lashes fluttered. For a moment he looked confused. Then, coming fully awake, he gave a small cry and launched himself into her arms.

"It's okay, sweetie." Hugging him close, she rubbed gentle circles along his back. "I'm here now. You're safe."

Walt wriggled away before she was ready to let him go. He startled both adults by wrapping his arms about Gideon's legs. Lifting her gaze, she noted the big man looked a trifle pale as he awkwardly patted Walt's shoulder. Conflicting emotions passed over his face like storm clouds racing across a turbulent sky. While it was clear he was as relieved as she was with the outcome of their search, shafts of sorrow glinted in his light eyes. More than ever before, Evelyn yearned to learn his secrets.

Walt lifted his arms in silent appeal. Biting her lip, she watched Gideon waver before giving in and effortlessly hoisting the child into his arms. The sight of them together—the aloof, tough-as-leather cowboy gazing at her innocent little boy as if he were the biggest, shiniest gift under the Christmas tree—cut up her peace. Something wasn't adding up here. Gideon's gentle ways, his genuine concern for Walt did not match the negative image her family had drawn.

"Walt, your mother and I were very worried when we couldn't find you. There are many dangers out here. I want you to promise that you'll never wander off again."

His round face somber, Walt nodded.

"Are you thirsty?" Gideon asked. Lowering her son to the ground, he removed the canteen and waited while he drank his fill. His eyes flashed to her. "Your turn."

Not arguing with him this time, she gratefully accepted the cool water. She'd forgotten her bonnet and the top of her head burned from the sun's rays.

"I don't know about you," he said to Walt, "but my belly is demanding to be fed. What do you say we go home and rustle up a quick lunch?"

Home. Did he realize what he'd said? Certainly Gideon viewed the claim as his home. He'd been there since day one, making plans and putting them into practice. But what of her and Walt? If the judge decided in their favor, it would be *their* new home. Gideon would have to leave it all behind and start over elsewhere.

Isn't that no less than a thief like him deserves?

The thought struck her like a lightning bolt. A few days ago, Evelyn had been convinced the middle Thornton brother was an underhanded crook. Now she had serious doubts.

"Ready, Evelyn?"

He stood by the horse, waiting to help her up. Gideon didn't look like a crook. He looked honest and good and…lonely. She shook herself out of her troubling reverie.

"I'm ready."

"I'm putting you in the middle this time, and I'll get behind you. You can hold on to Walt that way."

That meant a long ride home with Gideon's intimidating strength too close for comfort.

"You look flushed." Whipping off his Stetson, he placed it on her head and, without waiting for her response, circled her waist and boosted her onto Star's back. Ignoring her indignant yelp, he passed Walt up to her.

When he swung up behind her, she straightened her spine and squared her shoulders, determined to maintain her distance. But the afternoon's events had left her emotionally and physically spent, and before she knew it, she'd relaxed against him. His strong arms circled her waist. Heat that had nothing to do with the spring temperatures licked along her veins, shocking her. Certainly her reactions to this man were wholly disconnected from her common sense.

The sooner they got back to camp, the sooner she could put this entire episode behind her. And Gideon's surprising effects on her equilibrium with it.

Chapter Eight

Disturbed on many levels, Evelyn disregarded her chores in favor of whiling away the afternoon with her son. Fishing rod in hand, she lounged on the bank, letting the cool water rush over her bare feet and the rugged beauty of the plains restore her spirits. A mourning dove cooed overhead. Walt's happy giggles tickled her ears as he attempted to scoop up minnows with his hands.

She filled her lungs with the pleasant smell of ripe sunbaked grass. She should feel guilty for relaxing when there was work to do, but she couldn't summon the emotion. Not after the harrowing morning she'd endured. Her arms and legs were still limp, a strange lethargy lingering even though they were safe and sound.

For what seemed the hundredth time in the space of an hour, she offered her gratitude up to God. He must surely be tired of hearing the same words over and over. She couldn't help it. Every time she thought of what might've happened, tears threatened as emotion overwhelmed her.

I'm sorry for being such a ninny, Lord. It's just that he's my baby. My only child.

As a young woman daydreaming about her future, Evelyn had envisioned a loving husband and a cabinful of children. That dream was not to be. After her disaster of a first marriage, she would not contemplate a second, not even for the sake of more children. That was why she had to cherish the one child she did have.

Taking the pail containing four medium-sized fish onto her lap, she addressed Walt. "I think it's time to start supper. Remember, stay where you can see me, okay?"

His gaze flicking beyond her to where Gideon worked, he gave a firm nod. She'd washed the dirt and tearstains from his small face, and his cheeks were again suffused with healthy color. His fear had easily been set aside. Evelyn prayed he heeded her instructions and didn't wander off again.

Deliberately *not* looking toward the stable, she gathered the necessary tools for cleaning and gutting the fish. Gideon had retreated as soon as they'd ridden into camp, leading Star away in a cloud of silence. She knew why she didn't want to talk. What was his excuse?

Batting away annoying gnats, she quickly egged and floured the fillets and placed them in the skillet sizzling with bacon fat. Cooking in the open field on her portable stove was not a pleasant experience, but she was thankful for the supplies she did have. While they didn't have a roof over their heads, they had food and clothing and a place to sleep.

When she called Walt to supper twenty minutes later, he handed her an extra trencher. "What's this for?"

Brown eyes bright with entreaty, he jabbed a finger in the direction of Gideon's tent. Her lips parted in surprise.

"You want Gideon to eat with us?"

A wide grin split his face, and he did a little jig.

Only then did Evelyn realize she'd forgotten to thank Gideon for the part he'd played in finding Walt. Inviting him to supper would surely make up for the oversight. It didn't have to be a long, drawn-out affair.

"I suppose we could ask him. Wait here." Hurrying to the trunk containing her writing materials, she retrieved a small piece of paper and pencil and scrawled a note. "Take this to him and come right back."

She watched him race to find Gideon, not at all sure the cowboy would even agree to grace their table.

Gideon rolled up his sleeves and dunked his arms in the water, scrubbing the soap bar across his skin. His face and neck came next. Later, once he was certain Evelyn and Walt were asleep, he'd indulge in a real dunking to rid himself of the day's grime.

Quick footsteps alerted him to his young visitor. He wiped his face with a towel, then looped it over the rope to dry and turned to greet Walt. Seeing the boy hale and hearty, his expression open and smiling, filled his chest anew with humble gratitude. *I suppose I owe You my thanks, God.*

"What's this?" Taking the paper from him, Gideon unfolded it and read the precise handwriting. "Supper at our tent?" Hmm. Short and to the point. He would've thought, given the lovely widow's proclivity for speech, her notes would read more like novels.

Squinting, he gazed upstream. She was busy serving up the chow. Was this her idea or Walt's? In the end, it didn't really matter, did it? His growling stomach and the questionable appeal of beans and corn mush made the decision easy.

"I'd be happy to join you," he told Walt.

The boy flashed a smile and seized his hand. Allowing himself to be tugged across the grassy expanse separating their tents, Gideon couldn't fight the absurd grin kicking up the corners of his mouth. When Evelyn looked up and saw him coming, she almost dropped the coffee kettle she held. Her arrested expression, in turn, startled him. What had surprised her? That he'd accepted the invitation? His grin? Could his visage be so changed by a simple smile?

"H-hi." Her fingertips went white as she held the kettle more firmly. A self-conscious smile flitted across her face, and he had his answer. This had been Walt's idea.

"I hope coffee is all right? It's either that or water." She gestured to Petra. "I haven't milked her yet."

"Coffee's fine."

He supposed she had a reason to be flustered. Hours on horseback had hurtled them way past formality and into a personal zone fraught with land mines. He wouldn't be forgetting the feel of her arms around him or the silky glide of her hair against his neck anytime soon.

Gideon hung back, giving her plenty of space to work. She put him in mind of a high-strung filly who'd bolt if he made any sudden movements or tried to get too close.

She set the ceramic mug on an oversize trunk serving as their makeshift table. "You aren't allergic to fish, are you?" She swung around, regarding him with furrowed brow. "I had a cousin who broke out into a terrible rash whenever she consumed it."

Now he had to actually keep from laughing. "No, I'm not allergic to anything that I know of."

"Oh. That's good." Her delicate nose wrinkled. "It was a nasty-looking rash."

He eased forward. "Do you need any help?"

"No." As she shook her head, a glossy section of hair slipped over her shoulder to curve about her collarbone. In spite of riding across acres of wilderness and cooking over a hot stove, she managed to look as fresh as a rose.

"I'll just fill the trenchers and we'll be ready. Walt, can you please get us three forks?"

Gideon ran a hand over his hair, glad of the recent cut and shave. Resembling a wild animal was fine when he had only himself for company; not so much when a lady was in residence. She was the one forced to look at him day after day, after all.

"Please, have a seat."

When he'd settled his tall frame on the indicated stool, she placed a trencher of fried fish, sautéed greens and corn cakes in front of him. In the middle of the table, she set a jar of preserved peaches.

"For dessert." She waggled a finger at Walt, the action offset by an indulgent grin.

When every piece of cutlery and dishware was on the table and she had no other cause for delay, Evelyn took her place on the log beside the child. Situated diagonally from Gideon, she fussed with her skirts so she wouldn't have to look at him. Her discomfiture was plainly evident.

"Would you mind saying the blessing?" she asked, at last raising her dark gaze to his.

The request startled him. Him? Pray? Out loud? "I—I can't…." Heat seared his cheekbones. "I—I'm sorry."

She blinked, as if his words surprised her. Then she rushed to smooth over the awkwardness. "That's all right. Don't worry about it. I'm used to doing it."

What did that mean? How could she be used to doing it after only two weeks? Or had her husband not been a religious man? Gideon felt like an idiot. Still, he was barely able to utter silent, private prayers. He wasn't sure at this point if he could push the words out of his mouth.

Staring across at their bowed heads as she murmured a brief prayer, he felt his mouth go dry. This was too cozy, too close to what a family looked like for comfort. The mother and child were different, but he was the same. One part of a trio.

It's just food, Thornton. Relax.

Working to ease the tension from his muscles, he pulled in a deep breath. This would be a simple meal. Quick and painless.

"This is delicious," he told her once he'd tasted the crispy fish.

"It's nothing fancy." She shrugged and sipped her coffee.

"You have a talent, then, for transforming the simplest of fare into a first-rate meal."

Pretty color blossomed in her cheeks. She looked pained. "That's kind of you to say."

Sensing her unease, Gideon turned his attention to his meal. Evelyn Montgomery was a curious contradiction of bravado and insecurity. When it came to her family, she defended them without hesitation, battled with the courage of ten men. But not when it came to herself. It was as if she didn't see herself as worthy of being championed.

"Where did you find these greens?"

Swallowing, she swiped a napkin over her mouth. "The purslane? Walt and I discovered it upstream a little ways." She hesitated. "I know you said that you didn't care much about food, but a small vegetable garden might be worth the effort."

He balanced his forearms on the trunk edge. "I might plant a small one once the stable is finished."

"What about lodgings? You don't mind tent living?"

"I'll bunk in the tack room until I can get a cabin up."

Their gazes locked, and the specter of the court proceedings shimmered between them. Neither knew what the outcome would be, yet both he and Evelyn were assuming they'd continue on here. Foolish, considering one of them would be packing their bags.

For the first time, Gideon experienced a pang of misgiving. While he deserved the land—after all, he had planted his stake first—he couldn't help worrying what would happen to Evelyn if the judge confirmed his ownership. No doubt Theodore and the other brothers would take her in…but would she be truly content in that situation? He'd seen enough to recognize her drive for independence. The very same thing that drove him.

Walt gestured to his clean plate.

With a soft smile, she dished out a spoonful of peaches and cut them into manageable pieces. Gideon gritted his teeth until he thought they might crack from the pressure. How many times had he or Susannah done the same for Maggie? How he ached to see her again! *Why, God? Why did You have to take her from me?*

Rising abruptly to his feet, he carried his scraped-clean plate to the stream and dipped it in the trickling water burnished gold by the setting sun.

"You don't have to do that," Evelyn said softly behind him. "I'll clean them later."

"I don't mind," he grated, his throat thick. He didn't dare turn around. If he did, she'd see how upset he was and would question him about it.

"You don't want any peaches?"

"No, thanks."

"I'm going to finish my coffee, then. There's more if you want it."

He didn't respond, and she left him to gather his wits. This was what he'd been avoiding, these trip-ups that could so easily plunge him over the edge. He hadn't lost his control so far, and he had no plans to do so now. Especially not in front of a woman who detested him.

He should go.

He was walking back, a hasty goodbye forming on his lips, when he glimpsed her sitting alone. Her gaze centered on Walt, who was crouched in the tent opening drawing. She looked lost. Troubled. Forlorn. Emotions he could readily identify with. Disregarding his instinct to flee, he resumed his spot and wound his fingers about the cooled mug.

"Has he ever spoken?" he asked quietly.

"Oh, yes." A guarded smile touched her lips. "He was a typical child. Bright, curious. Always asking why this or why that. He especially liked to sing the silly nursery rhymes his babushka, Nancy, taught him. And then Drake died—" her brows met in the middle "—and he just stopped speaking." Head bent, she stared into her cup.

So this was a recent development. That meant there was a good chance he'd speak again. "You think it stems from the trauma of his father's accident?"

"I do." Her mouth flattened. "It makes no sense, though. Drake ignored him much of the time. He didn't even want us to come out here. He expected us to wait in Virginia until he sent for us. I refused because I had my doubts he'd ever make good on his promise." She pursed her lips, as if she'd revealed too much. "I simply don't understand how his passing affected Walt to this degree when they weren't even close."

Gideon digested that information, unable to understand how a man could treat a child as if he weren't important. Children were meant to be prized. Cherished.

If Drake had treated his son that way, how must he have behaved toward his wife?

His hands tightening on the mug, he let his gaze probe the shadowed depths of her eyes. "Was he ever violent?"

Inhaling sharply, she gripped the edge of the trunk, her knuckles going white. "No. Drake knew better than to lay a finger on either of us. My brothers would've killed him."

Instead of dispersing, the shadows merely deepened. He was suddenly very angry with a dead man. "There are other methods of cruelty, though. Is that not so, Evelyn?"

"I—" The color receded from her face. "I can't—"

He shouldn't have pushed. He had no right to intrude upon her privacy and sure wouldn't appreciate it if the tables were turned.

Pushing to his feet, he stared solemnly down at her. "I apologize. That was forward of me."

She followed suit, standing very close, her black skirt brushing his pant legs. "My marriage is not something I've discussed with anyone."

"You owe me no explanations." He gestured toward the dwindling fire. "Can I help you clean up?"

"No, but I appreciate the offer."

"I'll say good-night, then." Dipping his head, he started to move past her.

"Gideon, wait." Her small hand braced against his biceps, she stared up at him with an expression free of old prejudices. There was only a mother's gratitude. "If it weren't for you, there's a good chance I might not have been reunited with my son. Thank you." Leaning close, she rose up on tiptoe and kissed his cheek. A light, fleeting brush of velvet-soft lips against his skin. A kiss, innocent though it was, that sent him reeling.

Rendered speechless, he gave a halfhearted wave and backed away until his bootheel caught on a log and he almost tripped. Managing a gruff good-night, he strode away, eager for the darkness to swallow him up.

Chapter Nine

The memory of Evelyn's kiss stayed with him through the long, restless night, a sweet, wondrous moment in time that affected him far more than it should have. It was only a thank-you kiss, for goodness' sake. What intrigued him about the entire episode was the fact that she despised him. A lady didn't go around kissing liars and cheats. Did her behavior indicate her opinion of him was undergoing a change?

Does it really matter, Thornton? Who cares what she thinks of you? It wasn't as if the two of them would end up friends after the judge's ruling. They were on opposite sides. Always had been, always would be.

Hurrying through breakfast, he was emerging from the stable hefting a saddle for Snowball when he noticed Evelyn and Walt walking in his direction. They were decked out in their Sunday best—Walt in a gray-and-black pinstripe suit and Evelyn in her elegant black widow's weeds—a large Bible tucked beneath her arm. Lars's invitation passed through his mind. He smothered a groan. Surely they didn't expect him to escort them to church?

"Good morning, Gideon." Her guard was firmly in

place. No sign of the softness that had been in evidence last night. Her heavy mane was arranged in a severe chignon. Of course, it didn't detract from her beauty. She resembled a fierce warrior maiden. "Are you on your way to services?"

She wouldn't know of his aversion to anything God related. "I am headed over to Elijah's, but not for services. I plan to have a quick word with him afterward."

"Oh, I assumed…" Her black lace gloves flashing in the shimmering light, she gestured to the saddle in his hands. She looked resigned. "Would you mind terribly if we borrowed one of your mounts? Reid is supposed to bring one for me in the coming days, so it would only be this once."

"Let me get this straight. You want to attend *my brother's* church?"

"It's been a long time since I've heard God's Word preached. After what happened yesterday, I…" Her hand tightened around Walt's. "I feel the need to be around other believers. I'm desperate for encouragement, and if that means sitting in Elijah Thornton's congregation, so be it."

"I see." Although he didn't. Not really.

"Don't you ever feel that way?" she probed, her gaze searching for truths he'd worked long and hard to keep hidden.

"No." There was no help for him. No encouragement to be found.

She didn't appear to be satisfied with that answer. "Gideon—"

"I'll take you," he blurted, unwilling to deal with her curiosity.

Besides, not only was he fresh out of sidesaddles, but he felt responsible for their safety. He hadn't forgotten the soldiers' queer behavior and Private Strafford's marked interest in the widow. In fact, that was what he was intent on discussing with his brothers today. He adjusted the saddle in his arms. "Give me a few minutes to hitch up the wagon."

"I don't want to put you to extra trouble," she protested.

"No trouble."

When he'd hitched the wagon and handed them onto the smooth wooden seat, he circled around and climbed aboard, thankful Walt acted as a buffer between them. Gideon didn't need the distraction of her touch.

The picturesque ride passed in silence. Something must be weighing on her mind for her to be this quiet.

Was she already regretting her decision? He wondered what his brother's reaction would be to them showing up together. He didn't have to guess her brothers' reactions if they found out she'd willingly attended Lije's church.

He glanced at her profile. "You're not worried Theodore will find out about this?"

"I can hold my own with my brothers."

As the baby of the family and a girl at that, he could see where she'd had to develop a strong backbone.

"What's that?" She pointed to a rectangular log structure.

"That large oak we passed a few yards back marked the edge of Alice's property, Elijah's fiancée. That building is the Healing Heart infirmary."

"She's the nurse who tended to Drake?" Her voice lowered an octave.

Taking his eyes off the landscape, Gideon studied her profile. "Yes. You'll meet her today."

Lips compressing, she nodded but said nothing. He found himself wondering what was going on inside her head. It wasn't long before they crossed onto Elijah's claim and the large church tent came into view. They'd packed it up the night before the land rush and transported it here to use while their church was being built. Beyond it, on the western edge of Lije's property and the closest to town, the permanent church building was showing progress.

"That right there is going to be the church and schoolhouse."

To his surprise, he hadn't minded working with the men. Most of them were parishioners of Elijah's. They hadn't peppered him with questions, however, or acted as if his presence was a strange occurrence. At the end of his shift, he'd blurted out an offer to work again. The gratitude on his brother's face had been worth the time and effort.

After guiding his team alongside a handful of wagons, he set the brake, then strode around the rear and assisted Evelyn and Walt down. The boy's eyes were large as he took in his surroundings.

"I suppose I should introduce you to Lije," he said as he whipped off his Stetson and ran a hand through his hair. Dread pulsed at his temples.

"I don't expect you to babysit us." While her chin was set in stubborn determination, wariness pinched her forehead. "I can see you're about as comfortable as a baby chick in a nest of rattlers."

He couldn't suppress a small smile at that. Offering his arm, he said, "Are you comparing Lije's church members to reptiles, Evelyn?"

Surprise lifted her thick brows, and laughter trembled about her mouth. She lightly placed her hand in the curve of his elbow. "I would never dream of doing such a thing."

His trepidation momentarily forgotten, he escorted her across the lawn and into the tent's interior, where it was only slightly dimmer than the spring day outside. Walt tripped along behind them.

Gideon noticed his brother standing in the aisle greeting guests. When Elijah saw him, his jaw dropped. Not surprising, considering. He quickly recovered, however, and moved swiftly to clap Gideon on the back.

"Gideon, good to see you. Who do you have with you?"

Still in a stupor brought about by the rare appearance of Gideon's earth-moving smile, one that transformed his stark features into something truly beautiful and captivating, Evelyn vaguely noted the keen interest in Elijah Thornton's intelligent face.

Gideon quietly introduced them. Amidst rough-hewn rows marching along two sides toward the pulpit in front, people gathered to catch up on the latest news. A few cast curious glances their way.

Elijah took her hand in a firm grip. She'd seen him in town before. Ministers weren't all that plentiful in this start-up prairie town, their services in high demand to visit and pray for the sick and dying. The kindness brimming in his hazel eyes hadn't been visible from a great distance.

"I'm pleased to make your acquaintance, Mrs. Montgomery." His smile widened. "And young Walt. I'm glad you came today."

Clutching her hand, her son pressed closer to her side, shy in this new environment.

The pastor straightened and gestured behind him. "If you don't mind, I'd like to introduce you to my fiancée."

"That would be nice." She mentally grimaced at how

stilted she sounded even to her own ears. She'd wanted to come, yearned to hear a godly message, but now that she was here, awkwardness had set in. She was effectively in enemy camp. Gideon was right—her brothers would be spitting mad if they found out.

Tension radiating from his body, Gideon guided her down the center aisle toward the pulpit, his older brother leading the way. There were some similarities in the shapes of their faces, their dark hair and tan skin, but where Gideon was as solid as an oak, a man of the earth, Elijah was lean and compact, a man of wisdom and scholarly pursuits. One closed off, deflecting human interaction, the other engaging, seeking contact. Two devastatingly handsome men, two very different personalities. How did Sheriff Clint Thornton fit into the mix?

Snaking his arm about the waist of a petite redhead, Elijah interrupted her conversation with a quick word in her ear. She instantly turned into his embrace, and he smiled down at her with an expression of such pure adoration that Evelyn sucked in a painful breath. No man had ever looked at her that way. What must it feel like, to be the center of another's universe?

"Mrs. Montgomery, may I introduce my fiancée, Miss Alice Hawthorne?"

"How do you do?" she murmured, deeply troubled by the knowledge she'd never experience that kind of bond.

Alice was beautiful in a sky blue dress that mirrored her eyes. "It's very nice to meet you." She smiled in a way that put Evelyn at ease. There was no artifice, only sincere pleasure on her face.

Gideon gently extracted his arm from her grasp, his eyes questioning. Somber. "Will you be all right if I wait on you outside?"

She nodded mutely, surprised he'd ask her preference.

"You're not staying for the service?" Elijah's voice was rife with disappointment.

A muscle ticked in Gideon's jaw. "You know I can't," he bit out.

Evelyn watched the interchange with dismayed curiosity. Why was Gideon so upset? Why was he averse to staying? Questions pelted her mind.

"If you could try just once, maybe—"

"I'm leaving."

Walt lunged toward the big cowboy, grabbed on to his hand with both of his. His face bore a pleading expression.

"Someone sure wants you to stay," Alice commented in a hushed, awe-filled voice.

All four adults stared at Walt. From the look on Gideon's face, he was waging a fierce inner battle. She held her breath. What would he do? He seemed to possess a soft spot for her son.

After several drawn-out, tense moments, his mouth softened, his shoulders drooped slightly in defeat. "I'll stay." He held up a finger when Walt bounced on his toes. "But I'm sitting in the back."

The service was not a peaceful one. Evelyn couldn't fully concentrate on Elijah's words—something about extending mercy to others—because of the man beside her. He didn't sing along with the congregation, just stood there like a martyr staring straight ahead, his hands fisted at his sides. And when it was time for the message, he sat locked in a statuelike position, his arms folded over his chest and shoulders slightly hunched, as if deflecting an onslaught of bullets. How could she sense the turmoil raging inside him and not wonder about its source? Not be bothered by his suffering?

The more time she spent in Gideon Thornton's company, the less she thought of him as the enemy. Her family's accusations were growing fuzzier, their hatred harder to grasp. It would've been easier to maintain her hostility if he ignored her son or treated them with scorn. But no, he went out of his way to help Walt, to teach him things any loving father would teach a son. As worried for Walt's safety as she herself had been, Gideon hadn't hesitated to go off in search of him. She had no doubt he would not have given up until Walt was safely in her arms. And now he was sitting in this makeshift church against his will, all because of a little boy's silent plea that he stay.

Were these the actions of a bad man?

Stealing a glance at his granite profile, she noticed his pallor.

Elijah asked them to bow their heads for the final prayer. Before he'd uttered the last *amen,* Gideon bolted through the open tent flaps. She took hold of Walt's hand and together they quietly made their way outside. He was already at the wagon, black hat pulled low over his eyes, pacing.

Without speaking, she lifted Walt into the rear of the wagon and left him to play with his carved wooden horse and soldier. Then she turned and blocked Gideon's path.

A scowl twisted his lips and silver fire smoldered in his eyes, but she refused to be intimidated. Crossing her arms, she met his piercing gaze with calm resolve.

"I know it's none of my business, but I'd like to know what's bothering you. You're awfully upset over a mere church service."

Hands braced on his hips, he glared down at her. "You don't have to do this, you know."

"Do what?"

"Pretend to care."

She stiffened. "That's harsh."

"Is it? You've accused me of some rather heinous crimes, Evelyn. According to you, my word isn't worth the dust on my boot soles and I'm unscrupulous enough to take advantage of a dying man and his widow and child. So why are you surprised that I'd question your sincerity?"

"You're right," she conceded. "I did accuse you of some horrible things. And while I admit I'm not sure anymore what to think about what happened, that's not the issue here. You're obviously hurting, and you're lashing out to keep me from the truth." He flinched when she touched his sleeve. "What's wrong, Gideon?"

Kneading the back of his neck, he stared at his boots. "God let me down, okay? I trusted Him to take care of my family, trusted His *plan.* He could've saved them. Could have but didn't." He flung a hand toward the church tent, lifted a tortured gaze that slammed into her. "Being in there, listening to Lije wax on about God's love and protection, makes me want to hit something. Pointless to even go. I don't think I can ever trust Him again."

"You...you were married?" Evelyn stared at him, her mouth hanging open. Gideon Thornton, Mr. Lone Cowboy, once had a *wife?*

He clammed up. "I don't want to talk about it anymore."

"But—"

"Smile. The welcoming committee is about to descend." Curving a hand about her upper arm, he turned her to face his brother and his fiancée. Following them was a young Indian woman and a boy Evelyn had noticed slipping into the tent just before the start of the service.

Gideon spoke first. "I need to speak with you, Lije. Lars, too. Is he here?"

Concern lined the pastor's face. He would have had to be blind not to notice his brother's mood. "He's making his way through the crowd. Katrine is feeling under the weather this morning, and he's eager to return home to check on her. He won't be staying for lunch today."

"I'll make it quick, then."

As soon as the Dane reached them, the trio moved off by themselves. Alice turned to Evelyn with an apologetic smile. "I'm learning there are many issues involved with the establishment of a prairie town. They shouldn't be long. In the meantime, I'd like for you to meet a friend of mine." Drawing the young woman to her side, she said, "This is Winona Eaglefeather. And this handsome young man is her nephew, Dakota."

"Hello, I'm Evelyn Montgomery."

Winona smiled shyly. Outfitted in a print dress the color of orange blossoms, the statuesque beauty wore her coal-black hair in two thick braids that hung past her shoulders. She must be Cheyenne. There was a reservation not far from Brave Rock.

"Nice to meet you," she carefully enunciated each word, her musical voice heavily accented.

"Because Lars is fluent in Cheyenne, he is teaching Winona English," Alice supplied.

Winona's expressive obsidian eyes flicked to the big blond man. Admiration stirred in the dark depths. "He is very good man."

"I wish you could've met his sister, Katrine, today. She has become a particular friend of mine," Alice said. The breeze tugged a stray curl across her mouth, and she deftly dislodged it. "Maybe next week."

Evelyn wasn't sure she'd be back. For one thing, she

was risking her brothers' ire by coming here. For another, she felt out of place. These were Gideon's friends. No telling what they must think of her, despite their friendly manner.

Winona held out her open palm. A shiny red bead flashed there. "May I?" Her gaze slid to Walt, still hunkered in the wagon bed with his toys.

She agreed with some surprise. "He'll like that. Thank you."

Winona moved with effortless grace to the wagon's side and spoke softly to Walt. She held out her hand. Evelyn and Alice watched his face light up at the unexpected treat.

"You're welcome to join us for lunch." Alice waved a fan in front of her face. A misty sheen brought on by the overhead sun enhanced her peaches-and-cream complexion. "The Excelsior cast iron stove Elijah ordered arrived last week, and I've been breaking it in every chance I get. How does pot roast with all the trimmings sound?"

How she missed cooking on a real stove! Reid had ordered one from the mercantile, as well. She wondered if it had arrived. "Delicious. However, I'm not sure Gideon would want to stay."

"Stay for what?" his deep voice sounded at her right shoulder. Close. He was too close. Had that mesmerizing voice whispered words of love to his bride? Suppressing a shiver, she was stunned to recognize a seed of envy sprouting in her heart. Absurd! She wanted nothing from this man but to be left alone on her claim.

"I was asking Evelyn if she'd like to have lunch with us."

Gideon paused a moment, then said, "I appreciate the invitation. Maybe another time."

Relieved he'd declined—really, how comfortable

could a meal with the Thornton clan and their friends be?—she murmured her goodbyes.

One Thornton was about all she could handle, and even that was stretching it. Right now she needed a bit of distance from this troublesome cowboy. Maybe then her good judgment would be restored.

Chapter Ten

"Mmm. This fried chicken rivals my momma's."
Across the table, Evelyn tucked into a mound of green
beans with gusto. "She was one of the best cooks in the
county."

Gideon chewed on a buttery roll and marveled at how
he'd ended up in Brave Rock's only café with her. He'd
fully intended on rushing straight home so he could ditch
the widow and work out some of his frustration on the
nearly finished stable. The smell of fried chicken wafting down Main Street had proved impossible to resist.
That and the man-sized growl that had sprung up from
Evelyn's midsection.

Recalling her look of horror, he took a sip of coffee to
hide a smile. The sturdy cup in his hand sparkled, as did
the silverware and serviceable white dishes. Everything
in Molly Murphy's café was brand-new—red gingham
curtains hung at the windows overlooking Main Street
and wooden tables filled the space, a jar of perky orange
blossoms on each one—a far cry from the dirt-floor tent
restaurant she'd operated over in Boomer Town. Hers had
been the second establishment to open in Brave Rock,
right after the mercantile. Business remained steady due

to the simple, stick-to-your-ribs meals the Irish woman served up.

"Eat your carrots, Walt," Evelyn advised. When he wrinkled his nose in disgust, she looked at Gideon. "Were you a picky eater when you were a boy?"

"Couldn't afford to be. We were lucky to get what we got and Obadiah never let us forget it."

Her brows collided. "He doesn't sound like a very nice man."

"*Nice* is not a word I'd use to describe him, no." He sipped more of the fragrant brew. "Cousin Philomena tried to make our stay more tolerable whenever she could."

Her fork tines hovered above mashed potatoes and gravy. He noticed she ate all of one item before moving on to the next. "Your stay? You make it sound like a brief holiday gone wrong. Your father's cousins were your caretakers after he died, right?"

He grimaced. How had he gotten drawn into this conversation? Evelyn talked. A lot. But it wasn't frivolous or even annoying. Oh, no, he found he enjoyed listening to her. She was intelligent and witty and, despite her problems, optimistic. Her chatter was the only thing currently preventing Lije's disturbing message from echoing in his brain.

"Let's just say my brothers and I were eager to strike out on our own." They had, too, the very day Lije turned eighteen. Occasionally, he wrote to Philomena to let her know how they were doing, an acknowledgment for her small kindnesses.

"So you returned to Thornton Hall."

"Not immediately. We found work in Pennsylvania. Lived in a boarding house for a few years before deciding to return to Virginia."

What a catastrophe that had turned out to be. The truth of that was reflected in her big brown eyes, the tightening of her lips. Back then, it had felt like the town against the Thornton brothers, the Chaucers leading the charge. Theodore in particular had refused to let them be. He'd hunted trouble at every opportunity until, on the night of their altercation, he'd found it in the form of a broken nose.

Ready to halt the trip down memory lane, he asked, "Do you miss Virginia?"

Evelyn stopped midchew. Eyes narrowed, she studied him as if to gauge what had prompted the inquiry.

"Yes, actually, I do. I miss the green, lush neighborhoods, the trees everywhere, the hills and mountains." She glanced out the window and frowned. "Here it's so flat and there aren't as many trees. It's pretty in its own way, I suppose, but I'm finding it difficult to get used to."

"You must miss your friends." Evelyn was a social person. Unlike him, she seemed to crave companionship.

"I do. I miss my church most of all. The people there were like an extended family. We supported and encouraged one another. I've made a couple of acquaintances here, but it's not the same."

"Seems to me Alice would make a good friend. You should give her a chance."

"You're forgetting she's in the enemy camp along with you and your brothers."

Old contentions leaped to life in her eyes, and he despised her for refusing to see the truth. What about her admission that she was experiencing doubts about him and the issue of the stake? Clearly they weren't very strong doubts. She still saw him as the adversary.

"That's your loss, then, isn't it?" Tossing his napkin on his plate, he leveled a glare at her. "You're a grown woman. Maybe it's time you form your own opinions instead of letting your brothers do it for you."

Leaving her to fume, he wove his way through the crowded tables to find the waitress and settle the bill. Then he strode out the door, ruing the day her life collided with his.

Evelyn was putting the finishing touches on a sketch of a viceroy butterfly—she'd sat very still as it drank its fill of nectar from a nearby bloom, getting as many details as possible on paper before it flitted off—when a shadow fell over her. Recognizing Gideon's manly scent, she snapped the album closed. No one was allowed to see her drawings. The inevitable criticism would not only steal the joy drawing gave her, but it would make her question her skill. It was enough that she was satisfied with her work.

Gathering her pencils, she risked a glance upward. Gideon had steered clear of her the past two days, ever since he'd abandoned her and Walt at the café. Well, he hadn't exactly abandoned them. He'd waited to give them a ride, which had turned out to be one of the longest, most uncomfortable moments in his presence to date. She'd been hurt by his insinuations. Her desire to rail at him was kept in check only by the memories of his turmoil during and after the service. While she'd battled to keep her mouth firmly closed, he'd acted as if she didn't exist, as if she weren't sitting right there beside him on the swaying seat.

She'd revisited their exchange multiple times since then, continually snagging on the stunning revelation: he'd had a family. Certainly he'd had a wife. What about children? Her stomach did an odd little clench at the image of the big brawny cowboy cradling an infant to his broad chest. He'd accused God of not saving his family. The deep-seated sorrow on his handsome face warned her something terrible had happened.

Gauging by his expression now shadowed by his hat's brim, the frost had yet to thaw.

"Can I help you?"

She refused to acknowledge her heart's quickstep in response to the way his periwinkle shirt made his skin appear more golden, his eyes a striking gray, his hair a shinier brown. And she would be foolish to notice how his thick biceps strained the sleeves and the soft cotton molded to his muscular chest.

His glacial gaze flicked to Walt, who was curled up asleep on a blanket, hand tucked beneath this cheek. Lion stretched out nearby, lazy in the warm afternoon sunshine.

"It's time to pack your things."

Evelyn shook her head, certain she hadn't heard correctly. "What did you say?"

"I'll be glad to help you. Just point me to what you want moved first." He waved a hand to indicate the various trunks piled beside their tent. He was dead serious.

"I don't know what you're talking about," she huffed, scrambling to her feet, album pressed to her heaving chest. How dare he? "I'm not going anywhere, Gideon Thornton." She poked him in the chest. "Nothing has been decided. Where do you get off ordering me off this land? You're touched in the head if you think I'll jump to do your bidding!"

Gideon's impassivity and cool stare infuriated her, made her itch to shake him.

"Are you done?" he intoned.

"No, I am most certainly not done—"

When she went to poke him again, his large hand

seized hers and held it captive. "Would you be quiet and listen?"

Knowing it was fruitless to try to wrench free of his hold, she stilled, leveling the full force of her ire at him in a stinging glare.

"You and Walt are moving into the tack room for the time being."

"The tack room?"

With the help of his brother Clint, he'd finished the roof late yesterday evening and this morning had attached double sliding doors to the stable's entrance.

His grip loosened a fraction, the smooth heat of his palm almost a caress, scrambling her thoughts. What was that about the tack room?

"It's not the finest of accommodations, I know, but it'll be a roof over your heads. You'll have privacy and protection from the elements."

"I thought you were moving in there." She'd overheard him and Lars Brinkerhoff talking about it.

"I'm fine where I'm at." Shrugging, he released her and moved to stand beside the tent, fingers poised above the buttons. "How about I dismantle this so that you can gather your bedding?"

"I don't understand." Arms folded over her album, held against her chest like a shield, she met his unflinching gaze. "Why are you doing this for us?"

"For the boy," he corrected. "I'm doing it for Walt."

He'd said something similar the day he brought Petra to her. The distinction stung a little. "You didn't answer my question."

His chest rose and fell in a steadying breath. "Do I have to have a reason? Besides, I'm sure you'll pin your own meaning to it, no matter what I say."

Turning his attention to the row of buttons on the tent,

he effectively dismissed her. Apparently she wasn't going to get an answer. *Do you deserve one?* a voice wheedled. *How would you feel if you were in his position?*

Tucking her album into the trunk containing her books and writing implements, she woke Walt and explained what was happening. The idea of sleeping in the stable with horses didn't strike him as unconventional. He was downright giddy with joy.

Evelyn caught Gideon watching Walt bouncing on his toes, an affectionate smile softening his austere features. *He genuinely likes my son,* she thought, stunned, *and cares about his well-being.* Her heart expanded until it felt too big for her chest. The salty taste of tears reached her mouth, and averting her gaze, she concentrated on dusting off their blankets and rolling their pallets. Not surprisingly, Walt dogged Gideon's steps, eager to do his part. Also not surprisingly, the quiet cowboy invited the boy's help, patiently instructing him what to do.

Stop comparing him to Drake. Evelyn gave herself a stern lecture. *So he's kind to little boys. Lots of men like children. You just happened to marry one who didn't. Doesn't make this one special.*

She toted her rolled-up pallet inside the stable. This was the first time she'd been inside since its completion. The scents of fresh straw, elm sap and horseflesh hovered in the still air. All but two of the stalls were occupied, which meant soon smells of a more unpleasant nature would fill the rectangular space. She wouldn't complain, however. They'd been blessed with good weather, but she knew that wouldn't last. The thought of riding out a thunderstorm in that flimsy tent sent a shudder through her.

Lost in thought, Evelyn walked to the end of the wide center aisle and, turning to enter their temporary quarters, plowed smack into Gideon.

"Oh!" Her bundle tipped sideways and tumbled to the straw-dusted floor.

His hands shot out and gripped her arms, steadying her. Mere inches separated them. From this proximity, she could see threads of silver shot through his fog-gray irises. His lashes were pitch-black and spiky. Up close his lips looked incredibly soft and inviting. *You're staring, Evelyn.* Blushing, she jerked her gaze upward, amazement rippling through her at the answering longing in his face—a raw, unmasked need so great she was tempted to wrap him in her arms and console him.

Confused by the direction of her thoughts, the compassion he inspired in her, she looked down to where her fingers were clutching his front. "I, uh, seem to have wrinkled your shirt," she mumbled, uncurling her hands and smoothing out the material.

Big mistake. Beneath the cotton, his chest muscles flexed. He sucked in a startled breath, and his hands tightened on her, drawing her closer.

He's going to kiss me. Gideon Thornton. Wait a minute...I can't let a Thornton *kiss me!* The frantic thoughts raced through her mind, but her body was locked up, frozen, unresponsive. Shock, mingled with renegade anticipation, ricocheted through her veins. Her heart was the only movement, a wild fluttering in her chest as his head lowered a fraction.

Suddenly he stiffened, all emotion dissolving until his face was a blank mask. He dropped his hands and brushed past her in a hasty retreat.

Evelyn didn't move as his clipped footsteps faded into oppressive silence, sure of only one thing. Gideon Thornton was bluffing. The solitude and emotional distance he prized so highly weren't what he really wanted or needed. It appeared he was human after all.

Chapter Eleven

"Evelyn? Are you in there?"

Jumping up from the long cot tucked against the wall opposite the door, one she'd unearthed earlier this afternoon in one of the unpacked trunks, she left the tack room, rushing outside. "Brett." She smiled, impetuously throwing her arms around his neck and planting a kiss on his smooth cheek. She found she missed seeing her brothers every day. "What brings you here?"

Behind the wagon parked in front of the stable, she spotted Reid hoisting Walt into his arms.

Brett shoved the caramel hat farther up his forehead, then gestured over his shoulder. "We thought you could use some hens."

Moving to the wagon, she gripped the side and peered down at the cages, counting four Dominickers—good for meat and eggs. Wood planks were piled in beside them. She pointed. "Is that what I think it is?"

Brett came to stand beside her. "Can't have hens out here without a henhouse."

Again she hugged him, earning her a curious look. She wasn't usually so effusive in her affection. She must be lonelier than she'd realized. "Thank you, Brett." She shot her twin a smile. "You, too, Reid." An unsettling thought occurred to her and she frowned. "Wait. Shouldn't I get Gideon's permission first?"

Shifting his nephew against his hip, Reid scowled. "Why would you need that cur's permission to build a henhouse on *your* land?"

"He was here first—"

"Have you forgotten that it's your husband's stake in the ground?" he demanded, his coffee-colored eyes shooting sparks.

"Of course not." Toying with the buttons on her bodice, she wrestled with what to do. On one hand, she felt she owed it to Gideon to ask his opinion. Another part of her agreed with Reid—why should she have to check with him when it was essentially her land?

Brett gently nudged her with his shoulder, nodded his head toward their now-empty campsite. "Where's your tent?"

"Come inside and I'll show you."

The men shared a look of reluctance.

"Gideon's not here. He went into town to purchase more nails." Seemed he wasn't wasting any time starting on the cabin.

Evelyn worked to keep her expression bland as memories of their near embrace surfaced. If her brothers suspected anything at all friendly existed between them, let alone romantic, they'd throttle her. Then they'd whisk her away from there without stopping to ask her opinion on the matter. So long, sweet independence!

Gideon hadn't uttered another word as they'd worked together to transfer her things yesterday. Clothing, bedding and books had gone into the room, as had assorted personal items such as her mirror-and-brush set and a basin and pitcher for water. The unessential trunks had been lined along the front outer wall beneath the over-hang. When they'd finished, he'd disappeared for about ten minutes, then reappeared with a loaded weapon and an admonishment to be on her guard. Then he'd ridden out of there on Star as if a pack of rabid coyotes were nipping at his heels.

Tugging on Brett's arm, she hustled him inside. She watched him closely as he took in the chinked-log walls and broom-swept earthen floor.

Reid trudged in behind them, disapproval radiating from his lean frame. "What's going on, sis?" Walt shim-mied down and, grasping Brett's hand, pulled him over to the cot and motioned for him to sit. Brett complied, perching on the edge, his large hands clasped between his knees. While her twin looked as though he'd eaten a raw onion, her older brother wore an expression of grave concern.

"Don't you like my new accommodations?" Smiling, she waved her hands about.

"Please tell me you haven't fallen for his act." Reid stood stiffly in the middle of the space. Above his white shirt collar, his neck burned bright red.

Framing her face with her palms, she attempted to calm him with reason. "I haven't fallen for anything. Nothing's changed except for where Walt and I sleep. You should be happy." She looked to Brett. "Aren't you happy we at least have four walls and a roof over our heads?"

"Reid has a point, Evelyn." He sighed. "First the cow, now this…."

"Trust us to know what we're talking about," Reid in-terjected. "We know how the Thornton brothers operate. Even if he can't convince you to hand the land over to him, by softening you up, he may be able to get you to agree to share the land."

"That's ridiculous." A dry laugh escaped her. "He doesn't care what I think. He does, however, care about Walt."

Reid's jaw nearly hit his chest. "If you truly believe that, Evelyn, you're more naive than I thought."

Her chin came up. Anger simmered in her blood. "I am not naive. You're insisting I trust you, yet you refuse to show me the same courtesy. I've shared this land with Gideon for days now, and I'm telling you, he cares about my son." Folding her arms across her chest, she glared at each one in turn. "Walt wandered off the other day. The officers had paid us a visit to see how we were getting along, and neither of us noticed him slipping off."

Real fear lurking in his dark eyes, Brett pulled his nephew onto his lap and held him tight.

"I didn't have to ask Gideon for help. He just stepped in and took control of the situation. If it weren't for him, we might not have found Walt."

Reid's gaze slid to the boy, his mouth thin with displeasure. Neither man spoke. Of course they wouldn't readily acknowledge a Thornton might possess good qualities.

"He wasn't faking his concern," she insisted. Then she blurted a question that had been gnawing at her for days. "H-have you ever considered Ma and Pa were wrong about the Thorntons?"

"What?" Her twin spun around, looking ready to explode. She was beginning to suspect he had an even worse temper than Gideon. "First you defend the man standing in the way of your inheritance and now you're accusing our parents of misleading us? What's gotten into you?"

"The trouble between our families started when we

were kids. We don't know everything that went on, just what Ma and Pa told us."

Hadn't she always heard there were two sides to every story? What if the Thorntons weren't as bad as they'd been led to believe? What if jealousy and bitterness had colored her parents' view of the situation?

The condemnation in Reid's eyes stung. What kind of daughter thought such things about her own family?

"You know what? Forget I said anything." She shouldn't have brought it up. "Where's Theo?"

Reid looked as if he wanted to press the issue but ultimately relented. He rubbed a hand through his short hair. "He's had some trouble out at his claim. Three hogs went missing yesterday."

"Was it a coyote?"

"This wasn't the work of a four-legged predator."

"Someone *filched* them? Was anything else taken?"

"Not that we're aware of."

"We're keeping an eye out for more trouble, however." Brett gently nudged Walt off his lap and stood. "We should get started on that henhouse of yours so we can head back home."

"That's really not necessary," Evelyn protested. She calculated how long Gideon had been gone and when he might return. The last thing she wanted was for him to discover her brothers here. Reid, especially, was still hot about what she'd said.

Brett quirked a dark brow.

She blew out a frustrated breath. "I'm not completely slow-witted, you know. I can build a henhouse."

"It would go faster if he and I did it."

"That's true, but I want to do this. How do you expect me to manage my own claim if you insist on doing everything for me?"

"As much as I hate to admit it, she has a point," Brett said to her twin.

"Always was the most stubborn of the bunch," Reid groused.

Relief swept through her when they made their way to the wagon and, after unloading the supplies, took their leave. Waiting until they became a speck on the horizon, she retrieved her work gloves and transported the wood to a spot near the site where the cabin would be built. She had to admit Gideon had chosen well. Downstream from his tent, in the copse where she'd discovered him shooting arrows, stately cottonwoods and majestic elms would provide welcome shade from the summer sun and be a necessary buffer against bitter winter winds.

But who would ultimately inhabit this land?

Shoving aside the unsettling thought, she picked up her hammer and set to work. Walt tired of being her helper after a while and went to romp in the grass with Lion and Shadow. They were good companions for him. Playful yet gentle.

She was a quarter of the way finished by the time Gideon returned. Expecting him to be proud of her accomplishment, she was stunned to see him barreling toward her like an angry bull.

"What do you think you're doing?"

Jerking to a stop, he towered over her, his tanned hands furling and unfurling. His brows formed one dark slash above his eyes.

"What does it look like?" She pointed to the birds still in their cages. "I'm constructing a chicken coop."

"Why?"

"Because I have nothing better to do?" she retorted, irked at his affronted manner.

"Evelyn."

"To keep them safe from predators. Why else?"

"It didn't occur to you to ask my opinion on the matter, did it? I doubt the thought even crossed your mind. Who cares what a Thornton wants, right?" He threw his hands wide, his control slipping. "You don't care about my rights. You don't care that I've poured every last cent I have into this land, that I've spent every day since the land rush working to better this piece of land."

His accusation hit her wrong. What would he say if he knew she'd stood up for him in front of her brothers? That because of him, she'd questioned her parents' honesty, a move with the potential to create a chasm between her and the people she loved most?

"Gideon—"

Leaning down, he brought his face close. "Until the case goes to court, this is *my* land." He spoke slowly and succinctly. "I don't want you making any changes without my approval. Understand?"

Scrambling up, she matched his stance. "You've conveniently forgotten whose name is on the stake, Mr. Thornton. Just because you've been living here longer and have made improvements doesn't make it yours. I can do whatever I want. Understand?"

"My stake was in the ground when I left to get help for your husband. Someone switched it. Drake was the only one here."

"He was dying!"

"Your brothers came around to collect his body. In the chaos, my brothers and I weren't watching the stake…."

"What exactly are you insinuating?" she pushed out through clenched teeth.

"Think hard. I'm sure you'll figure it out. Unless you're incapable of thinking for yourself, that is." He smirked.

How dare he! The outrage churning inside bubbled up. That was the second and last time he insinuated she was a brainless female. Seizing the pail of water she'd brought with her, she dumped it over his head.

He flinched. Gasped. Water skimmed off his brim and plastered his shirt to his skin. Satisfaction pulsed through her at his dumbfounded expression. That would show him to insult her intelligence!

Then his eyes narrowed. His jaw clenched. Revenge heated up his eyes.

He took a step forward. She stepped back. He advanced again. She retreated.

"Gideon." Holding out her hands to ward him off, she injected a warning in her voice. He summarily ignored it.

Suddenly his hands were on her waist, and she was being lifted into the air, tossed over his shoulder like a flour sack.

Fists pounding his back, she gasped for air to hurl insults at his head. His shoulder wedged against her stomach made that impossible, however. Where was he taking her? She didn't have long to wait for the answer. One minute she was suspended upside down, the next she was sprawled in the stream, water soaking her backside and Gideon glaring down at her with his upper lip curled in disdain.

With a grunt of disgust, he stomped off.

"Don't you ever try a stunt like that again you…you big oaf!" she sputtered, mortified at such cavalier treatment.

Walt stood on the bank, his mouth forming a perfect O. Gideon's dogs sat on either side, seemingly smiling at her predicament.

How could it be that that beast of a man had ever managed to inspire softer feelings in her? Compassion?

Hah! Attraction? Never. From now on, she was looking out for her own best interests.

Gideon Thornton could take a flying leap off a tall cliff.

Had he really just dumped the widow Montgomery in the creek?

Stalking through knee-high grass, Gideon headed away from her and the cabin site, desperate for space. Perspective. Control.

He peeled the soaked shirt away from his chest and attempted to fan it dry. The last thing he'd expected was for her to upend a pail of water on his head! Evelyn's triumphant sneer had snapped his restraint, already spread thin from the treatment he'd received at the general store—thanks to her brothers' vile gossip—and he'd responded without thinking.

Why did she have to invade my life, Lord? he prayed out of desperation. *You know how much I crave solitude. All I want is to be left in peace, but that's impossible with her around. Please, I beg You, end this quickly. Before I lose my mind.*

A clap of thunder sounded in the distance. Glancing to his right, he saw purplish-gray clouds swollen with rain hovering over the wide prairie, a streak of jagged white splitting the sky. Wind gusted, whipping the grass stalks against his boots and tossing his hat into the air. Looked as if there'd be no avoiding this storm.

Seizing his hat, he pivoted and strode back the way he came. His horses would be safer inside the stable. So would the widow and her son. Despite all that had gone on between him and her, he didn't regret his decision to let them move into the tack room. He wouldn't have felt right staying there while they remained in their tent, vulnerable to the elements and wild creatures and unable to easily rouse him if trouble arose.

By the time he reached the stable, Evelyn and Walt were nowhere in sight. Not only had the coop been abandoned, the chicken cages were gone. Maybe she'd taken them inside when she went to change into dry clothes. Heat climbed up his neck at the memory of her sprawled in the water, gaping at him in disbelief.

At the corral Star and Snowball allowed him to guide them inside without balking. The others he had to coax into their stalls. Petra occupied the far one, meaning Evelyn had taken pity on the milk cow and brought her in with the chickens. He glanced with trepidation at the closed tack room door, half expecting it to swing open any minute and Evelyn to emerge and deliver a stinging set down. As soon as the last animal was taken care of, he quickly retreated to his tent.

Now that his anger had ebbed away, Gideon was beginning to experience a sweeping sense of shame. He knew better than to treat a lady like that. Even one who tested his last nerve.

Chapter Twelve

Please don't let him knock on the door.

She was not in the mood for another round with the infuriating cowboy. Jerking the brush through her damp hair, Evelyn stood before the pitcher stand in the corner and strained to hear his footsteps. Was it too much to hope he had already returned to his tent?

If he does knock, I won't answer it. I'll tell him to go away.

Setting the brush aside, she smoothed the serviceable gray skirt and tucked her white blouse into the waistband. Her wet clothes hung on nail hooks no doubt intended for the horses' gear, and her soggy boots sat beside the cot to hopefully dry before she had need of them. Like many women on the prairie, she had only one pair, and it wasn't as if she could do her chores in stocking feet.

I suppose that particular thought hadn't occurred to Gideon before he unceremoniously deposited me in the stream!

Walt looked up from his picture book at the sound of the wind whistling through the eaves. The clouds opened up then, rain pounding the roof with a ferocity that startled him. Book tumbling to the ground, he bounded off the cot and hurtled himself into her arms.

"It's okay, sweetheart." Hugging him against her, she finger-brushed his hair and caressed his cool cheek. "The storm won't last forever."

The words echoed in the still room. A verse slipped through her mind. "Weeping may stay for the night, but rejoicing comes in the morning."

She closed her eyes tight. *Are You trying to tell me something here, God?* The verse was a reminder that this storm she found herself in—not the literal one raging outside but the fight over this land—would pass eventually and that God would carry her through. He had promised never to abandon her. And He hadn't.

God had comforted her when her parents died. He had given her the strength and forbearance to endure her lonely, painful marriage. And when the shock of Drake's death and the prospect of raising their son alone had filled her with fear, the Lord had instilled her with His peace.

He would not abandon her. Somehow He would work this problem out.

Water slipped through the eaves and dripped to the floor, the splattering sound causing Walt to twist in her arms to watch. Suddenly she had to know where Gideon was, if he was safe and dry in the stable or riding out the fury of this storm in his flimsy tent.

"Wait here a minute, okay? I'm just going to see how the horses are faring."

His eyes big in his face, he nodded. She eased away from him and, crossing to the door, swung it wide and peeked out. The shadowed aisle was empty. She left the room and slowly inspected each and every stall. Petra looked bored. The chickens huddled together in the corner, quiet but alert. The horses, on the other hand, shifted in their stalls, ears pricked and tails swishing nervously.

Gideon wasn't here.

Chewing on her bottom lip, Evelyn debated whether or not to don her slicker and go outside and check on him. He really shouldn't be out there. What if lightning struck his tent? For certain the thin canvas wouldn't keep out the rain. What if he got sick?

What about your decision to worry only about yourself and Walt?

Going to the double doors leading to the corral, she laid a hand on the rough wood plank and peered through the sliver of an opening. Of course she couldn't see a thing. Indecision ate at her.

Gideon might be a thorn in her side, but that didn't cancel out those times he'd come through for her and Walt, expecting nothing in return. Take this shelter, for instance. No one forced him to give it up for them.

If she was honest with herself, she'd admit she cared about his welfare. About his safety. And although it wasn't easy to accept, she truly wanted to see him happy and at peace.

Strangely enough, the knowledge didn't make her feel like a traitor. It meant she was a human being capable of compassion.

Thunder growled directly overhead, shaking the walls, and Walt darted out the door, frantically searching the darkness for her. Snowball kicked the stall door.

"I'm here," she said, rushing over to him.

She couldn't leave her son. Gideon was a grown man able to assess his needs. He'd seek shelter from the storm if it got bad enough.

* * *

Evelyn woke later than usual the next morning. Without the benefit of a window and natural light to wake her, she felt disoriented and groggy. *That could be due to the disturbing dreams of Gideon that troubled you throughout the long night,* she thought grumpily. She'd dreamed all sorts of disturbing scenarios—his tent washing away with him inside, his tent catching on fire, trapping him inside.

Pushing the covers off, she shoved her feet into her boots and winced. Still slightly squishy. There was nothing to be done about it. Petra had to be milked, the chickens fed, breakfast tended to and the coop finished.

She dressed in the same gray skirt and white blouse from last night, hurriedly splashed her face with cool water, and brushed and plaited her hair in a single heavy braid. She left Walt sleeping in his bed. He'd had trouble falling asleep and could use the extra rest.

As she emerged from the room, her gaze fell on the row of empty stalls. The worry that had dogged her throughout the night eased up, the knot in her stomach loosening. Gideon had been here to let his horses out. He'd obviously survived the storm just fine.

No doubt he'd think her silly for fretting.

Deciding to skip her morning coffee, she made due with milk and a day-old biscuit. The day was a dreary one, thick fog coating the fields and a canopy of gray clouds hanging low in the sky. The air was slightly cool against her skin. Beneath her boots, the ground squished as she traversed the field between the stable and cabin site. She resisted the urge to check his camp. While she was relieved he was okay, that didn't mean she was ready for a friendly chat. Not that "friendly" really applied to them.

"Evelyn."

His steel-and-velvet voice washed over her, raising gooseflesh along her arms. Halting midstride, she looked up, right into a pair of devastating smoky gray eyes. His features, so familiar to her now, struck her as both tragic and beautiful.

I will not be distracted by this strange pull he has on me.

"Gideon." Her fingers tightening on the toolbox she carried, she walked right past him and continued on her way to the half-finished coop.

Setting the box in the damp grass, she rifled through the tools and fished out her hammer, keenly aware that he'd followed her. The tips of his brown boots edged her vision.

Focused on the box contents, she clipped, "If you're here to try and stop me, I'll just go and seek out Private Strafford's advice on the matter."

It was an immature threat and they both knew it.

His boots shifted once. Twice. A third time.

"I, uh, wanted to say I'm sorry for what happened yesterday."

She slowly lifted her head. An apology was the last thing she'd anticipated.

His hand massaged the back of his neck, and he wore a sheepish expression. The tips of his ears burned bright red. "I shouldn't have behaved the way I did," he said. "I hope you suffered no ill effects from the… Well, you know."

Standing upright, she folded her arms across her chest and cocked her head. She was enjoying his discomfiture far too much. "Are you referring to how you so rudely deposited me in the stream? On my backside, no less?"

He swallowed hard. "Yes."

Taking pity on him, she offered him a rueful smile.

"I owe you an apology, as well. My behavior wasn't exactly that of a mature adult."

The corner of his mouth kicked up. Not a full-fledged grin but awfully close. She felt a sudden longing to see the real thing.

His hand dropped to his side. "So we're good?"

"We're good." Until the next go-round. Considering the situation they found themselves in, she feared it was inevitable.

Gideon's gaze snagged on the widow's dazzling smile, her white teeth flashing against her burnished gold skin. Evelyn's exotic beauty floored him, rendered him weak. Tempted him to disregard the vow he'd made to steer clear of entanglements.

Take that near miss in the stable, for example. He'd come dangerously close to kissing her. He still couldn't quite believe it. He'd successfully held himself aloof since Susannah's passing, embracing the loneliness as his unique penance. Some men were meant to be blessed with hearth and home and a loving family. Not him. One failure had taught him that lesson.

He lifted a hand in the direction of the coop. "I'd like to help you."

Her rosy lips parted. "You would?" Clasping her gloved hands together at her middle, she cocked her head again in that cute way of hers, glossy braid slipping forward over her shoulder. "Are you sure that's a good idea? You and I working together carries a certain amount of risk, does it not? I wouldn't want to end up in the creek again."

Oh, being near her definitely risked his sanity. His composure, too. But after his sorry behavior yesterday, he owed it to her to help. "I promise to be on my best behavior."

One saucy brow quirked. Another potent smile flashed, and he found himself wanting to smile along with her. "In that case, Mr. Thornton, I accept your offer."

Inclining his head, he started forward and, crouching beside her tool crate, swiped a hammer for himself. "Let's get started, then."

Rinsing out his coffee mug, Gideon couldn't stop stealing peeks at the pair upstream. Likewise tending to after-supper dishes, Evelyn was bent near Walt over the shimmering water, her lilting voice singing a bewitching tune in a language he didn't understand. The disturbing ache deep inside grew.

As he'd sat by his fire and eaten tasteless corn mush and too-salty pork, he'd listened to her chatter and Walt's giggles, all the while battling the impulse to ditch his lonely meal and beg to join them.

Surprisingly their shared project that morning had gone well. Evelyn had told him she hoped her brothers didn't find out they had worked together, not when she'd rejected their offer of help. Intrigued, he'd thought about asking her the reason for her acceptance but resisted. It didn't matter. At least, that was what he kept telling himself.

Evelyn looked up and caught him staring. Her dark eyes widened a fraction before her pretty mouth curved in a smile and she waved.

Inclining his head, he deliberately turned away and, after replacing his mug in the proper trunk, retrieved his bow and arrows. The pastime never failed to restore his sense of balance and perspective, the intense concentration it required a good way to clear his mind of foolish thoughts.

He went through the motions of nailing the target to the tree trunk, rolling his shoulders to loosen the tense muscles and looping the leather quiver across his chest. Pacing away from the tree, he anchored the bow in the dip where chest met shoulder and took aim.

The first three shots hit square in the middle. The fourth went wide.

Evelyn had approached from behind, her footfalls masked by the grass, yet still he had sensed her presence, like a wolf recognizing a rival encroaching upon his territory. *Or a potential mate.*

Pivoting, he watched her come closer, dove gray skirts swirling about her long legs. Interest swirled in her eyes. *She wants to give this a try.*

Gideon extended the bow to her. "Your turn."

She halted. Trepidation wrinkled her brow. "We're just here to watch."

Belatedly, he noticed Walt trailing behind, his black hair mussed as usual. Gideon almost offered to take him into town for a haircut but reminded himself it wasn't his place. These two were not his responsibility.

That didn't mean he couldn't encourage her to try something new, however. "Come on, Evelyn. I can tell you want to give it a try."

Her teeth worrying her full lower lip, she shook her head. Escaped tendrils brushed her defined cheekbones. "I don't think so."

"Are you sure? I can teach you how, just like Lars taught me."

"Thanks for the offer, but no."

Troubled by the defeat in her stark gaze, he let the matter drop. For now.

He cocked his head to indicate the boy. "Would you mind if Walt gave it a whirl?"

"What do you think?" She bent at the waist, lightly touching her son's shoulder. "Would you like that?"

Pulling in his lower lip, the child nodded. Gideon held out his hand. At the light weight of Walt's hand in his, the unguarded trust visible on his round face, Gideon experienced an overwhelming desire to protect, to guard against danger, to ensure this sweet boy's happiness. But that was foolish in the extreme. He had no ties to Walt Montgomery. Even if he did, he knew from experience he had absolutely no power to keep him safe. He'd spent four years doing everything humanly possible to safeguard his precious Maggie and yet, in the end, he'd failed. Sickness had stolen her away.

Clamping down on the disturbing memories, he crouched to Walt's level and allowed him to examine and test the weight of the bow and arrow. Satisfied he had a healthy respect for the weapon, he helped him fire off the first shot.

"Good try," Gideon encouraged when the arrow landed in the bushes far left of the target. "This bow is too large for you. Maybe I can talk to Mr. Brinkerhoff about acquiring one more suited to a boy your size."

Walt's response was a blinding smile, one very similar to his mother's. His doe eyes gleamed with happiness.

What would it be like to have a son? One to teach manly things to? Maggie had been all girl, content with her dollies and ribbons and pretty dresses Susannah fashioned for her.

The longing for more children snuck up on him unawares and struck him with the force of a blow midsternum, all the more cruel because he knew it would go unfulfilled.

When Walt's attention was snagged by the dogs chasing a rabbit in the field behind them, he handed Gideon the weapon and took off like a cannon-shot. Gideon stood immobile, watching as the boy ran after the dogs, arms circling windmill-style.

"You're very good with children," Evelyn observed thoughtfully, lifting her skirts as she picked her way through the grass to join him.

Not trusting his voice just then, he shrugged.

"Have you considered marrying again?" she gently probed. "Having children of your own?"

He stiffened, fought to maintain a blank face. "Family life isn't for me. I'm better off alone."

"I don't believe that for a second, Gideon Thornton." She planted her hands on her hips and confronted him. "You may act all hard and tough and aloof, but in reality, you *want* to connect with people. And you have a lot to give. Look how much you've done for Walt. He may not voice it, but it's plain as day he adores you."

Gideon floundered for an appropriate response. He turned away. "You're wrong. I'm just fine on my own."

Her fingers slipped about his forearm, waylaying him, and she pressed in close to his side. Gardenias enveloped him, blurring his thinking. "I've been wrong about a lot of things, but not about this. Admit it—this whole hermit routine is just an act. You're scared of getting hurt again." Her features softened, voice lowering to a husky pitch. "I—I'm sorry about your wife. Did you love her so very much?"

His mouth went dry. "I didn't love her enough," he croaked. "I failed Susannah. Nothing I did made her happy."

Forcing his gaze to hers, he saw that she'd paled and her mouth had gone soft with understanding instead of judgment. What had happened to the accusations she normally hurled at his head? Where had his adversary disappeared to?

"I..." She hesitated, her thick black lashes sweeping down. "I know what you mean. I couldn't please Drake, either."

He couldn't imagine this woman failing to make any man happy. Evelyn was fierce in her loyalty, courageous, a loving, nurturing mother. Lovely in both appearance and spirit.

Drake Montgomery had been a fool.

"Then you understand my aversion to marriage? To relationships?"

Something akin to regret passed over her face. Releasing him, she stepped back, hugged her middle. "Unfortunately, I do." She looked away and murmured, "I suppose we're more alike than I realized. We both endured unpleasant marriages and because of that have chosen to live out the rest of our lives alone."

"There is something to be said for independence."

"And for loneliness."

"At least you have your son."

Her liquid brown eyes fastened on his face, she demanded softly, "What about you, Gideon? Who do you have?"

Chapter Thirteen

Her blurted question nagged Evelyn long into the night, as did the grief it had spawned in Gideon. He'd gone very still, his eyes tormented, before shaking his head and walking away. She regretted the entire conversation now, couldn't fathom what had possessed her to say such things to him. To breach the chasm separating them and to speak the intimate, painful truth.

When she slipped under the covers, rested her head on the pillow and began praying for him, she accepted that her opinion had altered, so gradually she hadn't been aware of it. And while a small part of her was fearful of her brothers' reaction if they ever found out, she experienced an inexplicable peace, a rightness in her spirit.

Sounds pierced the night stillness. Footsteps? But who? It must be three o'clock in the morning.

They grew louder, more urgent. Her heart in her throat, Evelyn bolted upright, wishing she'd kept Gideon's pistol. Feet tangling in the quilt in her haste, she tumbled to her knees, clapping a hand to her mouth to muffle her yelp. Somehow she freed herself and, snatching the porcelain pitcher from the stand, pressed into the corner. Whoever came through that door was gonna have a killer headache.

The latch lifted. The door inched open. Muted light spilled through the crack.

What kind of intruder carried a kerosene lamp?

Deerskin gloves curved around the wood. A scuffed boot planted itself in the dirt. She lifted the pitcher high above her head. *Lord, direct my aim. Please protect us.*

A dark head poked in. Her fingers tightened on the cold handle.

"Evelyn? Are you in here?"

"Gideon?" Shocked relief skittered through her. "What are you doing? Trying to frighten me to death?" she hissed.

Gray eyes glinting in the near-darkness, he cocked an eyebrow at her makeshift weapon. "What were you planning to do with that?"

She lowered the pitcher. "Offer you a drink of water?" she said too sweetly.

His expression grim, he straightened but remained in the doorway. "I didn't mean to startle you. I came to make sure you were all right. I heard men's voices. Horses. I was worried about you and the boy."

Unease rattled her bones. "Are they still here?" she whispered.

"I don't know," he admitted. In the weak light, the bristle along his jaws and around his mouth lent him a rakish air. Determination marked his features. "If they are, I'll find them." He lifted a Colt .45 from its holster and pressed it into her hand. "When I leave, I want you to scoot something in front of the door. Keep the gun ready."

She nodded mutely. Fear captured her in its cold, relentless grip. By going after these men, Gideon was putting himself in danger.

He made to leave. Reaching out, she snagged his sleeve. "Wait."

He stopped, gazing steadily at her but not really seeing her, already intent on the intruders' trail. Evelyn noticed belatedly that he'd dressed hastily, his shirt unbuttoned, hanging loose over a white undershirt. The column of his neck was strong and tan, the skin beneath his collarbone smooth and sleek, inviting her touch.

"How will I know if you're okay?"

"I'll be fine."

"You can't know that. What if—"

His hand cupping her cheek halted her words midstream. Warm and comforting, his rough palm against her cool skin temporarily drove the fear from her mind and replaced it with unwise awareness. He lightly skimmed a thumb over her trembling lips, and it was as if he'd strummed every tiny nerve ending in her body to life.

"Don't worry about me, Evelyn."

Her name again on his lips reduced her knees to jelly. "I want you to report back to me." Like her wits, her voice was scattered. "I won't rest until I know you're okay."

"Think of it this way. If something does happen to me, you'll have this land free and clear. No more Thornton standing in your way."

Then he disappeared into the night before she could slap him for saying something so despicable.

Nearly two hours later, Gideon's adrenaline was waning. Fatigue dogged his steps. He blinked in rapid succession in an attempt to rid his eyes of the grit. The men he'd overheard near his tent were long gone, leaving him with too many unanswered questions. They hammered against his skull.

Even more troublesome were the thoughts of Evelyn that refused to leave him be, distracting him from his purpose. Why he had to go and touch her he had no idea. She was a weakness, a source of fascination, like a thousand-year-old buried treasure to a treasure hunter, a priceless painting to an art collector, a wild, untamed mustang to a horse wrangler.

She's worried about me, which means she cares.

A thrill shot through him, one he ruthlessly suppressed. Evelyn had a big heart, he argued. She wouldn't wish ill on anyone. Her concern didn't mean he was special to her.

Of course you aren't. In her eyes, you're the bad guy. The man standing in the way of her future.

By the time he rubbed down Star and got him settled in his stall, Gideon could think only of his pallet and snatching what was left of this sorry night. He was unprepared then for the whirling dervish that assaulted him in the aisle.

Evelyn's wrath poured forth in a string of incoherent phrases, her small fists pounding his chest.

"Whoa, slow down." He captured her hands, forestalling her attack. "What's got you in such a tizzy?"

From the circle of light emitted by the lamp swinging on a nail above their heads, her eyes blazed accusation. Pink stained her high cheekbones. She jerked, trying to tug free of his hold. "Let me go."

"I don't think so. You might haul off and hit me again."

She jutted her chin, and her face was inches from his. "You are the most provoking, irritating man I've ever met, you know that? First you lead me to believe you're a horrible, underhanded liar. Then, slowly but surely, you disprove every awful thing my family ever said about you. And immediately before riding off into danger, you spout off ridiculous garbage, not giving me a chance to correct your skewed thinking. Then you stay gone for hours, leaving me to worry and wonder if you're lying somewhere hurt and bleeding. I debated whether or not to wake Walt and come searching for you or stay here and wait. O-only then it may have been too late."

Gideon stared into her eyes, trying to absorb the deeper meaning behind her speech. His heart pranced around in his chest like a saddle-shy mustang. "Do you really mean that, Evelyn? You believe my version of what happened the day of the land rush?"

Her shoulders sagged, bringing her weight closer so that she very nearly rested against him. "I misjudged you. I know now that you're honest to a fault. Good. Kind. Selfless. In answer to your question, yes, I do believe you."

Satisfaction rushed through him. *Finally.* Evelyn trusted him.

"My parents were good people," she continued, perplexed. "I don't understand why they would propagate falsehoods about your family."

Treading carefully, he suggested, "In the eyes of the town, my father betrayed the South. While he didn't escape the war—he lost his life for his beliefs—my brothers and I didn't have to endure the consequences of being on the losing side. Maybe your parents fell into the convenient habit of blaming him for their problems. Since he wasn't around, they channeled their anger and defeat onto us."

Pain twisted her features. "It's difficult to accept they wreaked such havoc on innocent lives. And I've been a willing participant, blindly accepting their lies as truth. I accused you of terrible things, Gideon. I'm sorry—"

He cut her off with his mouth on hers. Later he would blame his actions on the loss of sleep and the contentment spreading through him like a warm fire on a cold night. Right now he needed to shock her out of this sorrowful state, to steal this brief moment of connection she claimed he craved.

And what a connection it was. While her lips were soft and moldable beneath his, they were also bold and searching. Like the woman herself, the kiss was adventurous and thrilling, hurtling him into unfamiliar territory in one second flat. Evelyn challenged him on every level. Why be surprised by her reaction to his advances?

Breathing in her sweet floral scent, he tangled his fingers in the waterfall of silken strands. She leaned into him, her hands sliding upward to explore his nape, his hair, before coming to rest on either side of his face. The caress made him feel cherished in a way he'd never before experienced. Cherished and vulnerable. A treacherous position to be in if he planned to keep his distance.

Admit it, your good intentions flew out the window the first time you touched her. No, the first time you clapped eyes on the woman.

Gideon struggled with the voice of reason screaming at him to end the kiss. Holding her eclipsed the loneliness shadowing his every step. With Evelyn in his arms, he felt…*complete.*

His gasp severed their connection. She blinked up at him in confusion. "Gideon?" Sweet breath fanned his mouth even as her thumbs gently skimmed his bristly jaw.

Complete? It couldn't be. He was just fine on his own.

There were no other options for him. But the weak, needy part of him wasn't ready to let go just yet.

Mirroring her actions, he tenderly cradled her face and stared deep into her eyes, drinking in her loveliness. One dark brow wrinkled at his hesitation. Slowly lowering his head once more, he placed a brief, sure kiss upon her lips, a farewell of sorts.

He would not repeat this embrace. The knowledge made his hands shake a little as he drew back and disengaged himself.

Retrieving his hat from where it had landed in the straw, he avoided meeting her sober gaze. "I'll relocate my camp closer to the stable in case we have more visitors. Keep your weapon handy." He moved to the stable entrance. "Might not be a bad idea to barricade yourselves in each night."

"So this is how we're going to handle what just happened between us?" she asked softly. "Pretend it didn't happen?"

He closed his eyes. The sensation of holding her in his arms would stay with him until his dying day. "I doubt that's possible."

"Then why—"

"It can't happen again, Evelyn." He spoke without turning around, gazing unseeing out at the black night. "Surely you see the wisdom in that."

A long pause. "I do."

He sighed as he stepped outside. "Get some rest."

"Goodnight, Gideon," she called after him, the loneliness he called friend echoing in her voice.

Evelyn remained in the shadows long after he'd gone.

Like a brand, Gideon's touch lingered on her flushed skin, the sweet memories of his embrace burned into her consciousness. Wrong or right, she hadn't wanted it to end, had felt bereft when he pulled away.

No man had inspired such wondrous emotions in her. How ironic that her family's adversary—an untouchable cowboy who'd vowed to live out the rest of his life alone—should be the one man her soul recognized!

Movement outside startled her out of her reverie. She stiffened, and air whooshed from her lungs when she saw that it was Gideon, coming to set up his tent. Moonlight glinted off the silver-handled pistols in the gun belt riding low on his hips. His hair gleamed in the pale light, and she recalled how soft it felt sliding across her fingertips. What if she went to him now? There weren't any rules saying a woman couldn't initiate a kiss.

Where's your common sense, Evelyn? Forget the kiss. Forget emotions. They aren't reliable.

Gideon Thornton was off-limits. Not only because of who he was and the issue of the land and their respective futures standing between them, but because her marriage had soured her on ever trying again. All she had to do was remember how quickly Drake's interest and admiration had faded, his snide remarks about her appearance during and after the pregnancy, his complaints on everything from her cooking to the way she ironed his shirts, and she was resolved once again to carefully guard her independence.

Her husband hadn't loved her. Looking back, she wondered if she'd ever loved him. Maybe they'd both mistaken infatuation for something deeper, something true and long lasting. Whatever the case, she wasn't going to risk that particular brand of misery again. Not for any man. Not even one who in another place and time and in other circumstances just might've proved to be her soul mate.

Turning from the sight of Gideon, she quietly returned to her room and her bed.

Chapter Fourteen

Guiding the team to a halt alongside the Healing Heart infirmary—Brave Rock's one and only medical clinic, overseen by none other than his future sister-in-law—Gideon was glad he'd insisted Evelyn and Walt accompany him to Elijah's for a quick meeting. The evidence he'd discovered that morning made him uneasy. Tracks of four riders meant the middle-of-the-night visit hadn't been an accident. These weren't travelers who'd accidentally stumbled upon his property. They were after something...but what?

He set the wagon's brake and stole a glance at Evelyn's profile. She was in mourning clothes again. While the severe black dress didn't detract from her beauty, he preferred her in bright colors that set off her olive skin to perfection and brought a sparkle to her eyes. Besides, Drake hadn't done anything to deserve the honor.

"Are you sure you don't mind visiting with Alice while Lije and I meet with some of the townsmen?" Resting his gloved hands on his thighs, he regarded her from beneath his hat's brim.

Over Walt's head, who occupied the middle position and acted as a necessary buffer, troubled eyes touched on his and flitted away. Her nails dug into the berib-boned reticule on her lap. "I could stand for a little fe-male conversation."

What was troubling her exactly? The intruders? The prospect of a visit with Alice, a member of the "enemy camp"? Or was it the awkward tension arcing between them, the memories of last night hovering unspoken but visible in each other's eyes?

"I know you probably would've preferred to stay home." He paused on that last word, stunned to realize the claim felt more like home with Evelyn and Walt there than it had without.

"No, you were right. Gun or no gun, a woman alone would be an easy target for men intent on wickedness."

"It's not that I don't think you capable of handling yourself—"

"No need to explain." She wrested her gaze back to his. "Truly. I understand, and I appreciate your concern."

Gideon turned at the sound of light footsteps on the porch of the infirmary, which also served as his future sister-in-law's home. Alice turned the corner of the build-ing, her welcoming smile widening when she caught sight of his passengers. Waving, she twisted to speak to his brother, who'd followed her outside.

Watching the couple interact, Lije listening patiently, affection shining in his hazel gaze as he caressed Alice's porcelain cheek, Gideon's fingers curled into fists even as his heart squeezed with a thousand regrets. If anyone deserved to be happy, it was Elijah. He was the type of man who knew how to love a woman the way she needed to be loved. Unlike with Gideon, their father's untimely passing and their cousin's harsh treatment hadn't fatally flawed Lije or Clint, hadn't rendered them incapable of communicating love.

Forcing his gaze to his lap, he felt the seat give as Evelyn climbed down without his assistance. Walt scooted to the edge and let her swing him down.

Alice appeared on his side, that gentle expression she wore around him in full view. "I've got two apple pies cooling inside for when you return. Come hungry."

As Elijah settled himself in Evelyn's seat, Gideon forced a smile. "I'll be sure to keep the meeting brief, then."

Pushing an errant curl behind her ear, a knowing look stole into Alice's blue eyes. "Don't worry about Evelyn. We'll keep her entertained."

There was nothing he could say to that. He tipped his head. "Appreciate it."

Lije leaned forward. "Keep an eye on Dakota," he teased, referencing an incident when Winona's nephew first came to stay with the Gilbert family. Not realizing he'd be welcome to share the blueberry pie Cassie Gilbert had made, the eight-year-old boy had swiped it, eaten the entire thing and ended up with a terrible stomachache.

Alice laughed. "I don't think you have to worry about that."

"See you later, sweetheart." Lije gave a little wave.

"Be careful." She moved out of the way as Gideon took up the reins.

He couldn't resist a final glance at Evelyn. With Walt tucked tightly against her side, she looked uncharacteristically vulnerable.

Lije nudged his shoulder. "She'll be fine, brother. From what I've seen, the woman has spunk. Perfectly capable of taking care of herself."

Different from Susannah, who'd looked to him for everything. Once he'd admitted to Lije that sometimes he felt smothered by her neediness. Shame had filled him.

What sort of husband didn't willingly support and assist his wife? Only now that he'd encountered strong, independent women like Alice and Katrine and Evelyn, he wondered if perhaps he hadn't been right.

"Are we going to this meeting?" Lije motioned to their unmoving wagon, lazy humor coloring his voice. "If not, I'm going back inside for that slice of pie."

With a low growl he snapped the reins and called for the horses to head out, Lije's chuckles getting snatched away by the breeze.

No doubt because he was familiar with Gideon's moods, Lije didn't attempt to draw him into conversation. Instead, he regaled him with the minute details surrounding his upcoming nuptials, everything from the cake—Katrine Brinkerhoff had graciously agreed to bake it—to what type of flowers Alice planned to carry down the aisle.

"Alice wanted me to ask if you'd mind sporting a flower in the buttonhole of your suit jacket."

Gideon frowned. Alice had brought joy back into his brother's life. How could he deny her this small favor? "I suppose I could."

With a burst of laughter, Elijah clapped him on the shoulder. "Just checking to see if you were listening, brother. But I appreciate your willingness to please my future bride."

Gideon shook his head and remained silent the remainder of the ride into town. Clint's horse was tied up to the hitching post in front of the jail, along with several others. Beside him Lije's demeanor took a serious turn.

"What's the reason for this impromptu meeting, Gideon?"

"I'll tell you inside."

When they stepped into the jailhouse, Clint looked

up from his seat behind the desk and nodded a greeting, his pencil stilling above the pile of papers. Fatigue lined his unshaven jaw. The problems plaguing Brave Rock weighed heavily on his little brother's shoulders, Gideon knew. No doubt the prejudice against their family, fanned into flame by the Chaucers, made his job that much harder.

As Gideon and Elijah made their way into the center of the room, the hum of conversation gave way to silence.

"Morning, Preacher." Keith Gilbert, the deacon who'd initially taken in Dakota and cared for him while they searched for his family, stood and shook their hands. "Gideon."

Paul Ramsey, whose barn had been deliberately burned to the ground, leaned against the wall opposite the desk, along with Daniel O'Grady—a burly redheaded Irishman—Lenny Barton and Ben Hamm.

Tossing the pencil down, Clint leaned back in his chair and folded his hands over his vest. The star-shaped badge pinned above his heart winked in the sunlight streaming through the double windows.

"Let's begin, gentlemen. Gideon, you have the floor."

Moving to stand beside the desk, he held his hat in his hands as he addressed the group. "Four men stole onto my property last night. I woke to the sound of their voices. They must've heard me stir, because they moved out rather quickly."

"Did they take anything?" Ramsey's eyes narrowed.

"No."

Elijah's face was lined with concern. "Did you overhear their conversation?"

"No." In hindsight, he should've lain quietly and listened, but the instant concern for Evelyn and Walt's safety had driven rational thought from his sleep-muddled mind.

"What do you suppose they wanted?" Keith's wrinkles deepened.

"I don't know."

"Over on my sister's spread, four of her goats had their throats sliced from ear to ear last week. The scoundrels left them there for her to discover the next morning." Daniel O'Grady shuddered. "Gruesome scene. Leila's tough, but this was too much."

Lenny Barton spat a wad of tobacco into a cup. "Someone raided my henhouse and smashed all the eggs. My poor Sarah hasn't been able to sleep a wink since."

"Something has to be done, Sheriff," Ramsey fired at Clint. "You still haven't caught the scoundrels who burned my barn. What exactly are you doing to protect the citizens of this town?"

Clint, who'd been silently listening to the accounts, rested his forearms on the nicked desktop. "To answer your question, I've done everything in my power to find them. There's not much evidence to go on, however." He reached into a drawer and pulled out a scrap of solid black material. "Lars found this in the ashes of your barn. Looks to me like it's been ripped from a shirt or bandanna. Any thoughts?"

"I don't recognize it," Paul Ramsey conceded.

"Could belong to anybody," Daniel sighed.

Smoothing the material with his fingers, Clint said, "Sounds to me like these men aren't after anything specific. They're trying to scare people. The question is, to what end?"

"I hate to suggest it," Elijah darted a glance at Gideon before turning to address Clint, "but could it be that the Chaucers are trying to stir up trouble for you? They obviously aren't happy you've been appointed the new sheriff."

Gideon's gut twisted into a tight ball. If it turned out Evelyn's brothers were committing these heinous crimes, she'd be heartbroken. She'd suffered enough.

"Wouldn't be surprised," Keith grumbled. As a deacon in Elijah's church who clearly admired and trusted his preacher, he took the Chaucers' rumor-spreading personally.

Gideon spoke up. "While that's a possibility, we all know land for grabs can make men greedy. Is it possible someone is trying to intimidate the settlers into giving up their land?"

Clint's expression hardened. "It's happened before."

"What're you gonna do, Sheriff?" Ramsey asked.

"Simple. Lars and I will investigate the Chaucers. We'll set up watch on their spreads and track their movements." He lifted his gaze to Gideon's. "We start tonight."

Eyes downcast, Evelyn stirred a drop of honey into the fragrant tea, set the spoon aside and lifted the delicate china cup to her lips. Alice's fine dishes brought to mind the floral china set her mother-in-law had given her as a wedding present. They'd had to leave many valuable goods behind in Virginia, bringing only what was necessary and unlikely to be broken on the long, arduous trip out to Oklahoma. Although she knew it was foolish, she missed the comforts of a real home.

Across the table, Alice replaced her cup in its rose-emblazoned saucer. "I wish we didn't have to wait for the men to return to have a slice of pie. The smell is killing me."

Evelyn smiled. The cinnamon-scented breeze wafting from the desserts cooling on the windowsill tempted her, too. "I can't wait for a real stove," she said, then winced.

In order for her to have a real stove, Gideon would have to move. That wouldn't sit well with his friends.

"It's nice not to have to cook over a fire," the other woman agreed, either oblivious to Evelyn's discomfiture or too polite to make note of it. She gestured to this rear area of the clinic, which served as her home, sparsely furnished with a bed, wardrobe, stove and square table with four chairs. "It won't be long until the wedding. I'm looking forward to setting up a real home in Elijah's cabin."

The pretty redhead fairly glowed with happiness. At Evelyn's regard, her cheeks turned rosy. "I'm being a terrible hostess, boring you with incessant talk of my upcoming nuptials. Forgive me."

"There's no need to apologize." She smiled encouragingly.

With her considerate manner and the kindness evident in her eyes, it was impossible not to like Alice Hawthorne. If they weren't on opposite sides of an age-old, unfortunate feud, she'd count herself fortunate to have her as a friend. As it was, she was risking her brothers' ire simply by being here. "I don't mind hearing about it. I happen to like weddings."

Back in Virginia she'd relished the chance to attend friends' weddings. Didn't matter if they were simple or elaborate affairs. Watching a man and woman joining their lives, pledging to love and honor and obey for all their days, never failed to bring her to tears.

She should've known something wasn't right when Drake showed up for their nuptials slightly tipsy. She'd felt cheated somehow. As if he hadn't respected her enough to take their special day seriously.

Across the table from her, Winona lifted her head. Her pearly white teeth flashed. "You will make beautiful—" she paused, searching for the right word "—marry woman."

They both understood her substitution for "bride."

"I hope Elijah thinks so," Alice said.

"No doubt about that," Evelyn assured her, recalling the preacher's besotted expression earlier. He was clearly very much in love with the petite nurse.

Evelyn pointed to the leather moccasin Winona held. All throughout the visit, the young woman had quietly worked to attach colorful beads to the top and sides. "You are very talented."

Her slender shoulders shrugging, she held it out; she pushed the pile of beads toward Evelyn. "You try?"

She refused without a thought, accustomed to avoiding new and different things. Clasping her hands tightly in her lap, she shook her head. "I can't."

Slim black brows winged up. "Not so very hard."

"No, thank you. I'm really not a quick learner."

Alice looked at her in surprise. "Don't sell yourself short, Evelyn. Look at you…making a life out here in the wilderness for you and your son." She glanced at Walt playing on the rug, wooden horse and soldiers set up in a semicircle around him. "It takes guts and brains to do what you're doing."

Nonplussed, she focused on the honey-hued tea in her cup. This woman was set to join the Thornton family in a few short weeks. Didn't she know Evelyn was a Chaucer? Wasn't the fact she could potentially devastate Gideon's dream reason enough to dislike her?

A soft knock echoed through the long rectangular building. Alice stood and reached for the apron hanging on a hook on the wall behind her. "That may be a patient, although normally they ring the bell. I may be a while. Feel free to help yourself to as much tea as you'd like."

"Take your time," Evelyn managed as the redhead disappeared under the thick burlap curtain separating the clinic from the living quarters.

A man and woman's voices carried to where they sat waiting. Winona's head lifted from her task and a twinkle of anticipation stole into her obsidian eyes. She obviously recognized the visitors.

As they drew closer, Evelyn made out the singsong accent belonging to Lars Brinkerhoff. Speculation grew that the Indian beauty was interested in more than a teacher-student relationship with the Dane.

The big blond was all smiles as he entered the room. He circled the table and crouched beside Winona's chair, speaking rapidly in her language. Evelyn was so intent on observing the two interact that she didn't at first hear Alice or notice the stunning young woman standing slightly behind her.

"Evelyn?" she tried again. "I'd like to introduce you to Lars's sister, Katrine."

"Oh, I'm sorry. I was woolgathering." Pressing a hand to her chest, she scooted her chair back and stood to her feet. "Hello, Katrine. Pleased to meet you."

Lars's sister shared his Nordic coloring, with large sparkling blue eyes and flaxen hair arranged in a single neat braid that accentuated her delicate bone structure, the gentle curve of her jaw and full mouth. The robin's egg blue of her formfitting dress deepened the color of her eyes and lent her skin a healthy glow.

"Nice to meet you," Katrine said with a sweet smile, her voice more heavily accented than her brother's. "I have heard good things about you."

She had? From whom?

Alice gestured to Walt, who'd stopped playing and

watched the adults with curiosity, his horse clutched to his chest. "That handsome boy is Evelyn's son, Walt."

Katrine waggled her fingers. "Hello, Master Walt."

Pink staining his cheeks, he dipped his head.

She smiled. "Does he like stories?"

Evelyn nodded. "Very much."

"May I?"

"Of course."

While Katrine went to the boy, Lars stood and, eyeing the pie, rubbed his stomach. "Something smells good."

Glancing at the timepiece pinned to her bodice, Alice sighed. "The men have been gone over two hours. Winona, would you mind serving our friends while I prepare fresh coffee?"

With quiet grace, Winona bent her head in agreement and set about gathering dishes and forks. Beaded wristbands in intricate designs flashed with her careful movements. Moccasins much like the ones she was working on adorned her feet. In between questions after Evelyn's health and the state of things on the claim, Lars cast sidelong glances at his student. Male appreciation was there in his blue gaze, as was a healthy dose of respect, but caution superseded both. Was that due to their different heritages? The prejudice they'd face if they married and had children? Or was it religious views?

Considering the obstacles they'd have to overcome, Evelyn wondered if either would act on their obvious feelings.

A commotion outside caught everyone's attention. Katrine stopped her story midsentence when the back door opened to admit Elijah and Gideon. A third man entered behind them, the badge on his vest identifying him as Clint Thornton.

She'd seen him on the streets of Brave Rock, of

course. Close up, she noted he had the Thornton nose and strong chin, but his eyes were darker, chocolate-brown shot through with gold flecks. Like Elijah, Clint wore his strength in a tall, compact package. Unlike the preacher, he had features that held a promise of retribution if crossed.

Suppressing a shiver, her gaze naturally sought out Gideon, hanging back as his brothers greeted everyone. How was it possible she'd missed his quiet presence in the short span he'd been gone? Trouble—that was what he was. A threat to her impressionable heart. If only he hadn't kissed her....

But he did, and you're just going to have to get past it.

When his piercing gray eyes zeroed in on her, the pulse at the base of her neck leaped in response and she felt as if she'd just dashed full speed across the prairie. Beneath the tabletop, she twisted her hands into a tight ball.

A frown pulled his brows together. Storm clouds brewed in the pale depths. He was upset. Had the meeting not gone well?

Evelyn could hardly concentrate on the activity around her as the men accepted plates and consumed their pie standing up, insisting the women eat at the table. Conversation buzzed. Perched on her lap and happily indulging in the rare treat, Walt deflected much of the attention, for which she could only be grateful.

When they'd said their goodbyes and were leaving the yard, passing beneath the overarching branches of a large oak, she turned to study Gideon's profile. Seriousness cloaked him.

"How was the meeting? Did you get the answers you wanted?"

Gideon glanced over his shoulder to where Walt was

stretched out in the wagon bed. He'd probably be asleep before too much longer.

He shook his head. "There've been other incidents."

"Was anyone hurt?"

"No." His knee bumped hers when the wagon hit a dip. "One theory is that the perpetrators are trying to intimidate the settlers into leaving."

She gripped the edge of the seat. "Makes sense. Out here, land is more valuable than gold."

Squinting at the sun-washed horizon, he was quiet, seemingly preoccupied with his thoughts as if working a puzzle. Corded forearms rested atop worn-in denim stretched across muscled thighs. His Stetson shaded the upper half of his face, leaving only the harsh jut of his jaw in full view.

"What are the other theories?"

He swallowed hard. "I'm not sure you want me to tell you."

Dread clogged her throat. "If I didn't before, I do now."

"Some of the men think your brothers are the culprits." He paused at her sharp inhale and looked over at her.

"That's preposterous!" she sputtered, her temper rising. "My brothers aren't perfect, I admit, but they certainly aren't capable of such cruelty. They're God-fearing, law-abiding citizens."

"And yet they've made it their mission to slander our good name," he bit out. "To turn every single person in Brave Rock against us."

Deeply distressed, she scooted to the far edge of the seat, craving distance. As she did, the front right wheel hit a hole and she teetered.

"Evelyn!"

Gideon's gloved hand clamped down on her arm, yanking her back so that she fell against him with an "oomph." He jerked on the reins and set the brake.

"Are you crazy?" he demanded, his eyes spitting silver sparks as he gripped her shoulders. "You could've been thrown to your death!"

"Lower your voice." She angled her chin to where Walt lay sleeping.

"My heart nearly gave out."

"You're overreacting."

Charged tension permeated the inches separating them. His fingers tightened a fraction before falling away. He passed a weary hand over his face. "I suppose you're right. It's just— You didn't see what I saw."

She could imagine. While his concern cooled her ire somewhat, there was something she had to know. "Tell me something."

"What's that?"

"Do you believe my brothers are guilty?"

Gideon sagged against the seat, the reins going slack in his palms. "I honestly don't know."

"I see." Hurt by his frank answer, she again put space between them, careful this time not to go too near the edge.

"I do know this," he intoned. "I don't want you to get hurt again. For your sake, I hope they're innocent."

Chapter Fifteen

Gideon had hoped that by throwing himself into his work, he'd be able to forget the betrayal in Evelyn's eyes, the hurt he'd inflicted. But burning muscles and sore fingers weren't enough to distract him. Working on the rear cabin wall, he hoisted another notched log onto a stack that nearly reached his knees. The dense elm didn't go easily. When it at last shuddered into place, he straightened and tried to shake the stinging tension out of his shoulders and upper back.

A light breeze rustled the leaves. The quiet bothered him. There was no activity at the stable, only his horses grazing peacefully in the midafternoon sunshine. One thing about Evelyn's new quarters: he couldn't easily check on her. This time of day she was usually helping Walt catch crawdads or sitting on the bank with her nose in a book while he splashed around.

Funny, he didn't mind their presence anymore. He'd grown accustomed to it…even enjoyed it. *So what happens after they leave? Or you?*

He tugged off his gloves, mopped his face with a handkerchief and set off to check the tack room. Maybe they'd decided to seek shelter from the heat.

But the door stood ajar, revealing an empty room. He went back outside and, executing a complete circle, searched all directions. When he saw no sign of them, he tried not to jump to conclusions. They could've gone for a walk. Considering Walt's curious nature, that could take hours.

Just to be safe, he fastened on his gun belt. He whistled for Star, who met him at the gate, and hauled himself onto the palomino's broad back. Lion and Shadow did not like his command to stay put, but they did as ordered. He wondered what would happen when the judge handed down his ruling. The boy had grown attached to his dogs and vice versa.

He frowned, unhappy with the thought of Walt missing them. Dreaded the dogs' mournful eyes and mopey attitudes. *And what about you? Can't deny you'll miss the boy's smiles and spontaneous displays of affection. And Evelyn's singing. Her heart-stopping smiles.*

How had he come to this place? His goals used to be clear-cut, his stance on the stake and the claim unshakable, his view of anything Chaucer related set in stone. And now? Everything had blurred. The widow and child had tilted his world so that he saw everything at an angle, leaving him dizzy and disoriented.

Heading north, he covered about three acres before he saw them in the midst of a rolling field, shaded by a copse of trees. Drawing closer, he saw that they were sleeping, Evelyn propped against the trunk and Walt sprawled out on the blanket, his head in her lap.

He dismounted and quietly crossed to the edge of their picnic blanket. Evelyn's hair was loose about her shoulders, the black-brown waves a stark contrast to the filmy peach dress she'd changed into upon their return from the infirmary. A vision of graceful beauty. A delicate, exotic bloom.

Gideon's fingers itched to sample her exquisite skin again. How would she react if, like some fairy-tale prince, he woke her with a kiss?

Don't be nonsensical, Thornton. You must keep sight of your convictions.

His gaze fell on the open book just out of reach of her hand. She must've been reading it before she fell asleep. Careful not to disturb mother or son, he skirted the picnic basket and, squatting down, gingerly lifted the book. He recognized the maroon cover and gold lettering. He'd seen her guarding this tome on more than one occasion.

Gideon started to snap it shut when a riot of blues and greens caught his eye. A drawing of a dragonfly spread out across the page, wings spanning edge to edge, lifelike in its detail. Evelyn had done this? Feeling as if he was snooping in a diary but unable to quell his curiosity, he flipped to the first page and began to study the pages one by one. Flowers, trees, insects, animals.

He paused at a drawing of a stately mansion. Rose Hill. The former Chaucer home. He recognized the portico and columns from the brief time they'd spent in Virginia as young men. He wondered why he hadn't met her then. Knowing Theodore, he'd probably conspired to keep her hidden from them.

So intent was he on that particular drawing that he didn't notice her stirring.

"Gideon?" Her husky voice startled him. "What are you doing?"

Contrite, he lifted the book. "I came looking for you. You were asleep. This was open on the blanket."

The drowsiness fled. Her eyes narrowed. "And you saw that as an invitation to snoop?" Carefully shifting

Walt's weight, she scooted free and scrambled up. Extended an open palm.

"I— You're right, I had no business looking through your personal things."

"Please give it to me."

Only when he'd returned it did her shoulders relax.

"Evelyn, there's no need to be embarrassed. You're very talented. Who taught you to draw like that?"

"No one." Sweeping the cascade of hair behind her shoulders, she turned away to slip the book into the wicker hamper.

"You have a great eye for detail. And color," he continued, shifting his stance. "You should share your drawings, not hide them away."

"They're nothing special."

"I disagree. Not everyone is blessed with your natural ability."

She paused in her gathering of their things to quirk a brow his direction. "You're just being nice."

He'd noticed her doing that a lot, downplaying her abilities. And avoiding new situations, he realized, thinking of her reluctance to try her hand at archery.

"Who made you doubt yourself, Evelyn?"

The jar of pickled okra in her hands wobbled. "I don't understand what you mean."

Of course she did. She just didn't want to admit he was right. "Was it your brothers?"

Head bent, she worried her lower lip.

"Was it Drake?"

Flinching, she resumed packing as if a tornado were bearing down on them. "I don't know what you're talking about. I—I have to get back and start on supper. We've tarried longer than we should have."

Angry at the person responsible for shattering her

self-confidence, Gideon struggled against the need to press for answers. She obviously wasn't ready to divulge painful secrets. He couldn't blame her. Still, he foolishly hoped that one day she'd open up to him, that one day she'd stop believing lies about herself.

The persistent *thwack* drew Evelyn to Gideon's practice spot. She felt childish for avoiding him. Three days had passed since he'd discovered them sleeping, since he'd seen through her barriers to the truth, since he'd challenged her.

Coward. Odd—she'd always considered herself a brave person. Someone who met life's challenges head-on. Only now, looking back, did she see how she'd hidden parts of herself—her drawings, her singing—fearful of others' opinions.

Of course Gideon sensed her presence long before she announced herself.

Lowering his loaded bow, he turned and silently watched her approach, his expression unreadable. His eyes were watchful, seeing more than she really wished him to. But that was Gideon.

"Walt asleep already?" he inquired.

Nodding, she pressed her hands against her full indigo skirt. "He was tuckered out."

A tiny smile quirked his lips. "I'm not surprised. He splashed around in the stream for hours."

Evelyn hadn't thought he'd noticed, consumed as he'd been with erecting his cabin.

He hesitated, distracted by a pair of mockingbirds swooping beneath the branches. Dusk colored the world in an odd yellow light. "He hasn't spoken a single word?"

"No." Her fingers curled into her skirts. "I thought in

his excitement today he'd let something slip. Burst into speech. But nothing."

"It wasn't my intention to worry you."

A dry laugh escaped her. "I do that all on my own."

"Have you thought about taking him into Guthrie to see a doctor?"

"Theo doesn't think a doctor would help, but the longer he goes without speaking, the more I think I should take him. I have to try, at least. If he doesn't speak within the month, I'll make plans to go." While she respected her brothers' opinions, Walt was her son. She had to do what she thought was best. "In the meantime, I'll continue praying for God's healing."

His fingers flexed on the bow. Questions flashed in his eyes. "No one's around except you and me. Wanna give it a try?"

She debated. What would it hurt? Really? Gideon wasn't the type to criticize or make fun of her.

"Are you truly uninterested," he said softly, "or are you afraid to try?"

Her feet carried her to his side. The scent of campfire and leather and clean shirts stirred pleasant memories; his solid strength made her feel safe. Looking deep into his eyes, she said, "Imagine what it was like having three strong-willed, overprotective brothers. I had to fight for the chance to do things on my own. Is there such a thing as loving someone too much?"

His smooth brow furrowed, but he didn't offer an answer.

"I don't know the answer to that," she mused aloud. "All I know is that at some point, I started to question myself. And then I married Drake."

Gideon stood very still. His sculpted mouth pursed, and his eyes darkened to storm-cloud-gray. His dislike was plain. She wondered for the first time what her husband's final moments had been like and what, if anything, he'd said to this man.

"He, uh, was not easy to please." Oh, this was so hard. She hadn't spoken of this to anyone. Ever. But she forced the truth out. "He continually criticized my efforts, magnified every mistake. My cooking wasn't good enough. It was either too hot or too cold, too bland, too spicy. His clothes weren't ironed the way he wanted them. The house wasn't tidy enough. I wasn't a good mother." She cringed. That was the hardest to endure, the ridicule of her handling of Walt. "Eventually I became paralyzed, knowing that no matter how hard I tried, I couldn't do anything right in his eyes."

A muscle ticked in his jaw, his eyes now a fiery silver. "And you became afraid to try new things. Afraid to make mistakes."

"Exactly." A strange lightness expanded her chest. Gideon understood. Even more wondrous, there was no judgment in his expression. He didn't find her lacking.

"Drake Montgomery was an idiot," he pronounced, a fierceness to his tone she found fascinating. "You are an amazing woman, Evelyn. Brave and kind and smarter than I'll ever hope to be."

This elicited a self-conscious smile. She soaked up his praise like a flower striving for the refreshing rain.

"I've watched you with your son. You're a wonderful mother. You know how to balance love and affection with instruction and discipline. Don't let Drake's skewed views shackle you for the rest of your life. Don't let him win."

Evelyn knew it would take more than compliments to change her thought patterns, but it was a start. Gideon gave her hope. And courage to try.

Drawing in a steadying breath, she held out her hand. "I'm ready."

He smiled then, a full-fledged grin that hit her with the force of a gunshot. A happy and lighthearted Gideon Thornton was a sight to behold. Beneath that "keep your distance" scowl was a man of true beauty.

"You may not get it on the first try but I promise you this—you will have fun."

Then his arms came around her and a new thrilling sensation chased away her trepidation.

Her wobbly smile turned his heart to mush. Reduced his defenses to dust. Gideon was taken aback by the intensity of his reaction to her admission, the drive to encourage her, protect her, lo— *Whoa. Hold on a second.* Love was not on the accepted list of emotions. Not where Mrs. Evelyn Chaucer Montgomery was concerned.

Sure, holding her close resurrected memories of their kiss, made him long to repeat it, but that didn't mean he could lose sight of what was important. *Remember Susannah.*

He should never have married the lively, outgoing Southern belle. A wealthy socialite accustomed to having her way, Susannah had been bold and beautiful and determined, pursuing him in spite of the obstacles he'd tossed in her path. Ultimately, loneliness had triumphed over caution. The need for something deeper than what he shared with his brothers, the appeal of female companionship weakened him.

Unfortunately, their post-wedding bliss fizzled out quicker than a fire in a downpour. She became demanding, greedy for his time and attention. He'd thought having Maggie would change things, thought a baby would satisfy his wife. He'd thought wrong.

"Gideon?" Evelyn angled her head, bringing her luscious mouth to within inches of his.

He swallowed hard. "Uh, sorry. I was lost in thought."

Concentrating on the task at hand instead of the silky hair teasing his chin, the smell of gardenias washing over him and the brush of her back against his chest took a level of skill he hadn't known he possessed. As soon as he'd gone through the motions and she'd shot off the first arrow, he dropped his arms and stumbled back, wrestling the tornado of yearning into submission.

"Good try." His voice was gruff. "It may take several attempts before you come anywhere close to hitting the target, however."

Molasses eyes sought his. "How many did it take you?"

"So many I lost count."

Her smile had a devastating effect on his control. He backed up a couple of steps. "Remember to relax." He sounded anything but. "Concentrate."

Watching her, Gideon knew it would take everything in him not to fall hard. In the year and a half since Susannah's death, he'd admitted to himself that he hadn't truly loved her. Cared for her and wanted her to be happy, yes, but love hadn't been a part of the equation. It was different with Evelyn...his heart recognized the danger she posed and was susceptible.

Evelyn and Walt represented everything he desired but couldn't have—family, home, belonging to something bigger than himself.

He just had to be strong a little while longer. The cavalry soldiers had said to expect to wait a month or two for their case to be heard. Maybe in a couple more weeks they would know the outcome. One of them would leave. After that they'd never have to set eyes on each other again.

Chapter Sixteen

❧

"Your brothers are coming."

Gideon's pronouncement carried a hint of caution, reflected in how his stiff frame unfolded from his perch on a fallen log where he'd been observing her and Walt take turns with the bow. In the three days since that first lesson, she'd improved until she was able to at least hit the target's edges. One thing he'd been right about—she was having so much fun she wasn't as focused on getting it perfect. His encouraging, nonjudgmental attitude gave her the freedom to mess up.

Lowering the bow and arrow, Evelyn scanned the fields separating the stable and this small meadow behind the cabin site and spotted their three mounts approaching at a fast clip. Her stomach knotted with apprehension. All three wore matching grim expressions.

Had there been more trouble out at their spreads?

Then she intercepted the hateful glare Theo shot at Gideon. Foreboding skittered along her nerve endings as insight flashed. *They came to check up on me and are angry because I'm here with him.* She could only imagine how they'd interpret this seemingly cozy scene.

Please, God, I don't want trouble.

As Walt immediately set off to greet his uncles, she handed the bow and arrow to Gideon. Could he read the anxiety simmering inside her? He didn't utter a single word as he solemnly took the items from her, his gaze on her brothers—in his eyes, the enemy. She lifted the quiver over her head and handed that to him, as well.

Tugging her bodice down, she squared her shoulders and, walking away from Gideon, went to meet them. The farther away they stayed from him, the better. If she was lucky, she'd steer them back to the stable and distract them with talk of their progress on their claims.

"Hey, guys." She attempted a casual attitude. "If you'd come earlier, you could've had some of the fried fish I fixed for supper."

Brett lifted Walt into his arms and stared hard first at her, then beyond her shoulder at Gideon.

Theodore's boots hit the earth with a thud. He came around the front of his horse, his dark eyes smoldering, fists clenched at his sides. "What's going on here, Evelyn? I'm sure I speak for all of us when I say we didn't expect to find you cavorting with the enemy."

Reid slapped his hat against his thigh, frustration etched in the planes of his face. "Have you switched sides?"

"You are being ridiculous." She searched for the right words to deflect their wrath without revealing the true state of her heart. "Gideon was just showing Walt and me how to shoot an arrow. That's it."

"You can't fool me, sis." Reid drew closer, his sharp gaze probing hers. "You've completely tossed aside our warnings and have allowed yourself to be duped by this man."

Theo snorted. "Surely you haven't abandoned everything Ma and Pa taught us about that horrid family!"

Evelyn wavered. Did she pacify her brothers with half-truths, thereby possibly avoiding an all-out war? Or did she assert herself—defend her own stance? In the end, truth won out.

She looked at Walt. "Sweetheart, I want you to go to our room for a bit." When he hesitated, she added, "Perhaps you can draw pictures for your uncles."

Brett reluctantly let him go. She waited until he was out of earshot to continue. "I am a grown woman capable of making my own decisions. I have a mind that works just fine, thank you very much, and I've undergone a change of heart. The Thorntons are not our enemies."

Reid looked about ready to explode. Brett scowled. Theo spluttered.

Holding up a hand to forestall their responses, she said reasonably, "Think about it. Our parents' dispute was with Jacob Thornton, their father. We were kids when he chose to side with the North, as were Gideon, Elijah and Clint. They didn't cause our ruin. The war brought hardship to many, many people. Yes, our family suffered, but so did theirs. Just as we lost our brother in battle, they lost their father."

She barely remembered their oldest brother, Preston, who at fifteen had run off without their father's permission to fight for the South. She wasn't allowed to forget, however, the price he'd paid. Somehow her parents had found a way to blame even his death on the Thorntons.

"I won't stand here and listen to you be disrespectful to our parents," Reid growled.

Evelyn put a hand out. He flinched. She recognized then the chasm she'd created with her admission. "Please, Reid," she implored, hating that she was hurting them. "You know I loved them both dearly. The fact that I disagree with some of their assertions doesn't mean I don't respect them." She looked at Theo. "Don't think with your emotions. Try and be objective."

"Oh, that's rich," Theo snarled, "coming from you. Tell me you're being objective where that slime is concerned."

"That's not fair—"

"Evelyn?"

At the unexpected sound of Gideon's voice close behind her, she jumped. Three riled Chaucers swiveled to glare at the intruder. She turned on her heel, a warning spilling out. "You should go."

He didn't so much as blink. His honed body looked to be on high alert, and his attention was centered on her. "Are you all right?"

Reid pushed past her and got up in Gideon's face. "You got wax in your ears, Thornton? You're not wanted here."

As he edged sideways, his eyes held hers. "I want to hear it from her."

Evelyn's heart kicked with a giddy sort of pleasure, completely unreasonable considering the situation. Apparently her state of being was worth risking a confrontation. "I'm fine."

Then her brother shoved Gideon, and her knees went weak with fear. "Reid, no!"

As she sprinted to put herself in between the two men, he shoved Gideon a second time. Gideon raised his fists to return the favor just as she reached them. The knuckles of his right hand glanced off her cheek. Pain radiated along her cheekbone. Biting hard on her lip in a bid to keep silent, she covered that side of her face with her hand.

"Evelyn!" he gasped. "I'm so sorry—" He reached out to her, horror stalking his eyes.

The movement was halted, however, by Brett and Theo, who took hold of Gideon's arms, one on each side.

"I'll teach you to lay a hand on my sister," Reid growled. Rearing back, he planted a fist in Gideon's gut.

Almost dizzy with fear, she pounced on her twin, holding tight to his wrist. "Leave him alone, Reid!"

Adrenaline pumping, he easily shook her off. "Stay out of this."

Gideon struggled to free himself. "Go, Evelyn."

"No!" She refused to leave him to the mercy of her brothers. Tears stung her eyes. Begging silently for God's intervention, she cast about for a way to end this. They wouldn't listen to words. She had to take action.

Gideon grunted as Reid struck his face. Her body shuddered as if she had been struck.

The bow and arrow.

Racing over to where he'd laid it down, she seized it with trembling fingers and ran back as fast as her legs would carry her. Because of her nervousness, it took three tries to ready the arrow. She aimed it straight at Reid.

"Let him go or I'll plant this arrow in your leg!"

Her brother's eyes went wide. His fist hovered in the air. "Have you lost your mind?"

"No, but you have," she said, fury overtaking fear. How dare they act like heathens after she'd defended them to Gideon? Law-abiding citizens, she'd said. How dare they put her son's well-being at risk? "All three of you! Release him at once."

Not surprisingly, Brett was the first one to see reason. "She's right. We shouldn't be doing this." He dropped his hands and stepped back.

With one arm free, Gideon sprang into action, twisting free of Theo's hold. Fists up, he edged away from them. Closer to her.

Reid advanced a step, his face flushed with anger and telltale disappointment. "I don't know what to say, sis."

"How about an apology?"

"I'm not the one who's betrayed my family here today."

She winced at the sting of his words. "I couldn't stand by and do nothing while you beat a man who's innocent of wrongdoing. What happened was an accident, and you know it. You should've kept your distance instead of instigating trouble."

Gideon reached her side. Placing a steadying hand on her outstretched arm, he applied gentle pressure, silently urging her to lower the weapon. "It's okay."

Risking a glance at him, she sucked in a harsh breath. A slash of deep purple underscored his left eye, and the opposite jaw, red and angry looking, was already swelling.

"Let's go," Brett called, snatching his hat from the ground. "We all need a little time to calm down."

Muttering something under his breath, Reid pivoted on his bootheel and stalked off. Theo's eyes narrowed. "We aren't finished, Thornton. I promise you that."

Then, with a lingering reproachful glance at Evelyn, he joined his brothers and jerked himself into the saddle. When they directed their mounts toward town, her knees gave out. Gideon caught her about the waist, guided her across the grass to the fallen log he'd occupied earlier.

Tears spilled over and tracked down her cheeks. The enormity of her actions registered in her brain and a ripple of disbelief shuddered through her. Had she really threatened her twin with bodily injury?

"They'll never forgive me," she whispered.

His arm tightened about her waist, sheltering her, lending comfort. Gideon placed a finger beneath her chin and lifted her face to his. Admiration and compassion swirled in his eyes. "You're their sister. Of course they'll forgive you. Give them time."

"I didn't think." She swiped at the tears with the back of her hand. "I just reacted."

"I'll never forget what you did for me," he murmured.

Slowly registering his nearness, the heat of his upper body enveloping her in a warm veil, she studied his injuries. "Are you all right?"

He brushed off her concern with a lopsided smile. "I can handle a few bruised ribs." The smile faded. As he lightly curved his free hand over her sore cheek, the pale gray of his eyes deepened to gunmetal. "I didn't mean to hurt you. You believe me, don't you?"

Imprisoning his strong wrist, she held his hand in place. "What happened was an accident, plain and simple."

"I should've held on to my temper."

"You have the right to defend yourself." The hair covering his tanned forearm tickled her palm. "I'm sorry, Gideon. What my brothers did was inexcusable. I hardly know what to feel." She sniffled, then accepted the handkerchief he fished out of his pocket. "I'm angry, but I'm also frightened that I've pushed them away forever. I told them I no longer view the Thornton family as our enemy."

"That didn't go over very well."

"Not at all."

He caressed her cheek. "They love you, Evelyn. They'll come around."

"I hope you're right."

His touch scattered her thoughts until only one remained—kissing him again. When he brought his face close, anticipation zipped along her nerve endings. *You're in way over your head, Evelyn. Ahead lies forbidden territory.*

While her opinion of Gideon had changed, her decision to remain free and independent had not. Besides, being with him meant alienating her family forever. She could never give them up for the uncertainty of a relationship.

When his lips brushed a sweet, heart-melting kiss against her cheek, she experienced a stab of disappointment. Then reality set in. She couldn't have more, couldn't wish for more. Not if she wanted her heart to remain intact. Untouched. Unaffected. Unbroken by a man who'd turned out not to be the enemy after all.

Chapter Seventeen

"Would Master Walter like a lemon drop?" Polly Fairhaven, proprietress of Fairhaven's Mercantile, stood behind rainbow-hued jars filled to the brims with assorted candies.

His small hand gripping Evelyn's, he glanced up with hopeful eyes. Her smile twisted into a wince as her cheek still smarted. Fishing a penny from her reticule, she handed it to the lady while attempting to keep her face averted. Walt popped the yellow candy in his mouth, a look of pure pleasure brightening his countenance.

The older proprietress folded her pudgy hands atop the lid and turned her attention to Evelyn. "That's quite a shiner you have there, young lady."

Lightly touching the swollen flesh, she affected an airy demeanor.

"Yes, it was very clumsy of me." Hoping her self-conscious laugh would ward off questions, she tugged on Walt's hand. "Thank you for the assistance."

Mrs. Fairhaven opened her mouth to question her further but was sidetracked by another customer needing assistance. Relieved, Evelyn guided her son along the aisle to the back left corner, where the paper goods were displayed. He was out of drawing paper. She would soon need pencils but would need to consult the catalog, as they didn't carry them in stock.

Perhaps she should've waited a few days for her injury to heal. But Gideon had business in town, and she hadn't wanted to stay out on the claim alone.

The bell above the door rang, but she paid it no heed. Moments later an instantly recognizable feminine voice greeted her.

"Good afternoon, Evelyn."

Slipping the paper into her basket, she turned to greet the willowy blonde. "Katrine. How nice to see you again."

"I was passing by and saw you through the window." Blue eyes twinkling with good humor, she waved at Walt. "Hello, sir. I see you are enjoying a piece of candy. I think I would like one, too."

Walt's cheeks colored and he ducked his head.

"The rare treat makes shopping bearable for him," Evelyn said wryly.

Katrine's elegant, short-nailed fingers smoothed the thick braid sliding over her shoulder. Possessed of a fine figure, she made even the simplest of dresses look stylish. "My brother came to town on business, and I thought I would stop in at the café for a slice of Mrs. Murphy's ginger cake and some coffee. Will you join me?"

She hesitated. She was almost done with her shopping, and Gideon had said he might be a while. However, Katrine would surely ask how she'd received this injury. Evelyn wasn't sure exactly what to tell her. *If you didn't want questions, you should've stayed home.*

The desire for female company outweighed her reluctance. Although she didn't know the Danish lady very well, she sensed she wasn't one to gossip. And there was an absence of judgment in her eyes.

"I would love to. First let me pay for these items." Indicating her basket, she said, "Would you mind if I stopped in the sheriff's office to tell Gideon where I'm headed? We rode in with him, and I don't want him to wonder where we've gone."

"That is fine. I will wait outside." She bent at the waist. "Would you like to wait with me, Walt? Perhaps we can make up stories about the men riding by."

After a moment's indecision, he released Evelyn and took Katrine's outstretched hand. As she watched the two cross to the entrance, Evelyn was struck by a longing for the familiar so intense that it seemed to weigh down her spirit. If she missed their dear friends and family, their congregation and memorable town landmarks, how much more must her son? Maybe Drake's death wasn't the cause of his silence. Maybe it was the trauma of leaving his old life behind.

They were isolated here. Hadn't been in Oklahoma long enough for it to feel even remotely like home. *Spending time with Gideon's family and friends could help alleviate the problem.* The thought came unbidden. She liked Katrine and Lars, Elijah and Alice. Winona, too. She had a particular way with children. Evelyn wasn't as well acquainted with the sheriff, but he struck her as a decent sort. Fair-minded.

The matching expressions of censure on her brothers' faces pricked her conscience. After what happened yesterday, they would surely see her friendship with these people as another betrayal.

Torn, she offered up a silent petition. *Lord Jesus, I don't know what to do. The last thing I want is to alienate my family. On the other hand, my son and I need support. Good friends to replace those we left behind.*

When she'd settled her bill and joined Katrine and

Walt outside, the contented expression on her son's face, the trust shining in his eyes as he listened intently to the young woman, bolstered her resolve. His needs came first. On the off chance Theo or the others were to discover their association, she would simply explain the reasoning behind her decision.

They made their way slowly down Main Street, bypassing the line of people waiting outside the post office. The jail was located at the end, next to the barbershop.

Pushing open the heavy door, Evelyn led the way inside. Seated behind the desk, Clint looked up and his intense gaze stalled on her swollen cheek before sliding to Katrine following behind her. Because of his own visible injuries, Gideon surely would have already confided in his brother. She need not fear his questions. Clint lowered his boots to the floor. He stood up, tall and strong and all business. "Afternoon, ladies. What can I do for you?"

This was the man who'd been spying on her brothers. For a split second, she pondered whether or not the sheriff might possibly be tempted to frame the Chaucer brothers for the trouble that had stricken the town. That would certainly rid the Thorntons of their nemeses.

Then her gaze encountered Gideon, and she dismissed the idea. The Thorntons had done nothing to retaliate. Surely they would have already if they'd been so inclined. Elijah practically oozed compassion and mercy. Gideon was honest to a fault, and Clint was duty bound to uphold the law.

"I came to tell Gideon that we'll be at Mrs. Murphy's establishment whenever he's finished here."

His expression carefully blank, Gideon tugged at the hem of his pant leg where his ankle rested on the opposite knee. "I shouldn't be much longer." He nodded to Katrine. "You three enjoy yourselves."

"Would you like for us to bring something back for you both?" Katrine inquired, her accent curiously thicker than usual. Could it be she was nervous about something?

A slight smile touched Clint's mouth, softening the rugged planes of his face. "That's mighty kind of you to offer, but I think I'll pass this time. I'm still full from lunch."

Gideon also declined. As they were taking their leave, Evelyn caught the brothers exchanging a meaningful glance. Clint gave a barely perceptible nod. What was that about?

They had emerged into the overcast day and had started to cross the dusty street when Gideon called her name.

Closing the door behind him, he took a single step forward. "Can I speak to you for a moment?"

"I, uh—"

Katrine touched her arm. "I can take Walt over to the café, if you would like."

Curiosity burned in her chest. "I'd appreciate that. Thank you."

A pretty smile lifted her lips. "You are very welcome."

Lifting her skirts so that her hem didn't sweep the dirt, Evelyn closed the distance between them. The area around his cheekbone was still swollen and red, with a tinge of blue. "What did Clint say about your injuries?"

One side of his mouth quirked. "He said I don't look half-bad considering it was three against one. Of course I told him about my brave rescuer." His eyes sparkled, resembling the most brilliant stars. Gorgeous. "He was impressed."

"I don't think that's a story that should be circulated."

"Don't worry. Clint's as tight-lipped as they come."

The basket grew heavy in her hand. "What couldn't you say in front of Katrine?"

Growing serious, he cast about to make certain no one was close enough to overhear their conversation. "Clint and Lars observed your brothers' spreads three nights in a row. There was no suspicious activity. No one left the premises, and there were no late-night visitors. On top of that, another crime was committed on the third night."

Relief spread through her. "I knew they weren't responsible. Is Clint convinced of their innocence?"

"He is."

"What happens now?"

"We move on to the next theory."

"Which is?"

He shook his head. "Let us worry about that. Now, you don't want to keep your companions waiting, do you?"

"I can handle whatever it is," she huffed, put out by his refusal to confide in her.

"I won't argue with that," he surprised her by saying. "However, I feel you'd be safer at this point not knowing."

An older couple approached at a rapid pace, proving that a public street was not the place to argue the point. "Fine."

When she turned to go, his hand stole over her wrist, encasing her warm flesh in his steel-like strength.

"Don't be mad."

The pleading tone in his husky voice cooled her irritation. He was merely concerned for her well-being, doing what he thought best. He wasn't withholding information because he thought her a brainless female. Something Drake would have done. *Drake would not have hesitated to tell you that he didn't think you capable of rational thought.*

She lifted her gaze, allowing warmth to fill it. "I'm not."

Satisfied, he dropped his hand, waiting until the couple had passed to speak again.

"Enjoy your visit with Katrine. I'll try not to keep you waiting long."

"Take your time."

With a parting smile, she left him and made her way across the street to the Brave Rock café. Even though it was midafternoon, business was brisk, the one girl Mrs. Murphy had hired to serve her customers looking a bit frazzled. Katrine's blond hair gleamed, drawing her attention, and she wove her way through the tables to join her and Walt.

A steaming cup of coffee awaited her.

"I remembered you said you prefer coffee to tea." Katrine waved her fingers toward the sturdy ceramic cup.

Lowering herself into the chair opposite, she thanked her and took a sip of the bracing brew. They each ordered a slice of Mrs. Murphy's famous ginger cake. For Walt, a cinnamon cookie and large glass of milk.

Seeing the curiosity and concern in the other woman's eyes, Evelyn decided to broach the subject. "I suppose you're wondering what happened to Gideon and me."

An ever-so-slight smile lifted her lips. "It was—what is the word—*impossible* not to notice. However, do not feel as if you have to tell me." She frowned suddenly, secret shadows passing over her face. "I know what it is like to want to keep certain things to yourself."

Fiddling with the silverware, she said, "You will probably hear eventually. Gideon will tell Elijah, who will tell Alice and… I know how these things slip out." She sighed. "You are aware of the long-standing feud between our families?"

Katrine nodded.

"My brothers came to visit me and were not happy to see Gideon and me talking. Actually, Gideon has been teaching me to shoot a bow and arrow."

At this the blonde's brows rose. "That is generous of him."

Evelyn felt heat suffuse her face. Thankful for the interruption the arrival of their desserts created, she waited until the waitress had gone before continuing.

"Tempers flared. My brothers provoked Gideon. He was defending himself when I got caught in the fray."

Katrine cocked her head to one side. "Because you were trying to prevent the fight? Who were you trying to protect—your brothers or Gideon?"

Evelyn nearly spewed her coffee. She managed to gulp it down instead.

"I am sorry. That was—" she tapped her temple, searching for the right word "—*impertinent* of me."

"No, it's a fair question. It's just not one I've considered, so I'm not prepared to answer."

"Let us speak of other things." She smiled. "Otherwise, you may never agree to have dessert with me again."

Katrine entertained her with stories of her and Lars's journey to America many years prior. She was somewhat vague concerning the particulars of their first few months, but that was understandable. Who wanted to dwell on their hardships, much less divulge them to a new friend? Hadn't they had enough of that today, anyway?

As she savored another bite of the moist confection, she paused on the word. *Friend.* Yes, she had a feeling Katrine Brinkerhoff would make a very fine friend. She thanked God for bringing this godly woman into her life.

They had just finished their desserts when Katrine

checked the watch attached to her bodice. Dabbing her mouth with the pristine white napkin, she dug in her reticule. "Oh, my, I am supposed to meet Lars in five minutes. I was enjoying myself so much I completely lost track of the time." Placing coins on the table, she wore an expression of apology. "I am sorry to abandon you, Evelyn, but I do not want my brother to worry. He says there are unsavory characters in Brave Rock and that I must be careful."

Evelyn swallowed the last of her coffee. "It's okay. We're finished here, aren't we, sweetheart?" she asked her son.

Crumbs dotted Walt's mouth. His plate was empty.

"Drink the rest of your milk." To Katrine she said, "I'm glad we ran into you today. It's been a pleasant visit."

She smiled. "Soon you and Gideon must come and have supper with us. Our cabin isn't too far from town."

"I would like that very much."

After she'd gone, Evelyn was left with a hopeful feeling. Maybe, just maybe, she and her son could build a life here.

Emerging from the café, Evelyn smacked into a broad chest covered in military blue.

"Oh!" She stumbled back. "I apologize. I didn't see you."

A hand came up to grip her elbow, steadying her. "Well, if it isn't the lovely widow. Mrs. Montgomery." Private Ryder Strafford's smile had a predatory bent as he doffed his hat. "No need to apologize. You can run into me any day."

Shrugging away from his touch, she edged backward. Something about the man didn't sit right. She glanced at his companion, the one with the dirty-blond hair and bushy mustache. Private McGraw, she believed. The absence of all feeling in that man's eyes made him even more menacing than Strafford. Following his line of sight, she swallowed a gasp. His rapt attention was centered on Katrine's retreating form.

"May I buy you a cup of coffee?" Strafford's question distracted Evelyn. His blue eyes would've been beautiful were it not for the vulturine gleam. This was not a man who put a woman's wants and needs above his own. He was all about seeking his own pleasure.

She tugged Walt closer. How was it that she could feel threatened standing in the midst of town in broad daylight? She sensed these were not honorable soldiers. "I'm afraid I must decline. I'm late meeting someone."

A frown of displeasure pulled his brows together. Bending closer, he towered over her. "Can't they wait? I'm most eager to spend time with you."

Before she could reply, another voice sounded. "No, I can't wait."

Gideon. Sagging with relief, she turned her head to see him bearing down on them like a ravenous wolf homed in on his prey. His glacial eyes were narrowed to slits; his glare alone had the private straightening and stepping away.

Gideon ordered himself to calm down. Evelyn wasn't in immediate danger. That joke of a soldier was merely being too forward. But the sight that had greeted him when he'd come out of Clint's office had triggered at first jolting fear, then anger hotter than a poker left too long in the blaze.

Another soldier approached the group, openly curious. Gideon had seen him about town but did not know his name.

"What's going on here, Strafford?" that soldier asked.

"Nothing to concern you, Reeves," the dark-headed man replied, clearly irked at Gideon's untimely appearance.

Standing beside Strafford, Private McGraw belatedly pulled his attention from the other side of the street. He turned and stared curiously at Gideon's black eye. "What happened to your face, Mr. Thornton? And the lady's?"

"None of your business."

His mustache twitched. "Keeping the peace in this little nowhere town is my business."

Threading his arm through Evelyn's, Gideon leveled the other man a "back off" stare. "The matter has no bearing on Brave Rock's safety. Now, I have work to get back to. Good day, *gentlemen*."

He ushered Evelyn and Walt along the storefronts to where his wagon was parked. When he'd lifted the boy into the seat, he searched her face. Her color was slightly off. Blast those men for frightening her!

"Are you all right?" He worked to keep his voice calm.

Beneath her bonnet's stiff brim, uncertainty clouded her dark eyes. "I'm fine. It's just that— Gideon, I don't trust those men."

He blew out a breath. "Nor do I."

"The blond one, Private McGraw… He was watching Katrine. What if…he's interested in her like Strafford is in me?"

Strafford was a pest. McGraw, he sensed, could pose a serious threat. "I'll have a word with Lars."

He assisted her into the wagon. When he reached the corner of the bed, he spotted Private Reeves hurrying toward him. Reeves raised a hand to stall him.

"Mr. Thornton," he puffed, slightly out of breath, "I'm glad I caught you. I have a proposition for you."

"Oh, yeah? What's that?"

Glancing left and right, Reeves pitched his voice low. "I believe you could be of great assistance to my colleagues and me. We are in need of someone to do a few odd jobs for us. If you agree to help, we'd see to it that your court case is hurried along." His gaze flicked beyond Gideon's shoulder to where Evelyn sat waiting. "We have some influence with Judge Martin." He paused for effect. "I can guarantee an outcome in your favor."

Gideon stared at the private. Mind racing, he blurted, "What kind of odd jobs are we talking about?"

Reeves shrugged nonchalantly. "Whatever McGraw asks you to do."

Which translated into something underhanded, something no law-abiding citizen would do with a clear conscience. "Sorry, not interested."

He started to brush past the shorter man.

"Are you sure you don't want to think about it? You do want that claim, don't you? Or have you decided the widow should have it?"

At the sly innuendo, Gideon clenched his fists. "What I want, Reeves, is to do things the honest way. Coercion isn't my style. Nor will I take part in illegal activities." Rounding the bed, he uttered a terse, "Good day."

"If you tell your brother the sheriff about our little conversation, I'll just deny it."

Ignoring the threat, Gideon climbed onto the seat and, aware of Evelyn's regard, guided the team onto the street.

He wouldn't mention this conversation to her. It would only worry her. But he did intend on relating every detail to Clint. Those soldiers were up to no good.

Chapter Eighteen

"I was surprised to see Gideon at services again this morning." Alice hefted the pan of roast chicken from the oven and plunked it on the table. Her eyes were full of questions. So were Katrine's.

Stirring the green beans again, Evelyn lifted a shoulder. "I have no answers for you. He approached us in the midst of breakfast and offered to bring us."

She'd assumed he would wait outside the big tent while Elijah preached. Instead he'd escorted her to the back row and sat down on the other side of Walt. While he'd clearly been uncomfortable, at least he hadn't been tormented like last time.

Alice peeked out the window and Evelyn's gaze followed. From the looks of things, the Thornton brothers and Lars were discussing something of great import.

"Elijah can't help but be pleased," Alice was saying. "And hopeful that at least one of his brothers will come around and make peace with God."

Katrine, resplendent in a patterned dress of pastel blue and white, looked up from her task of placing silverware on the table. "Why do they stay away? Are they not followers of Christ?"

Resting her hands on a chair, Evelyn waited for the answer, glad Katrine had given voice to a question she hadn't had the courage to ask.

Tucking an errant curl behind her ear, Alice frowned. "Do you recall that Elijah lost his first fiancée, Marybelle, to influenza? An epidemic swept through their small Kansas town, killing nearly a third of the population. Both Clint and Gideon lost people they cared deeply about." She smoothed her apron, then picked up the carving knife, sadness stamped upon her lovely features. "I believe their loss and grief took a huge toll on their relationship with God."

"Gideon's wife died during the outbreak, didn't she?" Evelyn murmured without thinking.

Buried in the roast chicken, the knife halted midcut. "Susannah? Yes, I'm afraid so."

Her heart squeezed. No wonder he was resistant to connect with others, guarded his solitude so zealously. He'd loved his wife to distraction and hadn't been able to move past the loss. A tiny stab of jealousy stole her breath. It wasn't possible—or rational—to be jealous of a dead woman. Still, she couldn't help but wonder what Susannah had been like. *Must've been very special indeed to have lassoed the lone-wolf cowboy's heart.*

Gripping the smooth wood beneath her fingers, Evelyn gave in to her curiosity. "What was she like?"

"I confess I know next to nothing about her," Alice replied. "Elijah won't say much about Gideon's past. He knows how Gideon cherishes his privacy."

Disappointed, she gathered a stack of plates and, circling the table, placed one at each chair. Katrine poured coffee.

Alice stopped her carving to study Evelyn. "I know this land claim situation hasn't been ideal for either of you, but I have to say you and Walt have been good for Gideon."

Her mouth fell open.

Alice chuckled. "Don't look so shocked. Since you've been around, he's different. Less tense. I even caught a hint of a smile earlier. Wouldn't you agree, Katrine?"

The kettle hovered midair. Head tilted to one side, she considered the question, glistening braid sliding over one shoulder. "I do not know him very well, but the fact that he has attended church services two weeks in a row is significant."

"Exactly." With a triumphant smile and a knowing glance directed at Evelyn, the bride-to-be went back to her carving.

Footsteps clumped on the porch, followed by the front door swinging open and emitting four very large, very masculine men. And although their combined presence nearly overwhelmed the cozy interior, Evelyn welcomed the intrusion. Alice's suggestions pleased her too much. To think that she had had a positive influence on Gideon irrationally thrilled her. *Wrong. So very wrong.*

She deliberately avoided Gideon's gaze, fearful of what he might detect in her own. Because, despite the countless reasons that falling for him would mean disaster, she had a sinking feeling her heart was beginning to succumb to the pull he had over her.

At the last minute Winona and Dakota joined them at the table. Their arrival and the talk of Elijah and Alice's upcoming wedding made it easy for Gideon to remain lost in his thoughts. Not that anyone expected him to contribute to such a conversation. They were used to his brooding silences.

Inside his head, however, chaos abounded. What insane impulse had driven him to put on his Sunday clothes and offer Evelyn a ride to church? And why had he not waited outside the tent instead of subjecting himself to renewed grief? Perhaps most baffling of all was his agreeing to this cozy family scene where Evelyn fit like a long-lost puzzle piece.

Reaching to snag another roll, he made the mistake of intercepting Lije's gaze, the speculation there confirming what he'd suspected. His brothers thought the widow and her son meant something to him. He could hardly blame them. Showing up to church two weeks in a row was something of a phenomenon.

Walt's small hand landed on Gideon's leg, and he pointed to the basket of rolls. As rich brown eyes so like his mother's looked adoringly up to his, a tender, mushy feeling stole through his chest. Over the boy's head, Evelyn watched him carefully, the warmth and approval in her gaze inciting an irrational wish for a different future than he'd envisioned for himself.

Who was he kidding? Of course they meant something to him. In the past few weeks, they'd slipped under his defenses and planted themselves firmly in his head and heart. He cared about their safety and well-being. He wanted good things to come their way, wanted Walt to speak again and to have a father who showed interest in him. For Evelyn he wanted someone worthy of her, a man who would love her without conditions.

A shame he couldn't be that man.

Jerking his attention back to his plate, he forced the rest of its contents down—the formerly succulent chicken now sat in his mouth like a fist of splinters—and excused himself. There were too many happy pairings in this small room. Lije and Alice. If he didn't miss his mark, Lars and Winona. Clint and Katrine? No. Lars's sister hadn't shown any marked interest in his brother. Besides, Clint had determined not to marry. Lije thought he'd change his tune later on, but Gideon wasn't so sure. The youngest Thornton possessed a will of iron. Once his mind was made up about something, there was no changing it.

Outside he pulled fresh air into his lungs, soaked in the rugged beauty of the Oklahoma prairie. Thin layers of clouds hanging in the sky provided relief from the soaring mid-May temperatures and created contrast with the surrounding colors. A sea of green grass rippled into the distance, punctuated here and there by splashes of bright orange and golden yellow.

The door burst open, and Dakota, his shoulder-length brown hair swinging, darted into the field. Walt tripped after him. Whoops and giggles broke the silence. Lars approached, his knee-high moccasin boots masking his footsteps. A contented grin marked his features.

"Oh, to have the energy of a child."

Gideon nodded, steering his thoughts to calmer waters. "Sure would be handy." He thought of the endless tasks awaiting him, the chief of them being the completion of his cabin.

Dakota rushed up to Lars to show him a ladybug cradled in his palm. The Dane smiled and tousled Dakota's hair. Affection shone in his blue eyes. He'd clearly taken to Winona's nephew. And to the lovely Indian woman herself. But would he ever act on those feelings?

When the boy rejoined Walt, Lars shot Gideon a sidelong glance. "It pleases me to see you in services again, Gideon."

"Don't expect me to make a habit of it," he softly warned, breaking off a stalk of grass and chewing on it.

His hand settled on Gideon's shoulder. "Trust me, my

friend. In time you will find comfort in God's Word and in the friendship of other believers."

He swallowed a sarcastic remark, kept his gaze on the boys. "No disrespect, but I highly doubt that."

"Do you think you are the only one to suffer?" he calmly pointed out. "Dakota's father abandoned him. His mother died. Walt Montgomery also lost a father."

"Losing a child is altogether different," he pushed out, not at all happy about this conversation. He knew Lars meant well, but the subject was a painful one. One he'd rather avoid.

The Dane nodded. "I cannot imagine the sorrow you speak of. However, death and loss are a part of life on this earth, as are healing and joy and the prospect of new love."

On that last word, someone emerged from the cabin. Winona. A shy smile curved her mouth as her obsidian eyes settled on her tutor. Telltale color slashed Lars's cheekbones.

Glad of the reprieve, Gideon turned to greet her and, after a brief exchange of inane comments about the weather, eagerly made his escape. The subject of his lost daughter was off-limits. He didn't want to think about Maggie and the gaping, jagged wound her absence had carved in his soul. Healing? Joy? Love? They simply weren't possible in a world without her.

Evelyn stood in the tack room doorway, caught by the tender way Gideon carried her sleeping son, laid him gently on the cot and tucked the covers around him, hovering a moment to see if he would stir. *He seems awfully comfortable with the routine.*

When he turned to her he started, as if he'd been unaware of his surroundings. Walking swiftly past her, he left the stable. She followed him into the darkness.

"Is something wrong, Gideon?"

Because of his dark clothing and the lack of moonlight, his broad form blended with the shadows. "I'm tired, that's all. Long day."

Indeed, it had been a long day. Aside from the trying church service, however, it had been a pleasant one. The more time she spent with Alice and the others, the more she liked and admired them. They had reason to ostracize her, yet they'd generously drawn her into their circle.

Admit it, you like spending time with Gideon when he's around his family. You like watching him interact with his brothers, his polite deference to the nurse he'll soon call sister-in-law, his genuine fondness for his friend Lars.

With a small sigh, she folded her hands and gazed up at the navy expanse dotted with white sparklers. The air was warm and balmy against her skin, heavy with the scent of rain. Somehow the darkness made it easier to speak of difficult things.

"Tell me about Susannah."

Gideon's spine stiffened. He half turned to her, but she couldn't make out his expression. Part of her was glad of that.

"Why?"

Because I'm desperate to learn her secret...how she convinced you to open up your heart. She shrugged in feigned nonchalance. "I know very little about your life in Kansas."

Silence stretched to the point of being uncomfortable. "Not that much to tell."

"How did you meet her?"

"Evelyn—" Her name came out on a long-suffering sigh. She wasn't about to be put off. "I spilled my guts to you about Drake. The least you can do is answer some simple questions."

Her response was met by another too-long silence. Evelyn thought perhaps it was a lost cause. Recalling Alice's warning about Gideon's penchant for privacy, she was about to return to the stable when his low voice split the night.

"We met at church. She, uh, was up from Charleston visiting her aunt."

A Southern belle. She could never compete with that. "Let me guess—her beauty combined with her accent and charming manners led you to court her right away?"

He shifted his stance. "I didn't court her."

"I don't understand."

"Susannah came from an affluent family," he said, resigned. "She was accustomed to getting what she wanted. I guess she thought a rough-and-tumble cowboy would suit her fancy, so she set out to convince me that she was what I wanted, too."

Evelyn mulled this over. Their marriage did not sound like a love match.

"But you eventually fell for her?" she ventured, certain he'd put a stop to the questions.

"I haven't spoken of this to another soul." Wonder punctuated his words. She sensed his intense perusal. "Elijah surmised much of what went on between us, but he never guessed…I did not love Susannah. I married her because I was tired of being alone and, though I'm ashamed to admit it, all that heaping admiration boosted my confidence. 'Course, that didn't last. She soon learned what it was to be a lowly cowboy's wife."

Even though night cloaked them, she could see the defeat weighing him down. A soft breeze rustled through the distant trees, stirring the ends of her unbound hair.

Needing something to occupy her nervous hands, she gathered the mass in her hands and twisted it, finger-combing the ends.

"Why do you think you failed her?"

"I don't think. I know." His demeanor hardened. "I made the choice to marry her, so I determined to make the best of the arrangement. I did everything in my power to make her happy. It wasn't enough." He jabbed a thumb in his chest. "*I* wasn't enough."

"Oh, Gideon." Her heart breaking for him, she reached out.

He jerked away, warded her off with upheld palms. "Nothing you say will change the past. I was there. I saw how my inadequacies, my inability to love, destroyed her happiness."

Evelyn lowered her hand. There would be no convincing him of anything. He would have to figure things out for himself. Strange how they'd each dealt with similar issues in their marriages and come out the other side with scars.

"I wasn't going to try and convince you of anything."

"You weren't?" Stunned indignation marked his words. "You weren't going to tell me that I *am* capable of love? That it was her problem, not mine?"

"You wouldn't believe me even if I did."

Inch by inch, he lowered his hands. She had his full attention.

"My situation is somewhat similar to yours. I married for the wrong reasons. I found Drake's marked attention flattering. He was dashing, a little arrogant, I suppose, and the object of many a young girl's daydream. My brothers approved of him—a marvel in itself—and urged me to accept his proposal."

"I can see where their approval would carry a lot of influence with you," he observed thoughtfully.

Nodding, she continued, "The newness of married life wore off much too quickly, I'm afraid, and just as you weren't enough for Susannah, I wasn't enough for Drake."

"Evelyn—" He took a single step forward.

"There's something I've never told anyone." She rushed ahead before she lost her nerve. "Drake found his pleasure with other women. As soon as he found out I was expecting, which was not long after the wedding, he lost interest." She paused, inwardly cringing as the remembered shame and disgust washed over her anew. How undesirable she'd felt! How inadequate. "I hid it from my brothers, for I knew exactly what they would do if they found out. So I know what it's like to fail. I know what it's like to give something your best and have it still not be enough."

The confession left her strangely deflated, yet relieved, too.

"You didn't confront him?" Repressed fury rippled the air surrounding him.

That he was indignant on her account gave her hope that he cared a little. Just as she cared. Evelyn realized then she didn't need to see Gideon with her eyes; she knew him well enough to anticipate his reactions. She saw him with her heart.

"I considered it, but Drake wouldn't have changed his ways for the likes of me."

"The likes of—"

Suddenly, he was before her, his hands curving about her shoulders, his face hovering near. Sparkling awareness danced along her skin as his heat and strength enveloped her. Longing—that traitorous, willful, delightful longing for Gideon—surged through her, and she gasped at the potency of it.

"That man had no clue what a treasure he had in you," Gideon stated, a tremor shuddering through him.

Then he was kissing her, his hands sliding to her back to press her close against his chest. The kiss swept away past hurts and set her free to glory in the present. This man, her former adversary, had wrought a tremendous change in her. He'd challenged lifelong beliefs—about the Chaucer–Thornton feud and, more important, about herself—forcing her to form her own opinions, to set aside fear, to be as brave as he believed her to be.

There was a truth hammering at her heart, mind and soul, demanding to be named. A truth she dared not name, for once she did, she would not be able to ignore it, would not be able to stop herself from acting on it. And that would be a mistake.

Throwing her arms about his neck, she held on tight, shutting her mind to the future. A future that surely did not include Gideon.

Chapter Nineteen

Focus, Gideon. The wild bundle of horseflesh he'd just purchased was none too happy about his new surroundings. One second of inattention was all it would take to get kicked senseless. Murmuring in a low, succinct voice, he kept the rope taut as he coerced the big black into the new, smaller corral he'd erected yesterday with Lars's and Clint's assistance.

He was a gorgeous animal, powerfully built with a sleek black coat and intelligent eyes. Gideon itched to match wits with him.

Surely this new challenge would divert his mind from his troubles. Was it only weeks ago he'd claimed this land and set out to build a new life? A handful of days strung together since his only worries were filling his belly and erecting shelter for his animals as quickly as possible?

Now his future hung in the balance, all of it tied to one woman. He had a claim to defend. If Evelyn won, he'd be out a home. Weeks of hard labor down the drain. If *he* won, Evelyn and Walt would pack their things and return to her brothers. The mental image made him literally sick to his stomach. Did he truly have what it took to evict a widow and her son? On top of that, he had the troublesome Chaucers and their blasted rumors to contend with—again, connected to Evelyn. If he took them to task as he yearned to, she would ultimately be hurt, and he couldn't do that to her.

The worst of it was the constant awareness of her, the affection and deep regard that had sprung up without his consent. He didn't like how he could read her so well. Didn't like how his common sense flew out the window every time she was around and he spilled his guts at her first question. Took her into his arms as if it were his right, needing her as he needed his next breath.

Sensing his preoccupation, the stallion whipped his head to the right. The rope slipped through Gideon's gloves. At the last moment, Gideon clamped down on it, halting the movement.

"How 'bout you pay attention, Thornton, and try not to get yourself killed?" he muttered under his breath.

He had Thunder calmed and the gate tightly latched when Evelyn's mount snuffled a greeting. Swiping his rolled-up sleeve across his damp forehead, he leaned a hip against the middle rung and watched their approach. Relief at the sight of them safe and sound softened his muscles. He couldn't very well keep them prisoners here—although with faceless criminals roaming freely about Brave Rock, he wouldn't have minded doing just that—but he worried when they weren't with him. Something he was going to have to get over once their case had been before the court and they'd parted ways.

That was the trouble with this forced cohabitation… he'd gotten comfortable with the arrangement. Fact was, Evelyn was not his wife. Walt was not his son. They weren't his responsibility, but it sure felt as though they were.

Gauging from her expression, it appeared the visit

with her brothers must not have gone well. He hadn't expected any different. The Chaucers were a stubborn bunch, especially when it came to their stance on the Thorntons.

He strode to intercept her, then steadied the horse with a hand on his broad neck as she swung down from the saddle and then reached up to Walt.

"Theo and the others still upset about the other night?"

Toying with the reticule swinging from her wrist, she nodded, wisps floating about her temples. The stiff black bonnet that accompanied her widow's weeds framed her face, shading her dark eyes. He noted her cheek was no longer swollen, a slight redness the only reminder of the mishap. Thank goodness. Accident or no, Gideon hated that he'd caused her pain.

"Upset is putting it mildly," she said, pretty lips pulling into a frown. "Chaucer men don't easily forgive. They like to stew."

"I'm sorry."

"Like you said, they'll come around. Eventually. I just have to be patient."

Walt tugged on Gideon's pant leg and pointed at his new acquisition. Scooping the little boy into his arms as if it was the most natural thing in the world, Gideon walked to the corral, giving the animal plenty of buffer. Evelyn stopped beside them.

"Beautiful animal," she said with a touch of awe. "Isn't he rather large?"

"Yep. Rowdy, too." He touched a finger to Walt's chest. "Thunder is a pretty horse to look at, isn't he?"

The boy nodded, his big eyes fixated on Thunder.

"Well, he's not as nice as he looks. Not yet, anyway. Thunder hasn't been trained. He's used to running free and doing as he chooses, which means he doesn't like being cooped up in that corral. I'll have to teach him to obey my commands, but until then, I want you to stay away from him. If you want to look at him, I'll bring you over, but don't come by yourself, okay?"

Beneath the fall of raven hair, Walt's thin brows wrinkled. *He wants to ask questions,* Gideon thought, silently urging the boy to speak. When his little mouth pursed and he merely nodded, Gideon experienced a sharp prick of disappointment. A side glance at Evelyn revealed her mirroring disquiet.

Please, God, restore this boy's ability to communicate. I can only imagine the worry and uncertainty Evelyn must be feeling. If Maggie had clammed up for days on end, I would've pulled my hair out in frustration.

The prayer came naturally, his concern for Walt edging out the anger he felt whenever his thoughts turned toward his Maker.

Closing his eyes, he allowed himself to visualize his little girl healthy and happy, the blond ringlets and flushed cheeks and blue eyes full of laughter. The pain and grief were still there, still sliced deep like a razor-sharp ax, but they didn't threaten to cut him clean in two like before. Could it be due to Evelyn and Walt's presence?

A tiny, cool hand pressed against his cheek, and he opened his eyes and looked directly into innocent brown pools of curiosity. He smiled, wondering how the boy viewed him. As his mother's friend? As another uncle? *As a father figure?*

Whoa. Forget that last one. Fatherhood was not in his future.

He intercepted a tender smile on Evelyn's face as she watched the two of them, and his heart constricted. Regret tasted bitter on his tongue. Marriage wasn't in his future, either.

* * *

Evelyn turned the thin pork chops and long wedges of potatoes sizzling in the cast iron pan with a pronged fork, willing it to cook faster. The flames licking at the kindling upped the midday temperature by ten degrees at least. Perspiration dampened her neck and face, the hair at her temples and nape clinging to her skin. The shade cast by the stable overhang did little to ease the spring heat.

Balancing an arm on her bent knee, she twisted to see if Walt still chased Lion and Shadow in circles in the tall grass beyond the stream. She caught a flash of dark hair and tan shirt. He would miss those dogs once their case had been settled. She would have to ask Reid to look around for one. That is, *if* he agreed to help her.

Her brothers were all furious with her. She was angry at them, too. Why couldn't they at least try and have an open mind? Give the Thorntons a chance?

Her mind turned to Gideon. The image of him holding Walt against his broad chest, a loving smile curving his mouth, had stayed with her through the night and into the morning. His fondness for her son filled her with a peculiar contentment.

He'd surprised her by declining her invitation to supper. She'd thought to prolong the special moment. Evidently, his thinking had been clearer than hers. Evelyn needed to remember theirs was a temporary situation. Very soon the land's ownership would be decided, and one of them would leave this place.

The prongs sank into the potatoes, signaling they were done. Scooping them onto a trencher along with the meat, she wrapped a towel about the pan handle and set it off to the side to cool. Time to check the rolls cooking in the Dutch oven.

Evelyn glanced over her shoulder again to look for Walt. When she didn't see him or the dogs, she replaced the lid and stood, shading her eyes with a cupped hand. Lion and Shadow lay panting in the shade of a cottonwood. Walking to the corner of the stable, she searched the fields in vain.

Her pulse skipped. Surely he wouldn't wander off again. He knew how much he'd scared her the last time.

Just as she opened her mouth to holler for him, a masculine voice beat her to it. Gideon. But he and Lars were busy raising the cabin walls higher. Why—

"Walt!" The terror in Gideon's voice turned her blood to ice.

Whipping toward the new corral, she spotted Walt near the fence, frozen in fear as Thunder reared on massive hind legs, pawing at the air.

Feeling as if she were in a dream, she tried to scream a warning but her voice failed her. *Run, sweetheart, run!*

The ground seemed to shake as the stallion dropped to all fours and, tossing his head, made for the fence and freedom. Only, her child stood in the way.

No. I can't lose him, Lord! Evelyn forced her wobbly legs to move. *Faster. I'll never reach him in time!*

Out of the corner of her eye she saw Gideon sprinting for him. He was closer. He'd save him. *Please, God, let him save him!*

The instant he saw Walt at the fence and Thunder's furious reaction, Gideon's chest locked up with familiar fear. His muscles hardened into immovable stone; his feet restrained by iron shackles. He couldn't move.

For the span of a breath, he was back in Maggie's room, kneeling by her bed and begging God to save her.

Pleading with Him to take him instead. His wife had already succumbed to the influenza. Not his daughter, too.

You still have a chance to save Walt.

The nudge shattered the past's hold on him. *Walt. I'm coming, buddy.* Gideon burst into motion, drawing on his strength and speed to reach the boy in time.

Once again petitioning God for a child's life, he watched in horror as Thunder reached the fence and the rungs fell apart as if made of butter. Wrong. Something was wrong. That wood should've held.

Walt stood straight as an arrow, his mouth open, his face a colorless oval. He didn't seem to hear Gideon's shouted warnings. Pushing his legs beyond their endurance, he reached the boy in time to knock him to the ground and cover him with his body.

The earth beneath them trembled, hooves crashing against the ground like thunderclaps. Then those hooves found him. Striking. Pummeling. He gritted his teeth as waves of pain washed over his back and around his rib cage. He fought the swirling blackness stealing his consciousness.

Had to stay awake. Had to protect Walt. *Please, God...*

As his vision faded, Evelyn's frantic cries were eclipsed by a child's voice calling his name.

Chapter Twenty

Evelyn couldn't reach them. Couldn't save them. Couldn't stop the onslaught on Gideon's exposed body.

If only she had her gun, she wouldn't hesitate to shoot.

Lars's surprised shout filtered through her fear. Dropping a dish and cup onto the stream bank, he jumped up and ran toward them.

"Lars, do something!" she called, her voice strange and unfamiliar, laced with desperation.

She wrung her hands as Lars approached the animal, waving his arms as she'd seen Gideon do to get him to back off. The second Thunder stepped away and Lars seized his lead rope, she lunged to Gideon's side and fell to her knees in the grass. His shirt in tatters and blood marring his skin, he lay still. Too still.

"Gideon?" Her shaking fingers grazed a deep gash on his head. He didn't answer. She checked his wrist for a pulse. There. Faint. Erratic.

"We need Alice here now," she lamented. Peering under Gideon's large body, she saw small fingers clutching the grass.

"Walt?"

"Mama?"

At the startling sound of her son's sweet voice, she sat back, clutched her throat. "Walt, baby? Are you all right?"

Lars appeared at her side, chest heaving with exertion. "Do not worry about the horse. He is in the other corral alone." His eyes were solemn as he took in Gideon's injuries. "Let us lift him so little Walt can wiggle free."

Taking hold of his shoulders, she and Lars carefully eased him up enough so that Walt could scoot out from beneath him.

He threw his arms about Evelyn's neck. "Mama! Gideon saved me from the big horse." Drawing back, he looked at her with eyes full of worry. "Is Gideon gonna be okay?"

Awestruck, she caressed his smudged cheek. "You're talking."

His lower lip trembled. "I don't want Gideon to die."

Air hissed through her teeth. She shot a look at Lars. "I'll stay with him while you fetch Alice."

While she didn't have the right to order him about, she refused to leave Gideon. Was determined to be right here beside him when he opened his eyes. Reaching out, she gently smoothed his hair from his forehead. *He will open his eyes. I won't consider any other alternative.*

With a nod of understanding, Lars leaped nimbly to his feet.

"And, Lars?"

He twisted back.

"Please hurry."

Hot pokers seared every inch of his back. His head ached to the point it hurt to blink. Each breath sent shards of pain ricocheting through his chest.

The grass and soil beneath him had been replaced

with an equally hard surface, albeit cushioned with thick quilts. Hay. He smelled hay. And oiled leather and horses.

He was in the stable. Blinking, he tried hard to focus, barely making out the blurry cot legs and base of Evelyn's water pitcher table. Why was he lying facedown on the tack room floor?

Walt. The stallion. The fence failing. Why had it failed? Was Walt okay?

Sliding his hands beneath his chest to push himself off the floor, pain engulfed him in a fiery inferno and his vision blurred further. A groan slipped out.

Skirts swished. The strong odor of antiseptic invaded his nostrils. Cool fingertips brushed his bare shoulder.

"You need to lie still, Gideon. I'm tending the lacerations on your back."

Alice. Someone must've gone and fetched her.

Evelyn. He needed to see Evelyn.

He must've spoken aloud, for familiar black boots skimmed by an indigo skirt scooted into his line of sight. "I'm here, Gideon."

She knelt in the dirt near his head, her soft hand caressing his cheek. He closed his eyes, clinging to her gentle touch as to a buoy in the midst of a raging sea of agony.

"Why—" He gritted his teeth as Alice swabbed a wound near his waist. "Why are you crying?" He'd heard the silent sob. Then a horrible thought struck him. His eyes flew open, and disregarding the consequences, he lifted his head to search her pale features. "Was Walt hurt? Where is he?"

She swiped at the moisture on her cheeks, and a tiny smile flickered on her lips. "He's fine. He's outside with your brothers and Lars."

Gratitude flooded his soul, rendering him weak. *Thank You, God. Thank You.*

"You know, I—" Dizziness washed over him, and he lowered his head so that his cheek once again rested on the patterned quilt. "I could've sworn I heard Walt's voice just before I blacked out."

Her hand covered his and squeezed. "You didn't imagine it." Wonder filled her voice. "Gideon, Walt is speaking now. It was his worry for you that released him from whatever held him silent."

He hadn't imagined it? Walt really had spoken? Tears wet his eyes. *Thank You, Lord, for saving him in more ways than one.*

"I'll need to cover these wounds to keep them clean," Alice announced, her movements stirring the air as she stood and moved to the cot and her medical bag. "Then I'll need your brothers' help wrapping your ribs. From what I can tell, you have two broken on your left side and three on your right." Crouching beside Evelyn, Alice leaned her face near his, her sympathetic yet assessing gaze meeting his. "How is your head? I stitched up the gash while you were unconscious."

"Like I got kicked by a horse," he muttered, earning a slight smile from his future sister-in-law and a worried frown from Evelyn.

After she'd no doubt studied his mutilated back, she turned to Alice with a puckered brow. "Those bruises look pretty nasty. Could he have internal injuries?"

"Because of the repeated blows he sustained, we'll have to watch for warning signs. He's alert and coherent, which is good. His pulse has evened out and remained steady, and his skin, while pale, isn't clammy." She transferred her attention to Gideon. "Are you dizzy? Short of breath?"

Although he could've gazed upon Evelyn's lovely features for eternity, he closed his eyes against the brightness in the room. It aggravated his headache. "Just a little dizzy."

"That's most likely a result of the blow to the head, but we'll monitor it." Quiet descended as she worked quickly to cover his wounds. She touched his shoulder. "Gideon, I've procured a small amount of laudanum. You should take it now before we wrap you."

"I don't know…."

Boots thudded into the room. "You should listen to her, brother." Elijah's grim voice floated somewhere above his head. "She knows what she's doing."

"Hey, Lije."

Clint joined the group. "Glad to see you're awake. You had us all worried when you didn't come to right away."

Gideon searched for a response but came up empty. Exhaustion hounded him.

"Can you help me turn and lift him into a sitting position?" he heard Alice say. "I can administer the medicine and then we'll address those ribs."

Suddenly, strong hands were slipping beneath his armpits and hoisting him up, turning him. Tormenting him. A ragged groan filled his ears. His own?

"Sorry, buddy." Clint's voice, husky with apology, sounded near his ear. "Trying to be as easy as we can."

Weakness invaded his body as the darkness called to him again. His fingers searched for Evelyn's. He wanted to stay alert. Wanted her comforting presence nearby.

The sound of her weeping saddened him.

"Evelyn, darlin'?" he rasped. "Please. Don't cry."

And then a cup met his dry lips and he drank deeply, his fuzzy mind not registering the water was spiked with laudanum until too late. When the first strip of cloth was wound about his chest and pulled taut, the gloom stole over him and he slumped forward into relief.

He'd called her *darling*. Unintentionally, she was sure. Still, the endearment spoken in his velvet-soft voice had had a peculiar effect on her heart. And made the tears fall harder.

Elijah had looked over at her as if seeing her in a new light, speculation coming to life in his hazel eyes. She'd seen that discerning gaze before—as a preacher, he had a calling to assist people, to recognize their needs and meet them the best he could—but never had it been directed at her. Had he seen the hidden truth in her eyes? She prayed not.

It was a dangerous truth, one that could rip her life apart. Gideon would *not* be happy if he discovered her true feelings. His kisses had been born of the moment, spontaneous releases of pent-up emotion, not declarations of love. He was content with his solitary life. A smitten widow didn't fit in with his plans.

As for her brothers? They would disown her. No question about it.

Even now, seated beside the cot where they'd propped him up with pillows, she knew her actions betrayed her. Leaning close, she clasped his heavy, work-roughened hand in between hers and prayed for comfort and quick healing. She couldn't leave his side, however. Couldn't stop from comforting him.

Seeing Gideon in such terrible pain, knowing it was his brave rescue of her son that had gotten him hurt, was killing her.

Alice appeared in the doorway with Walt. Releasing the kind nurse's hand, his clunky shoes scraped the dirt as he came near, his troubled gaze on Gideon's pale features.

He pressed in close to Evelyn's side. "Is he sleeping?"

Having become used to his silence, she started whenever she heard his distinctive voice. "He's resting. Miss Alice gave him some medicine."

"I was scared, Mama."

Wrapping an arm about his small waist, she hugged him close. She'd come dangerously close to losing him. "You were very brave."

"Gideon saved me."

"He was brave, too."

Alice approached, her watchful gaze on the patient. "We're going to gather some more supplies from the clinic, along with bedding for Elijah. He'll camp outside in case you need for him to fetch me during the night."

"Do you think he'll wake up soon?"

His injuries required rest, she knew, but she needed to see those beautiful gray eyes of his.

"It's hard to tell. If he does, it's very important to have him take deep breaths and cough. This needs to be repeated several times an hour. You can support his ribs with a pillow."

Caring blue eyes shifted to her. "Thank you for offering to care for him. I would stay if Mrs. Carmichael's baby wasn't due any moment. From what I hear, she and young Sarah nearly died during her last delivery, and I want to take every precaution to ensure this one goes smoothly."

"I don't mind."

Alice opened her mouth to say something, then appeared to think better of it. "Don't worry about supper.

We'll stop by Mrs. Murphy's and bring plates for you both."

When she reached the door, Evelyn called out. "Wait a moment, please, Alice." After instructing Walt to choose a toy and play quietly on the rug, she joined her.

"He will be okay, won't he?"

Understanding dawned on the young nurse. She laid a comforting hand on Evelyn's arm. "He escaped the worst. Internal injuries would've required surgery, something our clinic isn't equipped for, something I'm not prepared to do without the assistance of a doctor. There's a possibility of pneumonia, but I'm hopeful that if we can keep him coughing and breathing deeply that we'll avoid that."

The image of the angry red gashes crisscrossing his back caused her to shudder. "And what of infection?"

"We're going to keep the wounds clean and covered with antiseptic." Stray red curls shifted as Alice tilted her head. "Evelyn, it's obvious you and Gideon have grown close. I know what it's like to watch someone you care about suffer. Last month, before the land rush, we almost lost Elijah."

Evelyn had overheard Keith and Cassie Gilbert speaking about his brush with death. How horrible that must've been for Alice. For his brothers. When Elijah and Clint had ridden in with Alice earlier, they'd worn matching frowns of dread, their pale countenances testament to their fear. And later, when they had assisted Alice in wrapping Gideon's ribs, it was as if they'd suffered along with him.

The Thornton brothers shared a bond that could not be broken. Whether forged by the loss of their parents, their troubled childhood or the challenges they'd faced together—including those presented by her family—

nothing could damage the love and respect they had for each other.

"Don't let worry consume you," Alice continued. "'Do not be anxious about anything, but in every situation, by prayer and petition, with thanksgiving, present your requests to God,'" she said, quoting the verse in Philippians.

"Thank you for the reminder." She dredged up a weary smile. "I admit I've neglected my Bible reading in the past weeks."

"When life gets busy," Alice motioned around her, "and yours is obviously unsettled, it's easy to let that slide. However, it's vital we make the time." She spoke without censure.

"Your friendship means a lot, Alice. Considering the situation with the land claim, not to mention my brothers' shenanigans, no one would've blamed you had you refused to speak to me."

"How could I judge you when I haven't walked in your shoes?" she said gently.

"Alice?" Elijah appeared behind her, his gaze seeking out Gideon's prone form. "He's still sleeping?"

"I'd say he will for the next few hours."

With a grave nod, he put a hand on Alice's shoulder. "We should go."

To Evelyn he said, "Are you sure you'll be all right?"

Interpreting the question for what it really was, she reassured him. "I won't leave his side."

Again, that penetrating look. "He's fortunate to have you in his life."

"I doubt he'd agree with you," she blurted, thinking how her presence had put his future in jeopardy.

"I wouldn't be so sure about that if I were you." Sadness carved deep grooves on either side of Elijah's mouth.

"You're the first person he's allowed to get close since he lost his wife and child."

"Child?" Shock knocked her back a step. "Gideon had a child?"

Chapter Twenty-One

Elijah and Alice shared a look of dismay. "I thought you knew," he said.

"He told me about Susannah. He never mentioned a child."

But he'd been a natural with Walt from the start, had known how to comfort, how to connect with a small child. She recalled being surprised at how comfortable he'd seemed tucking Walt into bed. Now she knew it was because he'd done it before.

Sorrow welled up, lodged like a boulder in her chest. Was the child a boy or girl? How old? How did it happen? When?

"I can see you have questions." Elijah wore an expression of regret. "But I'd best leave them to Gideon to answer. He wouldn't appreciate me talking about something that, for him, is an extremely difficult subject."

"You're right."

He was a private man. He certainly wouldn't appreciate others discussing him while he lay injured and vulnerable. Trying to absorb the revelation while choking back the burning need to know more, she returned to her chair and sat down hard.

Gideon. A father. One who'd buried his only child.

No wonder he kept people at arm's length. She looked at her sweet son building a fort out of wooden blocks and tried to imagine what life would be like if one day he were here and the next he were gone. *Empty. Meaningless. Desolate.* Tears smarted her eyes at the mere idea.

"Are you all right?" Alice's quiet inquiry shattered her thoughts.

Evelyn lifted her gaze to the couple still standing in the doorway. "I'm fine. It's just—" She broke off to study Gideon's dear face, ashen and fretful even in sleep, and her heart broke for him. "I hate that he's had to endure such tragedy."

"Death is a reality we must all deal with." From his resigned tone, Evelyn knew Elijah surely must've dealt with it more than most. "God gives us the grace and strength to bear it. All we have to do is accept His help."

Nodding, she threaded her fingers tightly in her lap when what she really wanted to do was take Gideon in her arms. He hadn't turned to God in his grief, had he? Instead, he'd turned away. Tried to shoulder his burden alone. *And suffered greatly for it.*

When they quietly took their leave, stating their desire to get to the infirmary and then to town and back before it grew too late, she took up his hand again and resumed praying for healing. Only this time she prayed for healing of a different kind.

A rustling of sheets and a low moan jerked her upright, out of a dreamless sleep.

Walt was quiet in his makeshift pallet on the floor. She must've drifted off sometime after midnight.

Gideon stirred, his spiky lashes fluttering as he

blinked and shifted on the cot, his arm immediately curling about his ribs.

She closed the Bible in her lap, placed it beneath her chair and scooted closer. Light from a single kerosene lamp washed the room in a soft golden hue. "You're awake."

His eyes shot open, gray irises cloudy with pain. "Evelyn."

Although propped up on pillows, he tried to sit up farther. The effort leached the remainder of color from his face. "Take it easy, swee—" She pressed her lips together. Sweetheart? Honestly? "Gideon." His name came out as a caress. "I'll get you a drink of water."

"*Just* water this time," he grunted, left arm bracing his wrapped ribs. His brothers had slipped a fresh white shirt on him but left the buttons undone so the material wouldn't pull over his wounds. Faint dark scruff lined his hard jaw and chin.

At the small table that Clint had carried in, she poured water into the cup and returned to his bedside. With effort, she kept her gaze off the expanse of smooth, tanned skin stretched over hardened muscle above the horizontal strips covering his midsection. His strength, his masculine appeal, could not be diminished by injury.

She lifted the cup to his lips, noting his hesitation. "No medicine. I promise."

His hazy gaze fastened on to hers, he unlocked his lips and drank the contents. Before she could stop herself, she smoothed locks of hair away from his forehead. His gaze cleared, roamed her features with an intensity that made her want to squirm.

"How did you get saddled with nurse duty?" he asked when he finished drinking. He shifted slightly, taking in slow, even breaths.

"I didn't get saddled with it," she said wryly. "I volunteered." When one brow arched, she quickly explained, "Alice needed to be at the infirmary, close to Mrs. Carmichael. Her delivery date has already passed."

The talk of babies had her thinking once more of his lost child. Would he ever tell her?

"How's Walt?"

Missing the weight of his hand between hers, she fiddled with the ruffled edges of her sleeves. "He's fine. Not a scratch on him. He's concerned about you, though."

"He asked about me?" Wonder filled his voice.

She smiled for the first time since the accident. "He did. You are his hero, Gideon." Emotion clogged her throat. "And mine," she admitted, her voice going scratchy. Unable to restrain herself, she covered his hand lying on top of the quilt and squeezed. "You put yourself in harm's way for my son. You saved him. I will never forget what you've done."

His fingers closed over hers, his thumb lightly grazing her knuckles. Her heart beat faster. She longed to hold him, to have his strong arms around her, sheltering her, reassuring her that everything was going to be all right. There was safety and comfort, as well as a thrilling sense of rightness, within those arms.

"Anyone would've done the same."

Evelyn thought of her deceased husband and wondered what decision he would've made. She immediately dismissed the thought. Drake was gone.

"I'm not so sure about that," she said.

Shaking herself mentally from such memories, she drew in a bracing breath and looked down at her patient. "Gideon, Alice left instructions." When she'd explained what they needed to do, he nodded solemnly.

Dreading seeing him suffer more than he already was

but knowing it was necessary in order to avoid complications, she retrieved a pillow and lodged it between his arm and torso. She supported his shoulder. He tried breathing deeply first, expanding his chest as far as he could stand it, then coughed a couple of times.

Lines of tension bracketed his mouth, but he didn't utter a sound.

Evelyn blinked away tears. It would bother him to see her upset, so she filed away her emotions to deal with later.

When he'd relaxed back against the pillows, she offered to heat up the soup Elijah and Alice had brought from the café. There was a fire outside next to his tent that could be easily stoked without disturbing Elijah. But he declined.

"I'm not hungry. Just feeling like I could sleep for a week."

She started to rise. "Would you like for me to lower the lamp?"

"No."

She sat back down, curious as to the cause of his uncertain expression.

He gave her a rueful smile. "I'd like it if you held my hand while I sleep. Not for long. You need your rest."

A giddy feeling shimmered through her like sparkles of sunlight on water. She returned his smile. "That is one request I will gladly fulfill."

Making herself comfortable in the chair, she leaned against the cot and threaded her fingers through his. Languid warmth suffused her limbs. This was right. And good.

Don't get used to it, a voice warned. *This is temporary. He's not himself.*

As soon as he was better, the wall would go back

up and he'd regret his vulnerability. He'd remember the
upcoming court case, the fact that his land and all he'd
worked for was at stake. Because of *her*.

As she watched him drift off, it hit Evelyn that somewhere along the way the land had come to mean less
than the man. Her independence less than his happiness.

If Gideon lost, where would he go? Where would he
rebuild? The available claims were all taken. Would Clint
or Elijah offer him half of their acres? Or would he return to Kansas?

If she lost, on the other hand, she had three homesteads to choose from. Would it be so terrible to move
in with one of her brothers? Walt would be around his
uncles more often. Theo, Brett and Reid missed having
him underfoot. They would be thrilled when they heard
him speak.

As for her…they loved her, too. It might take a while,
but they'd forgive her for taking sides with a Thornton.

"Where's Evelyn?"

Arms crossed over his chest, Clint crossed his outstretched legs and cracked a smile. "Well, good mornin'
to you, too, brother."

Gideon scowled. Every inch of his body hurt. "I'd expected to wake up to a different face," he drily pointed
out.

The smile widened. "Your lovely widow is enjoying
a late breakfast with Alice and Walt."

"She's not mine." He shook his head in protest, only
to cringe. Felt as if someone had buried an ax in the base
of his skull.

Clint quirked a brow. "You called her darlin'. Haven't
heard you call anyone that, not even…" He trailed off,
hesitant to speak Susannah's name.

Determined to avoid the topic, Gideon leveled his younger brother a "don't go there" stare. "Where's Thunder?"

That wiped the smirk off his face. "While you were out yesterday afternoon, Lije and I repaired the fence. He's back in his corral."

Gideon debated what to do with the horse. It wasn't as if the animal were mean-spirited. He was acting true to nature. Scraping a hand over the bristle covering his jaws, he said, "Would you mind taking him back to John Turner? Just until I'm on my feet again. I can't have an untamed animal on the property while Walt and Evelyn are here. That was a mistake on my part."

Abandoning the relaxed air, Clint sat up straight, all business now. "Gideon, Lije and I discovered something…disturbing. That fence didn't fail on its own. Someone tampered with it. Someone *wanted* it to fail."

A memory flickered. His gut tightened with unease. "I remember now. When I saw Thunder break through and head for Walt, I remember thinking it didn't make sense." Rage simmered in his veins. "That little boy could've been killed." He leaned forward. The bandages on his wounds pulled at sensitive skin. Pain screamed through his rib cage. "Uh," he grunted, and fell back, angry at his inability to even breathe without consequences.

He felt Clint's hand on his shoulder. Looking over at his brother, he saw determination, a promise. Clint would do everything in his power to deliver justice.

"Lars and I will look into it," Clint said. "We'll find out who did this and punish them to the full extent of the law."

"You're good for this town."

Shrugging off the praise, he said, "I know we ruled out the Chaucers as being responsible for the crimes plaguing Brave Rock, but considering what happened the other day between you and Reid, do you think one of them might've done it? To get back at you for influencing their sister?"

Gideon mulled it over. "I can't see them doing anything that would put Walt or Evelyn in danger. On the other hand, they could've assumed neither one would go near the stallion."

Please, God, don't let it be them. Evelyn would be crushed.

Communicating with his heavenly Father was slowly freeing him from his anger. The accident had opened his eyes to how wrong he'd been to turn away from the only one who could give him true and lasting peace. Comfort. Healing.

God was sovereign. The creator of the world, the director of all history. Who was Gideon to question His choices, His plan?

I'm sorry, Lord, for the past year and a half. Forgive me. Help me to mourn Maggie properly. And to celebrate the short time I had with her.

Clint brought him back to the present. "Or it could've been Reeves. You did decline to assist him and his cronies. He wouldn't have been too happy about that."

"Nor McGraw," he agreed, frustration setting his teeth on edge. Had the danger passed? Had the scoundrels gotten what they wanted? Or were Evelyn and Walt still vulnerable?

"How's the patient?" Alice breezed through the doorway, flame-colored hair scraped back in a sensible bun, bright blue gaze taking his measure. He didn't like the determined set to her chin.

Slipping between Clint and the cot, she deposited her medical bag on the quilt near his feet and placed a cool palm against his forehead. He felt like a child suddenly and scowled at Clint's amused expression.

When she retrieved a pillow and settled it against his midsection, his scowl deepened. And when he obeyed her instructions to breathe deeply and cough and fire engulfed his torso, Clint lost the amusement real quick.

"I need to clean those wounds and change the bandages," she said. "Clint, would you mind helping him remove his shirt?"

"Never thought I'd see the day when I had to have help getting dressed," he groused as Clint carefully helped him to his feet and tugged the sleeves down. He knew he was being a grump, but it was either that or weep.

His lawman brother's gaze was sharp, missing nothing, but he played along. "You think I'm enjoying this, do you? I'm not exactly nursemaid material."

By the time they had him on his stomach atop the pallet, which was wider and flatter than the cot, sweat dotted his brow and black edged his vision. Thankfully, Alice worked quickly and efficiently and, once she was done, suggested he rest there for a while.

"Thanks, Alice." He didn't know where he'd be, or Brave Rock for that matter, without her nursing skills.

"No thanks necessary. Get some rest."

When Clint made to leave, he called out. "Hold up a minute."

The scuffed boots stopped, pivoted, and then his brother's serious face entered his line of vision.

"I can't protect them like this," he said, "not with me in here and them out there in the tent at night. I need you and Lije to help me convince the women to move me to the tent. Evelyn and Walt can have their room back."

He didn't have to ask their opinions on the matter.

Alice would no doubt fret over dirt and exposure. Evelyn would refuse to switch places on principle.

Clint shook his head. "I'll try, but you know they can be mighty determined when they have a mind to. Besides, I don't think that's the best solution."

"It's the only one. If my cabin was finished, they could stay there. At least they'd have a locking door."

Clint's eyes lit with resolve. "Don't worry about a thing. I'll get it all figured out."

Chapter Twenty-Two

"Who are all those people, Mama?"

Such a simple word—*mama*—but it brought a smile to her face. Looking up from where she sat in the shade with her pile of clothes to be mended, her lips parted at the sight that greeted her. Wagons—had to be eight or ten of them—rambled across the open fields.

"I recognize some of them from church," she murmured. "Keith and Cassie Gilbert, the Lambert and Johnson families."

Elijah, who'd been quietly studying his Bible nearby as Alice tended to Gideon, stood with a pleased, expectant smile.

"Are we hosting some sort of church meeting?" she questioned, returning the pair of pants she'd been working on to the pile and thrusting the needle in the pin cushion.

A breeze ruffled his dark hair, pushing it across his forehead and lending him a boyish air. "You could say that." His sparkling gaze touched hers. "Actually, they're here for a cabin raising."

Clint's wagon led the pack. As they neared, she noticed the myriad tools filling the beds. Women clutched baskets on their laps. Food for the crowd?

Evelyn went to stand beside him, Walt following. "Are you saying all these people have dropped everything to come and build Gideon's cabin?"

"Yes."

It wasn't an uncommon practice, but up until two weeks ago, Gideon hadn't set foot inside the church. Granted, he'd helped out a time or two with the new church building. That these families would give up time—a valuable commodity when not only daily chores awaited but so did preparations for the winter—touched her deeply.

Overcome with emotion, she lifted Walt and whirled him in a circle, planting a big kiss on his cheek. He laughed, a happy, carefree cascade of sound.

"Why'd you do that?"

With a final squeeze, she put him down. "I'm so very happy you're my son, that's why."

And because in a few short hours, Gideon would have a home.

"Did you arrange for this?" she asked Elijah, fully expecting him to say yes.

"Nope." Brotherly pride ringed his smile. "Clint did."

Clint? She watched the stoic lawman park his wagon, jump down and begin directing everybody. It appeared that beneath that gold star beat a sensitive heart. The more she learned about the Thorntons and the more she saw them in action, the higher her respect rose for the brothers.

My parents were wrong. My brothers were wrong, and so was I.

Four men hastily set up a makeshift table to hold the bounty of food. Bringing up the rear, Lars and Jed Lambert carried a pole strung with a deer carcass, and already Keith Gilbert was starting a huge fire where they could roast it.

A pan of rolls in her hands, Cassie Gilbert hurried over. "Hello, Evelyn. Elijah, how is Gideon faring? It's just horrible what happened."

"He's doing as well as can be expected. Alice is taking excellent care of him."

Evelyn had gone in to see him earlier, but he'd already drifted off to sleep. He'd looked younger than his thirty-three years, wan and worn from his ordeal. Still handsome, though. Nothing could detract from his appeal. Not in her eyes, anyway.

"We're praying for him," Cassie told him.

"Thank you."

Dakota ran up then. "Hiya, Preechah." He greeted Elijah with dancing black eyes. "Hiya, Walt."

"Hi, 'Kota," Walt returned with a shy wave.

Dakota's jaw hit his chest. "You—" He pointed at Walt. "He—" He looked incredulously at the adults circling him.

Cassie's expression communicated her wonder. Elijah burst out laughing, reached out and ruffled the boy's shoulder-length brown hair. "Yes, Dakota, Walt is talking again. Isn't that wonderful?"

"When did this happen?" Cassie asked Evelyn.

"I'll explain later," she promised, reluctant to bring up the accident in front of Walt. He was still awfully worried about Gideon.

Dakota seized the younger boy's hand. "Come on, let's play by the water."

"Stay close," Cassie called after him. Nodding and waving, the two ran off.

"Winona is at the reservation today," she said, "so I'm keeping an eye on Dakota. Such a fine boy."

Other women trickled over to their group, and the conversation turned to how best to organize lunch for the crowd. Katrine barely had time to say hello before the older women began assigning tasks. It wasn't until after everyone had eaten and the bulk of the mess had been cleaned up that Evelyn was able to get away to check on Gideon.

He stirred when she opened the door. Entering the cooler, dimmer space, she set the bowl of stew on the small table.

"What's going on out there?" Voice husky from sleep, he rolled carefully onto his back and blinked up at her. "Sounds like an army. Are we being invaded?"

"Only by well-meaning church members," she returned lightly, going to stand beside the pallet so he didn't have to crane his neck. "My guess is that by this time tomorrow, you will have yourself a new home."

His eyes went wide. "What?"

"Your brother rounded up friends and neighbors. At this moment the walls are finished and they are starting on the roof."

"The folks of Brave Rock respect and love Elijah. They would do anything for him."

"That they would," she agreed. "However, it's Clint you'll have to thank. It was his idea, and he's the one who went door-to-door asking for help."

He looked stunned, then rueful. "I don't know why I'm surprised. He's good at mustering enthusiasm for a cause, bringing people together. That's what makes him such a good sheriff."

Gathering her skirts, she crouched beside him. "I understand completely. Elijah is our town's beloved preacher, and normally he is the leader. Clint is more reserved but no less effective in getting things done." Cocking her head, she threaded wayward strands behind her ears. "Do you want my opinion?"

His eyes warmed to soft gray. "Always."

"I think they're here to support all three of you. The Thornton name carries a lot of weight in this town, despite my brothers' attempts to sully it. People respect you."

"Thank you, Evelyn," he intoned. "That you would say that means a lot more than you think."

Feeling as if her inner thoughts were written across her forehead, she smiled and motioned to the table. "I brought you some beef stew and corn bread."

"Smells good."

He accepted her offer to help him to the cot. Sensing he tried not to rest his entire weight on her, she nevertheless gloried in the feel of his large body close to hers, warm and solid and more like home than she'd ever experienced. Calling herself all kinds of a fool, she tried to focus on anticipating his needs and not on how he made her feel.

About the time Gideon's spoon scraped the bottom of the bowl, Clint knocked on the open door, unnecessarily announcing his presence. His arrival was, in some ways, a blessing. She needed space to think, to regain proper perspective, to bury these fairy-tale dreams of Gideon, herself and Walt living on this claim as a true family.

Even if you and Gideon had met on different terms, he's made his stance on marriage clear. So have you. Or have you forgotten your miserable existence with Drake?

She had to concentrate on building a new life for her son. He was her priority. His love and companionship would have to be enough.

Exiting with as much equanimity as she could muster, Evelyn threw herself into the never-ending list of chores, losing herself amidst the cluster of workers. No one noticed her preoccupation. After a quick supper of leftovers, everyone departed for their homesteads, promising to return after breakfast in the morning to complete the roof and construct a front porch.

Coward that she was, she took Walt with her when she checked in on Gideon, allowing them to engage in conversation while she tidied up the room. Evelyn avoided his question-filled gaze and, when he caught her hand after she bade him good-night, attributed her subdued manner to fatigue.

"Tomorrow you'll have a roof over your head again."

Familiar determination settling across his features, he said, "I want you and Walt to sleep in the cabin. You'll be more comfortable there."

"Absolutely not." She tugged her hand free. "That's your home. Not mine."

Cradling his ribs, he shifted against the pillows, shot her an enigmatic look. "We don't know that for sure, do we?"

Suddenly the claim dispute hung between them. It was on the tip of her tongue to tell him to forget the court case, that he could have the land. But she didn't dare. That would invite speculation, questions she didn't want asked. She would have to answer to not only Gideon but her brothers. What in the world would she tell them?

"I won't do it, Gideon. The tack room is perfectly suitable for us."

One refined brow arched. "We'll see."

"Yes, we will." She stiffened her spine. Stubbornness wasn't only a Thornton family trait. "If there's nothing else you need, it's time for Walt to get to bed."

His narrowed gaze fell to her mouth. "I don't *require* anything else, Nurse Montgomery."

Tingles of awareness zipped through her, invading her limbs with a languorous warmth. Ruthlessly denying the irresponsible longing surging within her, she gave him a brisk nod.

"Good night, then, Gideon. Sleep well."

Evelyn was avoiding him.

She'd made herself scarce the entire day. Elijah had brought in his breakfast. At lunchtime she'd arrived with Alice and stayed only long enough to place his plate and silverware on the table. No doubt she hoped to avoid a continuation of last night's conversation.

He wasn't ready to let the matter drop, however, so when Lije came in midafternoon to inform him the cabin was finished and his bed was being put together, he demanded to speak with her.

Sensing something amiss, his older brother sank into the chair. "Evelyn is with the other women readying the mattress. Is there a message I can give her for you?"

"In other words, why don't I tell you what the problem is so you can weigh in on it?" Gideon said without bite. He couldn't fault Lije's inherent compassionate nature.

An amused smile flashed on his brother's face. "I do have a lot of practice, you know."

Gideon blew out a frustrated breath. "I want her and Walt to move into the cabin, but she refuses."

"On what grounds?"

"Because it's my cabin, not hers. But we both know that may not be the case for much longer."

"That's true." He crossed one leg over the other knee and toyed with his boot strings. "Why is it so important to you?"

"Isn't it obvious?" He spread his hands wide, instantly regretting the action. "The cabin is safer. Considering everything that's going on in our town, I'd prefer that she stay there. Besides, it's the gentlemanly thing to do. Would you let Alice sleep in a stable while you slept like a king in his castle?"

Elijah gave a commiserating grunt. "I see your point. However, I also understand Evelyn's rationale. In the eyes of the townsfolk, this is your property. They've just spent the last two days erecting *your* cabin. Don't you think tongues would wag if she moved in instead of you?"

"Let them wag. I don't care what anyone else thinks."

"You may not, but I believe she does. Try to see things from her point of view. She's spent the past three weeks in the company of your friends and family, knowing they're aware you're on opposite sides of a land dispute. Her brothers' actions have no doubt added to the awkwardness of the situation. I'm sure she doesn't want to call any more attention to herself."

Gideon let his head fall back against the pillows. Thank goodness the ferocious headache that had plagued him since the accident had lessened to a manageable ache. Closing his eyes, he pinched the bridge of his nose. "You're right. I don't like it, but you're right."

Clint skidded into the room. "We're ready for you, Gideon. Cabin's all been put to rights. I've two men waiting to help us carry you over."

Gratitude warred with embarrassment. Would the entire town be standing by to watch him being paraded across the field? He simply couldn't fathom being the center of all those eyes, not lying flat on his back, anyway.

"I'd like to walk."

His brothers shared a long look. Clint nodded. "Lije and I can each take an arm. We'll support you."

Relief flooded through him. And something deeper, truer. As they eased him to his feet, he admitted, "I don't say it often enough, but I'm a fortunate man to have you two for brothers. Couldn't have made it through without ya." They all knew he was talking about what happened in Kansas.

Accustomed to such sentiment from his parishioners, Lije simply smiled. Clint flushed and looked away, saying gruffly, "You're not so bad yourself, big brother." Then he plopped Gideon's black Stetson on his head. "Awfully bright out there."

Emerging from the stable, Gideon was glad of the hat. After being cooped up in the tack room, the cheery spring sunshine hurt his eyes. As predicted, folks had stopped what they were doing to watch. He searched the crowd for Evelyn.

There. Her silken hair flowing down her back, the top half pulled up and secured with a peach ribbon, she stood willowy and graceful on the cabin porch. An exotic bloom, lovely in a shade of apricot that set her olive skin to glowing and gave her large eyes a mysterious bent.

During the long, slow, excruciating trek, he kept his gaze trained on her as if she were a prize at the end of a race. Hopefully those he passed thought he was focused on his new home and not on the woman who'd stormed into his life not even a month ago, calling him every name in the book and vowing to fight him for this land, who along the way had taken up residence not only on his property but in his heart.

The admission—though it was only in his mind—made him stumble. His ribs protested. The pain jerked him back to reality.

Don't go there, Thornton. The feelings you have for Evelyn are merely admiration for her spirit and strength, bolstered by the chemistry that exists between you. Nothing more, nothing less.

Gideon clung to that rationalization of what she meant to him, praying he hadn't gone and done something stupid like falling for the Chaucers' sister.

Chapter Twenty-Three

Evelyn couldn't help feeling a tad sentimental. Walking through Gideon's new home, seeing the details Cassie and the others had seen to—blue curtains at the windows, crocheted hand towels in the kitchen, Gideon's Bible placed front and center on the rough-hewn coffee table—she experienced a bittersweet gladness. He deserved a home such as this and yet, if he followed through with his plan, he'd be living here alone for the rest of his life.

Once again her thoughts turned to his lost child, and she ached for him. Gideon should have half a dozen kids running around, little boys he could teach archery to and little girls he'd teach how to rope and ride.

Blond hair flashed in her peripheral vision and Katrine joined her at the window beside the kitchen table.

"You look…how do you say it? Oh, yes, lost in thought."

"Just admiring the view." From this vantage point, cottonwoods swept alongside the meandering stream, a sea of green grass stretching for miles.

"*Ja,* it is a nice view." Twisting slightly to admire the

cabin's bright interior, Katrine said, "And a cozy home. Home is everything, is it not?"

"Yes, it is." *And I don't have one. Not sure when or if I ever will have a home of my own.*

Turning back, Katrine trailed a finger along the shimmering glass. "I guess this cost a pretty penny. However, it is worth the cost. I should have insisted Lars put windows in our cabin."

At that moment the big Dane's boisterous laughter spilled from the single bedroom where he and a few other men had gathered around Gideon's bed.

Evelyn smothered a mystified smile. Three weeks ago Gideon would've been horrified at this invasion of his privacy, not to mention the townsfolk's charity. He'd changed, she acknowledged with some surprise, just as she had.

She recalled the strange intensity of his gaze as he'd hobbled as nobly as he could manage toward his home. She'd wondered if he meant to repeat his argument in front of everyone. But he hadn't. Upon reaching her, he'd looked momentarily uncertain, then uttered a soft thank-you for her ears alone.

Foolhardy as it was, she'd wished everyone away so that she could have him all to herself, just the two of them crossing his threshold for the first time.

"I should go and check on Walt." She turned to look at Katrine. "No doubt he needs a good washing before bed. The tack room will need to be put to rights, as well."

Katrine nodded. "It appears many are preparing to leave now that Gideon is settled."

The yard was a flurry of activity. While women packed up food baskets, their husbands loaded tools in the wagons. Walt and Dakota frolicked with the dogs, whooping and hollering with abandon. A delightful sound to her ears.

"Thank you for your help, Katrine. Lars, too. Everyone has been so wonderful."

"You are thanking us for helping Gideon?" A worried frown pulled her pale brows together. "I see that you care about him and he for you. What will you do if the judge grants him legal ownership of the claim?"

She squared her shoulders, determined not to heed the sinking sensation threatening to suck the life out of her. "I will return to my brothers."

And she would make the best of the situation, would build the best possible life for her son.

By midmorning the following day, boredom was setting in. Gideon had eaten a hearty breakfast of scrambled eggs, ham and biscuits—alone. He'd invited Evelyn to stay and eat with him but she'd declined, claiming a long list of chores to tackle. Afterward he'd read a week-old Guthrie newspaper from front to back. He'd napped an hour or so, and now here he was at ten o'clock, twiddling his thumbs and staring out the window.

While it offered a nice view of the side yard, it couldn't hold his attention. The quiet of his new home bothered him.

So when a short, dark-haired visitor knocked on the door and called his name, Gideon sat up straighter, ignoring the ache in his ribs.

"Come on in, Walt." He smiled encouragingly. The boy had seemed a mite intimidated by his injuries. "To what do I owe the pleasure of your visit?"

His eyes surveyed Gideon's chest, covered by a button-down gray shirt, and the rest of him, tucked inside a red,

white and blue quilt. His thin shoulders eased when he
didn't see physical evidence of the accident.

"Mama wants to know what you want for lunch."

"I have a choice?"

He held up two fingers. "Rabbit stew or fried chicken."

Gideon relaxed into the feather-stuffed pillows, satisfaction wrapping around him like a hug from a long-lost
friend. He was having a conversation with Walt, something he'd begun to think would never happen. *Thank
You, Lord.* "Hmm, let's see. How's your mama's fried
chicken?"

A smile cracked through the shyness. "Very good."

"Then that's what I'll choose. Thanks for the recom-
mendation."

"I'll go and tell her."

Gideon's gaze fell on a set of checkers he'd had since
he was a teenager. "Uh, Walt?"

He spun back.

"Do you like to play checkers?"

Nodding vigorously, he said, "Uncle Brett taught
me."

Smiling at the blunder, Gideon asked if he'd like to
play a couple of games once he'd spoken with Evelyn. He
barely replied before he shot out the door, boots pounding on the front porch. Walt was back in five minutes, his
eager presence chasing away the tedium of the sickbed.

They established a pattern over the next few days.
Walt joined him after breakfast for an hour of checkers
or cards and then again after lunch when they'd peruse
books together. The five-year-old climbed into his bed,
lugging the big encyclopedia that was his favorite. Evelyn had obviously worked with him, for he knew the
names and habits of many of the animals they read about.
Gideon was impressed with his knowledge.

By Friday he decided he'd had enough of Evelyn's evasiveness—something that had developed the day he moved into this cabin. He hauled himself out of bed, stepped into a clean pair of trousers and, because he couldn't manage a fresh shirt, wore the one he'd slept in. Socks were also out of the question, so he greeted her barefoot and in desperate need of a shave.

Her lips parted and her eyes rounded when she caught sight of him seated at the kitchen table. The tray in her arms wobbled. "Gideon, I didn't expect to see you out of bed." Circling the couch, she set it down with a thump, sloshing coffee over the mug's rim. Shoving a hand on her hip, she demanded, "Should you be up? Did Alice give you permission?"

"I'm tired of being in that bed. Tired of a lot of things, actually."

Her brows knit together. "How is your back?"

"Not bad." It itched and pulled and made him want to throw something.

Moving behind his chair, she leaned close, and the scent of gardenias enveloped him. Her fingers slid through his hair. His eyes drifted closed, and he clamped his lips around a sigh of pleasure.

"Your head wound looks to be healing well." Was that a tremor in her voice?

Putting the table between them once more, she clasped her hands behind her back. This morning she'd paired a serviceable black skirt with a gray-and-white paisley blouse, and her thick hair had been pulled into a tidy French braid. He'd thought her beautiful the first day he saw her, but she was even more lovely now that he knew her.

"If you don't need anything else, I'll leave you to your meal."

"Stay."

Her head bowed. "I shouldn't."

"Why not? Evelyn, have I done something to offend you? Have I hurt you?"

"We have a court date," she blurted, her eyes a swirl of emotion.

Gideon slumped in his chair. *A court date.*

"A soldier stopped by. He said our case will come before Judge Martin in two weeks."

"I see."

The aroma of bacon and johnnycakes slathered with butter and molasses turned his stomach. No wonder she'd been distancing herself. In a few short days, their futures would be decided. This…friendship would come to an end.

"This soldier… It wasn't Strafford, was it?"

"No, someone else. A man I haven't met before."

Why wasn't he excited? Clearing his throat, he searched her features and came up blank. The emotions in her eyes were too muddled to distinguish one from another. "This is what we've been waiting for all along."

"Yes. It will be good to have things sorted out," she said carefully. "We can finally move forward."

Forward. Without Evelyn. Without Walt. Why did such a notion slice deeper than any of the wounds he'd sustained? And why didn't he care more about losing the land than he did about losing them?

Evelyn tipped the dirty wash water out of the pail, squinting in the afternoon sun. The hours since their morning conversation had dragged by, her mind replaying Gideon's stunned response to the news. How different things were compared to that first day and their heated confrontation. Recalling the hateful slurs she'd hurled at him then, she blushed with shame.

She couldn't have been more wrong about him.

Glancing toward his cabin tucked amidst the trees, the verdant backdrop lending the rough-hewn logs a golden hue, sunlight glancing off the windows, she wondered what was keeping Walt. His hour-long visit had stretched into two. What if Gideon was tired and in need of a nap?

She was a mess—dirt smudges clung to her hem and her skirt was damp from washing clothes—but there was no time to change.

There was no answer to her soft knock on the front door. Easing it open, she called for Gideon, her gaze going immediately to the bedroom. Propped up against the pillows, Gideon pressed a finger to his lips, then pointed to the boy curled up on the quilt beside him. She walked through the living room and stopped just inside the bedroom. Walt slept soundly, round face innocent and peaceful.

The moisture glistening in Gideon's eyes caught her off guard.

She rushed to the bed and smoothed locks of hair away from his forehead. "Are you in pain? Should I get the medicine Alice left for you?"

Capturing her hand, he held on tight. "I am in pain, but it's not what you think."

Ignoring the internal warnings to keep her distance, she returned the pressure. "Tell me what's troubling you."

"I—" He visibly swallowed, blinked. "I had a daughter. Her name was Margaret, but I called her Maggie from the beginning."

Her pulse sped up. His anguish became her anguish. Gently lowering herself onto the mattress so as not to disturb Walt, she said quietly, "What was she like?"

Gideon's sudden smile twisted with grief. "She was a ray of sunshine, always giggling and dancing about. Maggie was never still. When—" He swallowed, as if struggling to get the words out. "When she smiled, her entire face lit up and her eyes sparkled. It'd make you happy just to look at her."

The love he had for his daughter shone through his tears. If Walt hadn't been there between them, Evelyn would've been tempted to recline beside him and take him in her arms, hang propriety's rules. Instead, she attempted to offer comfort through their joined hands.

"She sounds like a delightful little girl."

"She was my whole world," he gruffly admitted. "When I lost her, I wanted to die, too."

Her own tears threatening, she ventured, "How old was she when…?"

"Four."

Nodding, she broke eye contact to gaze at her precious son. Being around other children must be a terrible reminder of what he'd lost.

As if he'd read her mind, he said, "At first I didn't want anything to do with Walt. I hadn't spent time with any kids since Maggie. Too painful. But I found I couldn't resist his beseeching brown eyes, the sense I got that he wanted to communicate but just couldn't. Spending time with him the last few days, *talking* with him, has been wonderful. You have a special little boy, Evelyn."

Her smile wobbled. Gideon loved Walt. The evidence was there in his eyes. And the fact he'd risked his life for him. What she wouldn't give for a father such as this for her son!

"He is a gift from God."

Grief marred his features. "I was angry at God for a long, long time. It hasn't been easy, but I've come to accept that railing at Him, cutting myself off, won't bring Maggie back. She was a gift, one I wasn't ready to let go of. I've had to remind myself that Jesus loves her more than I ever could."

Tears slipped down Evelyn's cheeks. She freed her hand from his grip, then caressed his stubbly jaw. "I'm sorry. So sorry."

"Talking about her, with you, makes it a little easier to bear."

Evelyn cried harder then. Walking away from this man was going to be the hardest thing she'd ever had to do.

Chapter Twenty-Four

Gideon and Evelyn rocked on the porch in chairs that were a gift from his brothers. He'd avoided his bed as much as possible the past three days, preferring this chair, where he could breathe fresh air, listen to the birds chime overhead and watch squirrels darting up and down the tree trunks. He could never tire of this view—never-ending fields that would eventually produce wheat and corn, the stream that supplied the ranch with valuable water and fish, the corral where his horses grazed.

You may be leaving this soon. Ever since she'd informed him of the court date, the unknown niggled at his peace, forced him to consider his options—none of them easy.

"Mama! Gideon! Watch me." Walt waved his hands in the air to get their attention. He'd been romping in the grass with Lion and Shadow the past half hour, no doubt hoping to postpone bedtime. The supper dishes were cleaned and put away, and the sun nearly kissed the horizon.

"You have ten more minutes before bed, young man," Evelyn called in warning.

Gideon glanced at her profile, noting the tension about

her mouth, the whiteness in the knuckles gripping the armrests. The stress of their situation was showing. They didn't speak about the dispute, but it hovered in the air like an invisible poison.

He could scarcely believe he'd told her about Maggie. He hadn't told anyone.

Must've been the compassion in her eyes, the knowledge that she shared his hurt, his grief, in a way that no one else ever had. What that meant in the way of his feelings for her he was afraid to face.

"Look, Mama! Uncle Theo and Uncle Brett are coming."

Evelyn's anxious gaze shot to Gideon, then sought out the two approaching riders as she eased to her feet. He stood more slowly, praying a confrontation could be avoided. He wasn't fit to tussle with a groundhog in his current state, let alone two Chaucers. His gun belt hung just inside the doorway, out of reach.

One positive was that Reid hadn't accompanied them. Brett was the most levelheaded Chaucer, and while Theo carried a grudge for the broken nose Gideon had gifted him with all those years ago, he was smart enough to know when to back down from a fight.

They didn't immediately dismount. Theo's upper lip curled. "Well, isn't this a cozy scene? I have to hand it to ya, Thornton, I underestimated your charm. Our sister fell for your act, hook, line and sinker."

"Please, Theo. I don't want any trouble." Evelyn edged sideways so that she stood between her brothers and him. She thought she could protect him?

Gideon could've kissed her. Instead, he rested a hand against her lower back and moved to stand beside her. "It's all right, Evelyn."

Worry for him, for herself and Walt, for her brothers warred in her eyes. "You can't know that," she murmured.

Taking in the exchange, Theo growled, "Oh, what, are you a couple now? What are you thinking, Evelyn, aligning yourself with this pile of rubbish?"

Walt's expression communicated his confusion. Of course he wouldn't understand the tension between his favorite adults. "Uncle Theo, Uncle Brett, did you bring me any candy?"

Both men jerked in their saddles, eyes going wide and jaws dropping. Brett's gaze shot to Evelyn. "He's talking?"

Theo slid to the ground and rushed over to his nephew, crouching to his level and pulling him into a hug. Brett joined them, tenderness wreathing his features as he playfully ruffled the boy's hair. Their love for Walt shone in their eyes.

Gideon shouldn't have been surprised that a Chaucer was capable of feeling. Walt was their flesh and blood. There was a very real possibility he'd be going back to live with them. The thought made him sad.

I love that little boy as if he were my own son.

Beside him Evelyn stood as taut as a strung bow, one hand clapped over her mouth.

Theo stood, his gaze a mix of accusation and hurt. "When did this happen? Why didn't you tell us?"

Her hand dropped to her side. "I'm so sorry, Theo, I—" She gestured to Gideon. "There was an accident. Things have been in an uproar."

Theo and Brett shared a look. That they didn't appear surprised bothered Gideon. "You did hear about the accident, didn't you?" he challenged.

Theo kicked up a shoulder. "We heard talk in town."

Evelyn gasped. "You heard but didn't bother to come

and check on us? Walt nearly died. If it weren't for Gideon, he would've gotten trampled by that wild stallion."

"We knew Thornton was hurt," Brett said, "but we had no idea of the danger to Walt."

"Is it possible you stayed away because you're the guilty party? Someone messed with that fence with the ultimate goal of harming me." Gideon fished for information. To this day, they still had no idea who'd tampered with the fence. He needed to gauge their reactions to such a suggestion. Ignoring how Evelyn bristled, he said, "We all know how you feel about my family. Me especially. Admit it, you hate that your sister and I have grown close."

"Gideon, how can you suggest such a thing?" Evelyn gasped. He risked a glance at her. Betrayal beamed back at him. Anger, too. "These are my brothers. I told you before they aren't the type of men who would break the law. To suggest they'd put Walt or me in danger is ludicrous. This is low, even for you."

"Even for me?" His own temper flared. "What's that supposed to mean?"

"Walt," Brett said in a voice loud enough for everyone to hear, "why don't you go on over to the tack room and play? We'll be along shortly."

Although clearly reluctant, he did as he was told, calling for Lion and Shadow to follow him.

Blazing mad, Theo thrust a hand in the air. "You see, Evelyn? You've been duped. He may act all friendly and protective, but deep down, he'll never trust you, because of your heritage. Thorntons and Chaucers don't mix."

Brett rubbed a weary hand down his face. "We should never have let her stay out here alone. That was a mistake."

"I never did get an answer," Gideon snapped. "And while we're at it, how about we discuss the issue of the stake?"

Evelyn sucked in a harsh breath.

"Someone discarded my stake," he continued, "and replaced it with Drake's. Was it Reid? Or was it you, Theo?"

Evelyn slanted him a "how could you" look, a look that pierced the haze of wrath enveloping him but didn't dispel it entirely. His gut told him the Chaucers knew more than they were letting on. He wouldn't back down until he got some answers. Not even for her.

If they didn't get to the truth, there could be more accidents. Who knew what the outcome would be then?

"Why, you sorry—" Theo surged in their direction. "I'll make you wish you'd never opened that trap of yours."

Gideon braced himself, knowing he was doomed but determined to defend himself the best he could.

"That's enough," Evelyn bolted off the porch and planted herself in her older brother's path, her small hands pushing at his chest. "I won't have more violence here. Think of Walt, Theo!"

"You expect me to stand by and listen to this?" Taking hold of her shoulders, Theo moved her out of the way. But she seized his wrist and held on with all her might. "Gideon's angry. Don't let him bait you."

Her scathing glare cast his way pained him more than the ribs, the head and the back wounds combined. He was propelled back to that first day, easily recalling her animosity, her accusations ringing in his ears. *Liar. Cheat. Scoundrel.*

Brett grabbed his brother's arm and hauled him around. "She's right."

"Please, I'll pay you a visit first thing in the morning," she pleaded with her brothers. "I'll bring Walt so you can spend time with him. We can discuss what happens next."

That had an ominous ring to it, Gideon thought.

The muscles jumping in Theo's rigid jaw, he jerked a nod. "Fine."

Still braced for a fight, Gideon watched mutely as her brothers left.

Managing to appear irate and sorrowful at the same time, she marched over to the porch, skirts swirling and her hands thrown wide. "I can't believe you! I thought you trusted me. Trusted my judgment. How could you suggest they'd put us—their family—in danger?"

"They have motive, Evelyn."

"You're too angry and biased to see they are good, decent men."

"Those good, decent men despise me, or haven't you noticed?"

"You haven't exactly made it hard for them, have you?" she retorted. "You've made no effort whatsoever to mend the breach between our families."

"Right. It's *my* fault." He pinched the bridge of his nose to ward off the headache blooming behind his eyes. "It's clear where your loyalties lie, Evelyn. Wednesday can't come soon enough."

She jerked back as if he'd struck her. "I agree. The sooner we can move on with our lives, the better."

In other words, the sooner she didn't have to deal with him...

The fight drained out of him, leaving his knees weak and his spirit weaker. Gideon found he didn't have the strength to do this, to swap cruel words with her. Wounding her only ended up wounding him more.

"I think we've said enough, don't you?" he muttered. Without waiting for a response, he turned and walked away.

Shaking with emotion, Evelyn stared at the closed door. He'd turned his back on her. Dismissed her. Practically slammed the door in her face!

Beneath the outrage, hurt wrapped her heart in an excruciating grip. The sense of betrayal rushed through her veins. She was a fool. She'd begun to believe he actually cared for her. His actions today proved that, despite his stirring speeches about being true to herself, he didn't respect her at all. Just as Drake hadn't.

The kicker was her heart hadn't thirsted after Drake as it did Gideon.

"I love him," she whispered aloud, turning and walking dazedly across the field, leaving the cabin and the man inside it behind.

There. She'd said it. Put a name to her feelings for him.

It didn't change anything, of course. They had always been on divergent paths. Her brother was right. Chaucers and Thorntons didn't mix.

In the tack room, she carefully explained to Walt that Theo and Brett had had to return home and that they would visit them after breakfast the following morning. He went to sleep plotting out his day with his uncles.

Evelyn hardly slept and woke feeling groggy, weary in both body and soul. She went through her morning routine with lethargy and finally readied herself and her horse for the trip to Theo's homestead. As she and Walt rode past Gideon's cabin a while later, she couldn't resist a glance. The rocking chairs sat empty. Concern flared. Had he suffered a setback?

She tamped it down. Gideon was on the mend. He was fine. Besides, his welfare wasn't really her responsibility, was it? They weren't a couple. She wondered now if they were even friends.

Her brothers met her with varying degrees of disappointment and resentment. They were seated around Theo's extra-long kitchen table finishing up breakfast when she and Walt walked through the door.

Reid popped a sausage patty in his mouth, chewing angrily. "Ma and Pa must be turning over in their graves. Never thought I'd see the day a Chaucer turned on her own flesh and blood."

She tossed her reticule on the table and went to help herself to a cup of coffee. Maybe if she had a cup to occupy her hands, she wouldn't be tempted to strangle them all. On her way she told Walt to take his toys in the bedroom to play.

"Don't be so hard on her," Brett said. "She's recently lost her husband. Of course she would be lonely over there all by herself, vulnerable to Thornton's advances."

Theo snorted. "You'd think she'd be too heartbroken over Drake's passing to give Thornton a second thought. But that didn't seem to faze her one bit."

Evelyn set the mug down with a thump. *Please, God, help me not to lose my temper.* Twisting to face them, she said, "Don't talk about me like I'm not in the room. You want to know why I wasn't heartbroken? I'll tell you why. It's because I didn't love Drake. I married him for the wrong reasons. I wanted to please you and, like other young girls with stars in their eyes, I was eager to experience married life for myself."

"You didn't love him?" Reid demanded, stunned.

"He didn't love me, either. He spent the bulk of our marriage in other women's beds."

Brett paled. Theo slumped in his chair, dumbfounded. "Why didn't you say anything, Evelyn?"

Reid looked ready to burst. "I would've put a bullet through his cheatin' heart."

"That's why." She pointed at him. "I kept quiet because I couldn't risk such an outcome."

"I can't believe it." Theo hung his head as if it were his fault.

"I'm sorry, sis," Brett pushed his chair back and pulled her into his arms. "You deserve better than that."

Tears stung her eyes. Considering everything that had happened since she moved out to Gideon's, she'd half expected them to call her a liar. Hope sprung up. Maybe her moving back here would work out after all. Maybe they could move past this and find peace. She loved her brothers dearly and hated the discord between them.

Reid hurled his napkin on his plate. "To think we plotted with that snake to take Thornton's claim out from under him."

Brett's hand rubbing her back stilled midmotion. He stiffened and pulled back, apprehension brewing in his dark eyes as he searched her face.

Evelyn's breath caught. Dread pummeled her temples. "W-what did you just say?"

Chapter Twenty-Five

Pushing out of Brett's arms, Evelyn looked at each of her brothers in turn. They actually looked scared.

"Please tell me you didn't just say what I think you said." Fists clenched, her entire body shook and her face felt hot.

Reid held up a hand. "Calm down, sis. It's not as bad as it sounds."

"Tell me the truth," she bit out.

Her twin shot a questioning glance at Theo, who gave a reluctant nod.

Shifting from one foot to the other, Reid had trouble holding her gaze. "About a week before the land rush, Drake found out the Thorntons had scouted out plots on the survey maps. We discussed it and came up with a plan. Drake was to follow Gideon to his claim and challenge him for it. Not only would he get a claim on a well-chosen parcel of land, he'd get rid of a Thornton in the process."

"Drake didn't anticipate his horsemanship letting him down," Theo inserted. "He underestimated Gideon's abilities."

Reaching blindly for the nearest chair, Evelyn sank

into it and buried her face in her hands. Nausea threatened. From that first day when she and her brothers had ridden onto his land, an army soldier in tow, Gideon had proclaimed his innocence. He'd insisted all along that he was the one who'd planted that first stake. But she'd chosen not to believe him…because he was a Thornton.

She'd bought her brothers' theory—that Gideon had actually plotted to steal a dead man's claim. Infected by their lies, she'd accused an innocent man of vile crimes. Angry tears slipped down her cheeks.

A hand settled lightly on her shoulder. "Don't cry."

Shying away from Brett's attempt at comfort, she glared at them through her tears. "I trusted you. All of you. Like a mindless idiot, I ignored my own qualms regarding our family's allegations against the Thorntons and accused Gideon of horrible things." Her voice broke.

Gideon. Although innocent of any wrongdoing, he'd endured her intrusion into his life with amazing equanimity. Images scrolled through her mind's eye…. Gideon rescuing her from her miserable attempt to erect the tent, stepping in to defend her against the too-familiar soldier, searching the prairie for Walt as if he were his own son. Moving her things into the tack room so that she and Walt would be safe and dry. He'd treated her far better than she deserved…eventually treating her as a friend, worthy of his time and regard.

How could she ever face him again?

"I would've expected such a mean-spirited plan from Drake, but not from you. Our parents taught us better than that."

"It wasn't mean-spirited." Reid sat down in the chair opposite her. "It was a matter of strategy."

"But you accused him of something you knew he

didn't do." She threw her hands wide. "I defended you three to him."

Reid's fist hit the table. "We didn't tamper with that fence."

"What about the stake? Did one of you switch it? Was that in your grand plan, too?"

Theo spoke up. "We didn't touch the stake. If you recall, the three of us were busy staking our own claims."

Sincerity blazed from his eyes. It was true. The day of the land rush, they'd raced to stake these plots—on the opposite side of town from the Thorntons—and hadn't left until a soldier arrived to inform them of the accident, summoning them to identify Drake's body. She'd been here with them the entire time.

"When you went to identify the body, you didn't switch it then?"

"No." Her oldest brother managed to look hurt at the suggestion. "The stake was the furthest thing from our minds. All we could think about was you and Walt and what would happen now that you'd lost Drake. We didn't know about…" His gaze slid away.

The affairs. The sorry state of their marriage.

"Besides, we couldn't have even if we wanted to. Clint Thornton was there, and he watched us like a hawk. He didn't trust us any more than we trusted him."

"Who did it, then?" Brett said quietly. "Drake was injured."

"Yes." Evelyn smoothed nonexistent wrinkles in her skirt. "But to what extent? I know him. To Drake, winning was everything. He would've done everything in his power to make sure he triumphed over Gideon."

"You think he switched them out himself?" Reid asked Theo.

"It's the only thing that makes sense."

Better than anyone, Evelyn knew Drake was cunning. Cunning enough that he would've replaced the stake and, after discarding Gideon's, dragged himself back to his original position. By using up his energy and straining his injuries, he had probably pushed himself too hard and died before medical help could reach him. Getting one over on the Thorntons had driven him to his death.

"This feud has poisoned our lives for too long. It's time to let it go. We have to stop blaming others for our own misfortune." Making eye contact with Theo, she said, "Haven't we inflicted enough suffering on ourselves? On them?"

Theo appeared to waver. Then Reid snorted. "This land dispute issue is an isolated incident. So Gideon was in the right this time. So what? That doesn't mean he or his brothers deserve our respect. This feud ain't over, Evelyn. As long as there's breath in my lungs, I'll hate what they did to our family."

Evelyn sagged with disappointment, the futility of trying to change their minds weighing on her spirit. "That's just the thing. They didn't do anything to our family."

Gideon was watering his horses when Elijah rode up in his wagon. His brother's grim expression filled him with dread. He dropped the bucket and strode to intercept him, ignoring the pain shooting along his rib cage.

"Has something happened to Evelyn?" He'd woken to find them gone this morning. "Is Walt okay?"

Swinging down from the high seat, Lije pulled an envelope from his pocket and held it out. Gideon took it, stared at his name scrawled across the ivory paper. "What's this?"

"Evelyn came to us this morning. She was very distraught." He paused, his eyes dark with concern.

"Gideon, she's asked to stay in the infirmary until she can arrange for a more permanent living situation."

"What? Why?" Something akin to panic seized him. Evelyn was leaving?

"I believe she put everything in the letter." He shifted uncomfortably. "I'm here to load her stuff into the wagon."

Ripping into the envelope, Gideon skimmed the lines. "Her brothers. Drake. They plotted to take this claim from me."

At last…vindication. Evelyn had confessed she believed him innocent long before this. Still, their confession freed him, confirmed his version of events in her eyes and the eyes of the townsfolk.

Upon the heels of jubilation came a slow, simmering rage. "I've always known they hated us, but to embroil Evelyn in their schemes is unforgivable."

Lije's hand came down on his shoulder. "Nothing is unforgivable, Gideon. Take Maxwell Peterson, for instance," he said, referring to the scum who'd tried to force Alice to marry him last month. "It would be easy to hate him for what he did to her, but that would only poison my own soul. I'm not saying I've completely forgiven him, but with the Lord's help, I'm working on it day by day."

"I know you're right," he grated out. "But it's gonna take time." Just as healing from Maggie's loss would take time.

As he scanned the remainder of her letter, Gideon's heart sank. The remorse she felt practically leaped from the page. "She blames herself. She doesn't feel up to seeing me right now, if ever." His fingers trembled, jostling the paper.

"Once Alice got her calmed down, she sat and talked with us for a while. She deeply regrets that you got caught up in this mess. From what I understand, she and her brothers have had a falling-out. That's why she came to us. I have to admit, I feel like I've been placed in a tenuous position. As a preacher, it's my duty to assist the needs of my parishioners. But as your brother, my first loyalty is to you." He paused, searching for the right words. "If our helping her hurts you, I will look for somewhere else for her to stay."

Humbled by his words, Gideon said, "I appreciate your thinking of me, Lije. But I want you to help her. I know that with you and Alice, she'll be looked after properly."

"Do you love her, Gideon?"

The direct question rocked him back on his heels. For the second time in the space of a few minutes, panic seized him. Only for a different reason.

"No."

Lije's brows lifted.

"Don't get me wrong, I care what happens to her. I want her to be happy."

He couldn't love her. He'd been so careful to guard his heart.

"What do you think will make her happy? She clearly has feelings for you. Deep feelings."

"It's not what you think, I'm sure."

The denial hadn't left his lips before he found himself fascinated with the notion of Evelyn loving him. Could she…? Did she…love him?

"Furthermore, what will make *you* happy, Gideon?" Lije pressed. "Will living here alone make you happy? I know losing Susannah and Maggie took a toll on you. I know because it's how I felt after losing Marybelle. It's frightening to think of experiencing that pain all over again, but even a single day with Alice would be worth it."

Turning away, Gideon gazed at the quaint cabin set amidst the cottonwoods, the prairie grasses swaying in the spring breeze, the ribbon of water bubbling a lazy tune. He'd poured his life into this place. Felled trees. Built a stable one log at a time. Dreamed of a long life here spent taming the land and raising his horses, all by himself. Independent. Alone. Above all, safe.

Now he could easily picture Evelyn rocking on the front porch and drawing in her journal, wading in the stream with Walt searching for lizards and frogs, standing in his kitchen cooking breakfast, heavy with his child....

No. If he ever lost her—

"I need time to think," he told Lije. "Besides, she's made her wishes clear. She doesn't want to see me. Maybe that's the wisest course."

"Gideon—"

He pivoted and brushed past him. "I'll help you load her things."

Evelyn sat on the narrow cot in the rear of the infirmary after supper, running the brush through her hair, stroke after mindless stroke. She couldn't seem to summon the energy to arrange it. In fact, she couldn't summon much enthusiasm for anything. Food held no appeal. Drawing, a pastime that normally soothed her, was not the distraction she'd hoped it would be. She was lucky to get her chores done.

Four days without Gideon. That was ninety-six hours since they'd said spiteful things to each other, two days and two nights since she'd learned the truth about the stake. About her brothers. About Drake. About herself.

Glancing out the window she saw that the sun hung low in the orange-and-pink sky. Dread settled in the pit of her stomach. The nights were the worst. Lying on her cot in the darkness listening to Alice and Walt's soft breathing, all the cruel things she ever said to him playing over and over in her mind. Taunting her.

Alice pushed the curtain divider aside and emerged from the infirmary, where she'd tended to a patient with a deep cut that had needed to be stitched. Lifting the crisp white apron over her head, she hung it on a nail and proceeded to wash her hands.

"Would you like a cup of chamomile tea, Evelyn?" she offered, her gaze bright with concern and, above all, kindness.

She and Elijah had welcomed her and Walt into their lives and homes with a generosity of spirit she'd never forget.

Smothering a sigh, she set her brush on the stand and folded her hands in her lap. "No, thank you."

"Are you hungry? I noticed you didn't eat much at supper."

"The pot roast was delicious." She rushed to assure her hostess. "It's just I've a lot on my mind. I'm afraid I have some major decisions to make in the coming days."

She and Walt couldn't live here indefinitely. After the wedding, Alice's mother would be joining the newlyweds and would likely stay here in the infirmary until more permanent housing could be built.

Swiping a bright strand behind her ear, Alice came and joined her on the cot they'd brought in and put beside Alice's, placing a hand atop Evelyn's. "Don't rush into anything. You're welcome to stay with me for as long as you'd like." She glanced around with a rueful smile. "It's a bit snug, but cozy, too."

Evelyn dredged up a smile for the other woman's sake. "Thank you for everything you and Elijah have done. I don't know what I would've done without you."

"I've enjoyed having you around. Walt, too." She glanced at where he was crouched on the rug with a crate bearing three tiny turtles.

"Mama, can I take my turtles out and give them fresh grass and water?"

"Sure. Stick close to the house, though."

"Okay." Cradling the small crate to his chest, he scooted through the door. Unhappy about their move to the infirmary, he'd repeatedly asked when they would see Gideon again.

Taking advantage of his absence, she said, "I've been thinking about returning to Virginia. I have cousins there who'd gladly take us in."

"Pray about it first. I'm confident God will direct your steps." Alice frowned. "We sure would miss you both. Elijah and I thought… That is, you and Gideon…" She bit her lip. "I shouldn't pry."

Sadness pulsed through her. "It's all right. You're aware we quarreled."

"I saw him at services Sunday morning," she confessed. "He left before the final prayer was said. I wondered if you'd seen him."

A shard of icy pain pierced her heart. Gideon was at church? He'd sat yards from where she'd sat and yet he hadn't said a word to her. He must loathe her.

Pressing a hand to her chest where a dull ache had set up, she said, "I don't blame him for avoiding me. I would avoid me, too."

Alice squeezed her hand. "He cares about you. That much I'm sure of. Give him time to sort through this."

Even if he ultimately forgave her, he wouldn't want

her like she wanted him. For so long, she'd tried to convince herself that she didn't need anyone. How wrong she'd been. She needed Gideon. Needed his strength, his companionship and, most of all, his love.

She sighed. "Maybe I will take that cup of tea."

"Certainly." But when the redhead moved to the kitchen and pulled down the canister, her brows knit together. "Oh, I didn't realize I'm all out. I'll run over to Elijah's for some of his. I'll be right back."

Shortly after the infirmary door closed, Walt burst through the rear door waving a folded piece of paper in the air. "Mama, Mama! For you!"

"What's this?"

"A note."

Bouncing from one foot to the other, he held it out to her.

"A note."

He nodded rigorously.

"From who?"

"You'll see." His smile reached from ear to ear.

Unfolding the paper, her pulse skittered as she read, "Care to share an evening stroll and a slice of ginger cake with me? G."

"This is from Gideon?" By now her hands were shaking. "Gideon is *here?*"

"Yep. Right outside. Can you believe it?"

No. She couldn't believe it. She'd assumed he wouldn't want to see her again.

Chapter Twenty-Six

She flipped the note over, took up a pencil and hurriedly wrote, "I'll meet you at the stream."

"Take this to him. Then I want you to go next door to Elijah's and wait with him and Alice until I come for you. Understand?"

His brown eyes filled with hope. "Does this mean we can move back to Gideon's stable?"

"I honestly don't know, Walt."

She didn't know what Gideon would say. It could be something as simple as "You forgot a trunk in the stable and I've brought it to you." Or "Writing a letter was the coward's way out. I want a face-to-face apology."

How was she supposed to face him and act normal? How was she supposed to resist throwing herself at his feet and begging forgiveness, not to mention doing her best to convince him to give them a chance?

After Walt had gone, Evelyn hurriedly slipped into the peach dress—Gideon's favorite—and left her long locks hanging free. Feeling dizzy and not a little bit out of control, she prayed for equanimity. Poise.

Pausing at the door, she took a deep breath and emerged into the lazy spring evening. There in the distance stood Gideon, gazing at the water trickling past, his broad back to her as she silently approached. On a low rock near his boots sat a plate with two forks, a napkin protecting the favored dessert from insects.

Maybe the cake was a thank-you. *For what, Evelyn? Wreaking havoc with his life?*

Of course he sensed her presence. Pivoting sharply, he stared hard at her. "Evelyn."

The audible caress raised goose bumps along her skin. His black shirt, paired with the black Stetson, made his eyes glitter like silver in the pastel light of late day.

"I found something." From behind his back, he produced a wooden stake flaked with dirt.

"Your stake," she breathed. He released it into her hand without a word. *Thornton, Gabriel A.*

"I went searching yesterday. Came upon it by chance, really. The top edge was sticking out of the ground and my boot grazed it."

"Where was it? Near where Drake lay injured?"

He nodded, wincing in apology.

Coming close, he lifted his hand and gingerly fingered a lock of her hair. His knuckles grazed her collarbone.

She shivered. It took Oklahoma-sized willpower to keep her arms at her sides.

"I've missed you," he murmured, intense yearning blazing to life in his beautiful face.

"You have?" The breath whooshed out of her lungs. He had?

"Everywhere I look, I see *you*."

There was no condemnation, no distaste in his frank gaze. For the very first time, Gideon was allowing her to see everything. He held nothing back. And it humbled her.

"When I think of all the rotten things I said to you—"

Her voice broke. Overcome, she buried her face in her hands.

His gentle fingers trapped her wrists, tugging downward, urging her to look at him. "That's all in the past. We didn't know each other then." He gifted her with a wry smile. "You're not the only one who said things worthy of regret. I'm not completely innocent here."

"No," she countered, "you were so kind and good. You endured our onslaught with a noble spirit few men would've displayed."

Releasing her wrists, he cupped her cheek. "I didn't come here to say goodbye. I came here to tell you that I don't care about the land. I don't care about the feud. All I care about is being with you." Setting his shoulders as if gearing up for battle, he took an unsteady breath. "I want you with me always. Till death do us part."

The sorrow and uncertainty of the past four days began to ease. His wonderful, simple words unraveled her determination to remain calm. Sliding her arms up and around his neck, she pulled him down for a kiss. An eager, messy, uninhibited kiss fueled by pent-up longing for the man she adored.

Gideon snaked his arms about her waist and held her fast, ignoring the twinge in his sore ribs. Against his chest, he detected her heart beating wildly, like a bird trying to take flight. Her fingers playing in his hair sent delicious tingles along his spine. He matched her fire with a fire of his own, letting her know without words just how deep his feelings went.

That Evelyn had initiated the embrace shouldn't come as a surprise. His beloved was nothing if not bold and courageous, a woman with a lion's heart, a woman who'd make him a fine wife and partner. *If* she agreed to his proposal.

Easing his mouth from hers, he breathed words he'd never thought to utter. "I love you, Evelyn Chaucer Montgomery. What do you say we get hitched?"

Her beautiful brown eyes cleared. Laying her palms flat against his chest, she carefully searched his gaze. "I thought you'd decided marriage wasn't for you."

He smiled. "That was before a lovely, spirited widow came into my life."

"Be serious, Gideon."

"I am deadly serious, sweetheart. I love you, and I want to build a life with you and Walt. If that's what you want, too."

"I do. Very much. I love you, Gideon Thornton."

Thrilling in the love and affection shining in her eyes, he said, "I can't deny a part of me fears losing you, but I realize there are no guarantees in life. My brother made me see that I have to accept each day as a gift. I'm determined to live each one to the fullest, making sure those closest to me know how much I love them."

When Evelyn cradled his face and gazed at him as if he were a priceless treasure, his heart expanded with gratitude and wonder. "The answer to your question is yes." She smiled tenderly, "I will happily marry you." She cocked her head. "Do you know of a preacher who could do the honors?"

Laughing, he lowered his mouth for a lingering kiss. "As a matter of fact, I do."

Epilogue

"Where are they?"

Gideon checked his pocket watch. It was only three minutes later than the last time he checked. He couldn't very well get married without his brother to stand up with him.

Unconcerned, Elijah nodded his head toward the horizon. "Relax. I told you they'd be here."

Spinning at the stable opening, he waited as Clint and Lars raced across the lush fields. The instant they drew near, he knew they'd discovered something. Something huge.

His brother swung down from the saddle. At least he'd had time to wash up and change into a proper Sunday suit. Gideon blinked at the sight of Lars wearing pants, a button-down shirt and a string tie.

"You were almost late to my wedding," Gideon accused, hands on hips. "This better be good."

Clint and the big Dane exchanged a look.

"You'll never believe what Lars witnessed today." Clint gestured for him to proceed. "I'll let you tell them."

"I discovered a cave outside of town. This cave contains a large amount of ammunition. I decided to watch this place. Just before dawn, I saw two men enter. Private Reeves and Private Wellington."

Elijah exhaled sharply. "I can't believe it."

"I can." Gideon felt familiar anger rise up. He'd never cottoned to those men, and Reeves's proposition had confirmed his suspicions. They weren't to be trusted. "What are we gonna do?"

Again his sheriff brother exchanged a look with Lars.

"We have a plan to smoke them out."

"And that is?"

"Sorry." Clint's gaze was unflinching. "The fewer people who know the details, the better."

Another wagon entered the yard, a straggler arriving for the wedding. Evelyn hadn't wanted to wed in a tent, and with Brave Rock's church still lacking a roof and bell tower, they'd decided to have a simple affair here on the ranch that would be their home. After sharing the news of their engagement with Elijah and Alice, they'd gone straight to the land office to withdraw their complaint. The hearing had been canceled, of course.

Elijah settled a hand on Gideon's shoulder. "Time enough to worry about all that. Right now I have a wedding to officiate. And you, dear brother, have a lovely bride waiting for you."

Clint cracked a rusty smile. "Never would've guessed you'd beat Lije to the altar."

"Evelyn didn't need a fancy ordeal."

"And you couldn't wait to make her yours, am I right?"

"Just wait," Gideon warned with a wicked grin. "One of these days a little filly will lasso your heart."

The humor fled Clint's eyes. "You know that's not going to happen."

Aware of his younger brother's stance on marriage,

he said lightly, "'In his heart a man plans his course, but the Lord determines his steps.' Look it up. Proverbs 16."

"Gideon, quoting Scripture?" Lars grinned big. "Now this is a good thing, *ja?*"

Gideon glanced at Lije, who wore an expression of relief and brotherly pride. "It's a very good thing."

As a group, they made their way to the wide front yard where guests milled about waiting for the ceremony to begin. It was a gorgeous Saturday afternoon. Many of Brave Rock's residents had turned out, some even donating food to feed the crowd. Mrs. Murphy had generously supplied the cake. The Gilberts had brought their biggest hog to be roasted on a spit. Jars of lemonade and sweet tea lined one table, while beans and corn and other dishes occupied another.

Their friends stood at the front of the crowd. Lars was flanked on either side by Katrine, Winona and Dakota. Off to the side, Lion and Shadow lounged in the shade, white ribbons tied about their furry necks.

At the sight of the preacher and groom, the crowd parted to make way. There beneath the cottonwoods stood Evelyn, filmy white dress framed by the green grass at her feet and the leaves hanging overhead, and by the cerulean sky hovering over the prairie and the shimmering silver stream winding past. Tiny white blossoms were woven into the lustrous dark locks skimming her shoulders, the top strands caught at the back with flowing white ribbons.

With each step that carried him closer, his heart thundered louder in his ears. This was his future. His forever love.

When he reached her, he took her hands in his and whispered, "I've never seen you look more beautiful." And then, because a touch of sadness tinged her smile—

despite her invitation, her brothers had chosen not to attend—he tacked on, "Except maybe when I dumped you in the water."

Her eyes widened in surprise. Then a happy laugh bubbled forth. "I'll get you for that."

When he felt someone tug on his pant leg, Gideon looked down to see Walt, dapper in his brown suit, beaming up at them. Crouching to his level, Gideon placed a hand on each shoulder. "Are you ready to stand up with me, little man?"

"Yes, sir."

As soon as Evelyn had agreed to be his wife, they'd gone in search of Walt and talked to him about their decision. His reaction couldn't have been better. He'd hugged Evelyn first. Then he'd thrown himself into Gideon's arms and exclaimed, "I have a new pa!" Both adults had had tears in their eyes.

Standing here now with his new family, Gideon offered another prayer of thanks to the Lord for His provision. For him the ceremony marked a genesis of sorts, the beginning of a life he'd never dreamed would be his. While a part of his heart would always mourn his first family, Evelyn and Walt filled his days with love and laughter, joy and delight.

A throat cleared nearby. Lije bent close. "The crowd's getting restless. And hungry. We'd better get started."

Straightening, Gideon locked gazes with Evelyn. "We're ready."

Coming up behind Gideon, who was crouched on the stream bank, Evelyn dipped her fingertips in the bucket of water she carried and sprinkled droplets on his neck.

"You look like you need to cool off," she teased, his

pre-wedding quip—and the skirmish that had spawned it—springing to mind.

Twisting around, he eyed the bucket swinging in her hand. Even as a smile flashed, straight, white teeth sparkling against golden skin, one dark brow arched. "You wouldn't dare."

She shrugged a shoulder, affected an air of nonchalance. "I seem to recall a certain groom who had the audacity to bring up a particularly humiliating incident to his bride on the most important day of her life."

"I was trying to distract you," he said, smile widening.

Her taciturn cowboy was no more. In his place was a man who knew how to laugh, how to enjoy the ridiculous, silly moments in a day, a man with a ready smile and wicked sense of humor. How she loved him!

"Oh, I was distracted, all right." Relishing the exchange, Evelyn slowly lifted the bucket. "It sure is a scorcher today. If it's this hot at the end of May, I wonder what June has in store for us."

"As long as I have you and Walt by my side," he vowed with mock seriousness, "I don't care what the weather does."

"Nice try, cowboy." Acting fast, she tossed the water at him, dousing his entire back. Then, dropping the bucket, she ran.

"You'll pay for that, Mrs. Thornton!" he called, already gaining on her.

Exhilaration shooting through her veins, Evelyn didn't run as fast as she could have, because a part of her wanted to get caught. As long as she lived, she'd never tire of Gideon's strong arms around her, his sheltering embrace.

She squealed the instant he stopped her forward motion, scooping her up as if she weighed no more than a feather pillow and carrying her to the water.

Clutching his shirtfront, she repeated his earlier words. "You wouldn't dare."

He burst out laughing, a rumbling, happy sound that was music to her ears. "The water isn't deep. You won't drown." Sparkling gray eyes devouring her, his voice dropped an octave. "You look overheated, wife. You should cool off."

Stopping at the bank, he clutched her tighter so that she was pressed against his chest. His perfect mouth hovered above hers. He cocked his head. "If I agree not to release you, what will I get in return?"

"A slice of Mrs. Murphy's ginger cake?"

"Not good enough."

"A bowl of my rabbit stew?" While he praised all her meals, he seemed partial to her stew.

Extending his arms, he made as if to drop her. "I don't think so."

"All right, all right." She clutched at his biceps. "I have something else."

Stepping back from the edge, he said, "What's that?"

Suddenly shy, she lowered her gaze to where his collar opened at the neck. "I drew a picture for you. It's in the cabin."

Gideon promptly lowered her, gently setting her feet in the grass. All seriousness now, he said simply, "Can I see it?"

Nodding, she took him by the hand and they walked to the shaded porch. "Wait here."

When she returned, she handed him the picture and, heart hammering against her rib cage, waited for his reaction. His gaze soaked in the drawing of himself cradling a little girl, her face hidden against his chest, long curls flowing over his arms. His jaw worked and his Adam's apple bobbed.

He hated it. "I'm sorry, Gideon, I shouldn't have—"

"No." He reached out and, taking her hand, tugged her close to his side. "If you hadn't, I would've missed out on a wonderful reminder of Maggie. It's beautiful, Evelyn," he said, his voice husky and his eyes full of emotion. "I'll treasure this always."

Then he placed a tender kiss on her lips, one of promise and of a love that would endure all things.

"If God wills it, one day I hope to give you more sons and daughters," she told him, emotion clogging her throat. While theirs was a recent union, she was already dreaming of expanding their family. Gideon was a terrific father to Walt, as he would be to any children they had together.

He lightly caressed her cheek. "That would please me more than anything. However, if God doesn't see fit to give us more children, you and Walt are enough. You are the family He gifted to me."

Evelyn blinked through misty tears. "I love you."

"I love you, darling wife."

Arm in arm, they entered their new home, aware of their many blessings and ready for the future, whatever it might hold.

* * * * *

Dear Reader,

I sincerely hope this second installment of the Bridegroom Brothers continuity series entertained and encouraged you. This was my first time participating in a continuity, and while the process came with unique challenges—for instance, making sure we authors each didn't give a character different hair colors!—I'm thankful to have been a part of it. As soon as I read about the land rush and the resulting dispute between a taciturn cowboy and a lonely widow, I knew I'd enjoy bringing their love story to life. The characters of Gideon and Evelyn were a joy to explore. I have to admit I'm gonna miss spending time in Brave Rock, Oklahoma, as well as working with fellow Love Inspired Historical authors Laurie Kingery and Allie Pleiter. Don't forget to catch the conclusion of this series, Clint Thornton's story, out next month!

If you'd like more information on this series or my Smoky Mountain Matches series, please visit my website, http://www.KarenKirst.com or email me at karenkirst@live.com. You can also find me on Facebook or follow my Twitter account, @KarenKirst.

Karen Kirst

Questions for Discussion

1. Have you, like the Thornton brothers, ever been blamed for others' misfortunes? How did you handle the situation?

2. Evelyn initially bases her assessment of Gideon's character on her family's opinions. How are our views influenced by those close to us?

3. God's Word warns against judging others. Why, then, do you think we sometimes fall into this trap?

4. 1 Samuel 16:7 says, "The Lord does not look at the things people look at. People look at the outward appearance, but the Lord looks at the heart." What are some of the things we tend to focus on when meeting someone new?

5. Because of Drake's criticism, Evelyn is afraid of trying new things and of making mistakes. Have you ever felt this way? What did you ultimately do about it? Can failure be good for us? If so, how?

6. Gideon is angry at God for not sparing his young daughter. Have you ever been angry at Him for not answering a prayer the way you wished? What can we do for those close to us who, like Gideon, are grieving the loss of a loved one?

7. The Thornton brothers choose not to retaliate against the Chaucers. What would you do if someone was spreading lies about you or your family?

8. Gideon and Evelyn both admit to marrying for the wrong reasons. What motivates people to marry in this day and age?

9. Lars and Winona obviously harbor feelings for one another, but several obstacles stand in their way—cultural backgrounds, language, religious views, potential prejudices. In your opinion, are those same issues still affecting couples today?

10. What are some other challenges couples face today that weren't present in the late 1800s?

11. Have you ever known anyone who, like Gideon, closed themselves off from others following a tragedy? What, if anything, did you do to draw them out?

12. Due to Evelyn's change of attitude concerning the Thorntons and her growing feelings for Gideon, Evelyn's relationship with her brothers becomes strained. Have you ever been in a similar situation? How did you handle it?

13. Have you ever stood up for the right thing and suffered for it? What was the situation?

COMING NEXT MONTH FROM
Love Inspired® Historical

Available June 3, 2014

LONE STAR HEIRESS
Texas Grooms
by Winnie Griggs

Ivy Feagan is headed to Turnabout, Texas, to claim an inheritance, not a husband. But when she meets handsome schoolteacher Mitch Parker on the way to town, will she become both an heiress and a wife?

THE LAWMAN'S OKLAHOMA SWEETHEART
Bridegroom Brothers
by Allie Pleiter

Sheriff Clint Thornton is determined to catch the outlaws threatening his town. When his plan to trap them requires conspiring with pretty settler Katrine Brinkerhoff, will this all-business lawman make room in his life for love?

THE GENTLEMAN'S BRIDE SEARCH
Glass Slipper Brides
by Deborah Hale

When governess Evangeline Fairfax plays matchmaker for her widowed employer, he agrees on the condition that she give him lessons in how to court a lady. Soon Jasper Chase longs to focus his newfound courting skills on Evangeline!

FAMILY ON THE RANGE
by Jessica Nelson

Government agent Lou Riley thought of his housekeeper Mary as a sister—until now. As they work together to save an orphaned child, will they find that love was right in front of them all along?

LIHCNM0514

REQUEST YOUR FREE BOOKS!

2 FREE INSPIRATIONAL NOVELS
PLUS 2
FREE
MYSTERY GIFTS

Love Inspired
HISTORICAL
INSPIRATIONAL HISTORICAL ROMANCE

YES! Please send me 2 FREE Love Inspired® Historical novels and my 2 FREE mystery gifts (gifts are worth about $10). After receiving them, if I don't wish to receive any more books, I can return the shipping statement marked "cancel." If I don't cancel, I will receive 4 brand-new novels every month and be billed just $4.74 per book in the U.S. or $5.24 per book in Canada. That's a saving of at least 21% off the cover price. It's quite a bargain! Shipping and handling is just 50¢ per book in the U.S. and 75¢ per book in Canada.* I understand that accepting the 2 free books and gifts places me under no obligation to buy anything. I can always return a shipment and cancel at any time. Even if I never buy another book, the two free books and gifts are mine to keep forever.

102/302 IDN F5CN

Name _____ (PLEASE PRINT) _____

Address _____ Apt. # _____

City _____ State/Prov. _____ Zip/Postal Code _____

Signature (if under 18, a parent or guardian must sign) _____

Mail to the Harlequin® Reader Service:
IN U.S.A.: P.O. Box 1867, Buffalo, NY 14240-1867
IN CANADA: P.O. Box 609, Fort Erie, Ontario L2A 5X3

Want to try two free books from another series?
Call 1-800-873-8635 or visit www.ReaderService.com.

---

* Terms and prices subject to change without notice. Prices do not include applicable taxes. Sales tax applicable in N.Y. Canadian residents will be charged applicable taxes. Offer not valid in Quebec. This offer is limited to one order per household. Not valid for current subscribers to Love Inspired Historical books. All orders subject to credit approval. Credit or debit balances in a customer's account(s) may be offset by any other outstanding balance owed by or to the customer. Please allow 4 to 6 weeks for delivery. Offer available while quantities last.

Your Privacy—The Harlequin® Reader Service is committed to protecting your privacy. Our Privacy Policy is available online at www.ReaderService.com or upon request from the Harlequin Reader Service.

We make a portion of our mailing list available to reputable third parties that offer products we believe may interest you. If you prefer that we not exchange your name with third parties, or if you wish to clarify or modify your communication preferences, please visit us at www.ReaderService.com/consumerchoice or write to us at Harlequin Reader Service Preference Service, P.O. Box 9062, Buffalo, NY 14269. Include your complete name and address.

LIH13R

SPECIAL EXCERPT FROM

Love Inspired
SUSPENSE

The marshals are closing in on the illegal adoption ring, and Serena and her partner Josh must team up to bring it down for good.

Read on for a preview of the exciting conclusion to the **WITNESS PROTECTION** *series,* *UNDERCOVER MARRIAGE by Terri Reed,* *from Love Inspired Suspense.*

U.S. marshal Serena Summers entered three-year-old Brandon McIntyre's room with a packing box in hand. Her heart ached for the turmoil the McIntyre family had recently suffered. Danger had touched their lives in the most horrible of ways. A child kidnapped.

But thankfully rescued by the joint efforts of loving parents and the marshal service.

The McIntyre family no longer lived in Houston. The U.S. marshal service had moved them for a second time when their location had been compromised.

Only a few people within the service knew where Dylan, Grace and the kids had been relocated.

Serena and her partner, Josh, were among them. It was their job to pack up the family's belongings and forward them through a long and winding path to their final destination.

Serena's fingers curled with anger around a tiny tennis shoe in her hand.

So many deaths, so many lives thrown into chaos.

The thought that someone she had worked with, trusted, had stolen the evidence and had been leaking information to the bad guys sent Serena's blood to boil.

If her brother were alive, he'd know how to compartmentalize the anger and pain gnawing at her day in and day out.

But Daniel was gone. Murdered.

A sharp stab of grief sliced through her heart. Followed closely by the anger that always chased her sorrow.

"Hey, you okay in here?"

Serena glanced up at her current partner, U.S. marshal Josh McCall. He'd taken off his navy suit jacket and rolled the sleeves of his once crisp white dress shirt up to the elbows. His brown hair looked like he'd been running his fingers through it again, the ends standing up. She'd always found him appealing. But that was before. Now she refused to allow her reaction to show. Not only did she not want to draw attention to the fact that she'd noticed anything about him, she didn't want him to think she cared.

She didn't. Josh was the reason her brother had been alone when he'd been murdered.

Turning away from Josh, she said briskly, "I'm good."

Taking the two ends of the sheet in each hand, she spread her arms wide and attempted to fold the sheet in half.

"Here," Josh said, stepping all the way into the room. "Let me help."

He reached for the sheet, his hands brushing hers.

An electric current shot through her. She jerked away, letting go of the ends like she'd been burned. "I don't need your help."

His hand dropped to his side. "Serena." Josh's tone held a note of hurt.

Glass shattered.

Someone else was in the house.

Pick up UNDERCOVER MARRIAGE by Terri Reed, available June 2014 from Love Inspired® Suspense.

Love Inspired
SUSPENSE
RIVETING INSPIRATIONAL ROMANCE

Hometown secrets

Was the explosion that took the lives of Sarah Russell's parents an act of murder? Her teenaged daughter thinks so and is determined to seek answers in their sleepy small town. Sarah fears her daughter will uncover a secret she's not ready to share: everyone—including Sarah's daughter—believes the girl is Sarah's kid *sister.* Even the child's father doesn't know the truth. But as Sarah reunites with Nick Tyler to look into the mysterious deaths, she knows she'll have to tell him—and her daughter—the truth. Yet someone wants to ensure that no one uncovers *any* long buried secrets.

COLLATERAL DAMAGE
by
HANNAH ALEXANDER

Available June 2014 wherever
Love Inspired books and ebooks are sold.

LIS44599